LIGHTFALL

A Novel by

Christian Carvajal

Fear Nought Publishing
A division of Fear Nought Productions LLC
1025 Black Lake Blvd. Ste. 3A, Olympia, WA 98502, USA.
Website: http://publishing.fearnought.net

Manufactured in the USA
First published in USA 2009

ISBN-10:   0-9824855-2-2
ISBN-13:   978-0-9824855-2-1

Cover Illustration by Fear Nought Publishing

Lightfall is lovingly dedicated to my mother, Barbara Shelton, who deserves a thousand books.

THE LIGHTFALL IS COMING

Sugar Roses, Oklahoma, population eighteen thousand: a sleepy, conservative college town known—though not widely—for its Christian infotainment company, Saving Grace, and a misguided police prosecution. Nothing much ever happened here worth knowing about...until now. Sugar Roses is about to become a flashpoint for the prophesied End of the World.

Meet the eyewitnesses:

Shay Veracruz—a frustrated customer service rep at Saving Grace, widowed mother to four-year-old Lacey.

Zack Heath—a theatre professor at Southern Oklahoma State University; currently sleeping with Shay...and a number of his students.

Buddy Sims—a mentally retarded adult paperboy who converses with his own personal Jesus.

Amanda Quinlan—an angst-ridden nineteen-year-old blogger, who shelves books at the Sugar Roses library while fretting she may be pregnant.

Scott Glass—local boy made good, a Hollywood screenwriter come home to write about the Sugar Roses police department.

Phillip Mars—the openly gay book department manager at Bayeux Books, Music and Video.

And *Danny Murcheson*—a redneck, domestic beer enthusiast, and avenger-in-training who takes orders from a bloodthirsty Voice in his head.

"This is our Apocalypse," Amanda writes. "Tell me you can't feel it coming. Does anyone hear me calling for help?" Together this cross section of America's Bible Belt will face a series of unprecedented catastrophes. Are these events truly supernatural? Do they presage the foretold Apocalypse? And who will be moral and strong enough to survive? Only one thing is certain as we begin Earth's final story:

The endgame has already begun.

Part One
Παρουσία

Presence

Reprinted by permission of Global NewsNet, 10 March 20--:

Bee Gone: The Mystery of the Missing Millions

Story by Meredith Keguchi-Feinstein

VISALIA, CA—Farmer Jeff Crundy has seen mysteries of nature in his 42 years, but even the crop circle he found on his property in 1996 couldn't prepare him for a new and disturbing enigma: Hundreds of millions of bees have gone missing in America over the last few months. Whole colonies have vanished, some seemingly overnight. Farmers in Texas and along the east coast report over 70 percent losses. The mystery has been reported in fully half the states in the union, and no one seems to know exactly where the bees have gone.

"It's the dangedest thing," Crundy sighs, wiping his forehead with a John Deere cap. "I need these bees for pollination. This is going to make things a mite tricky, I can tell you that." The American Beekeeping Federation claims bee pollination is essential to a full third of our diet. The cost of a replacement hive has risen from $45 to $135 in less than three years. "[Bee] suppliers have tripled the cost," Crundy laughs. "Thanks a lot, guys. Have fun sleeping at night." His math checks out. A queen bee alone costs $15, and populations are limited across the board. The number of beehives in America has dropped by 25 percent, while the number of beekeepers dwindled by half.

The phenomenon is clear and pronounced enough that researchers have given it a name: "colony collapse disorder." Rapid die-offs have been variously attributed to global warming, mite infestation, suburban sprawl, pesticides, even a plague of insect immunodeficiency. "All I know is, there ain't no bees," Crundy shrugs. He is literally correct. Bees usually dispose of their dead by shoving them out the front of the hive, yet there are no piles of honeybee corpses in front of depleted hives. The hives are full of

1

honey and pollen, like the legendary half-eaten breakfast discovered aboard an abandoned sailing ship. It's as if the bees have simply vanished from existence....

A

If and when the Rapture exploded over the planet like a sunrise, it would not come to Sugar Roses first—but then again, nothing ever had. An hour southeast of Norman, three hours north of Dallas, ten years behind either coast, the small town clutched a few thin inches of epidermal topsoil over Oklahoma's red clay muscle. Deep below, veins of black arterial sludge enabled Sugar Roses' faltering "oal well bidness." Clouds the color of sidewalks drifted on the dusty wind above, ominous tall ships laden with the energy of a plundering piratical storm.

Sugar Roses is known, except it isn't, for three things.

First, its lovely name. Originally saddled with the less melodious moniker Bugfuskee, the town was renamed in honor of a grandiose wedding between John Calloway Walton, then governor of Oklahoma, and Madeleine Orick in June 1923. To this day a faded mural of the event could be ascertained from the paint flakes on Mertham's Mercantile downtown. Less reminisced about was the shameful impeachment of John Walton four months later; the governor was charged with disregard of the state constitution in the aftermath of the Tulsa Race Riot.

Second, miscarriage of justice. Of Sugar Roses' eighteen thousand citizens, approximately ten thousand bought, shoplifted, or otherwise acquired copies of Scott Turow's recent nonfiction opus *Court of Law*, which describes the unfair incarceration and torture of one Poke Duncan in 1987. Mr. Duncan's alibi, that he was too busy trying to date rape a chubby Stars Drive-Thru counter girl in Holdenville at the time to murder anyone in Sugar Roses, didn't sway an angry jury, especially since the vengeful attempted rape victim refused to back his story. Mr. Duncan came within twenty minutes of being partially ionized in Old Smoky, the famous electric chair in McAlester State Prison, before the Innocence Project freed him on DNA evidence in 1998. Turow's book disappointingly described Sugar Roses as "rural, churchy."

Third, the international success story that is Saving Grace, Incorporated. Saving Grace, of course, is the well-known Christian book and novelty manufacturing company headquartered near the

3

intersection of Highway 19 and I-35 at the northwest corner of town. The joke around Sugar Roses is it'd take a dang sight more than an interstate and parallel railroad tracks to keep the busy Christian soldiers at Saving Grace away from the Choctaw Raindance Casino on the other side. Even Southern Baptists appreciate an eight-dollar Sunday brunch buffet. And the chicken fried steak is outstanding!

The garage-door-sized plaque outside reads, "Godliness With Contentment—I Timothy 6." Most Christians in town knew the rest of the phrase: "...is great gain." And so it was.

The *Christian Soldiers* series of apocalyptic novels sold over seventy million copies, and its media-savvy authors were only eight books into their twelve-part saga. Movie effects spectacle *Christian Soldiers IV: Beasts Full of Eyes* opened the Thanksgiving before to over twenty million dollars, eventually pulling in a respectable hundred and twenty million take. It was rumored *Episode V: Whore of Babylon* might be a musical, with lyrics by Tim Rice and singles from Amy Lee and Richard Marx. Faith Hill and Tim McGraw released a successful Christmas album, *Do You Hear What I Hear*, on the Saving Grace label.

The company also co-produced the popular *Li'l Warriors* DVD series, in which computer-generated chipmunks and other woodland creatures fought the forces of unholy darkness with moral sentiments from the New Testament. (Most of the proceeds went to World Vision International and Rough Draft Korea.) All in all, about one in nine Garvin County residents worked for Saving Grace, and the company pulled in combined revenues of close to half a billion dollars a year.

Wendell "Buddy" Sims, a lumpy blond stump of a man in his early thirties, looked up at the phalanx of oncoming weather as he waited for Mr. Holcomb to finish bagging his day's bundle. Buddy worked twenty hours a week delivering papers for the *Sugar Roses Sentinel*, an unthreatening daily that still bore the Emersonian legend, "The wise man prays, not for safety from danger, but deliverance from fear." The Church News sat directly across from the pagan horoscope at the end of each day's dozen or so pages. There were over forty churches in Sugar Roses, everything from gleefully Freewill Baptists to resignedly predestined Calvinists, with a few defensive Mormons and Jehovah's Witnesses bridging the dogmatic gap. It was possible to get naked, drunk and saved on a Saturday night, just so long as the sinner wasn't caught by anyone who mattered before Sunday morning.

The God experience was more personal and elemental for Buddy Sims. Buddy drowned in the pond at Byrd's Mill when he was twelve, ten years after doctors diagnosed Buddy with fetal alcohol syndrome and mild mental retardation. Panicked by a roiling tangle of water moccasins, Buddy swallowed two lungfuls of water and sank upside-down. As he crawled over slimy rocks, terrified into mental paralysis, he found himself warmed by a heart-shaped concentration of light. The golden, ethereal valentine melted scales from his eyes. Jesus sauntered toward him, affected by the green water only to the degree that it wafted the bleachy white sleeves of his Messianic bathrobe. Jesus the Nazarene looked much like circa-1985 Kenny Loggins.

"Buddy," he said, smiling. "I love you, Buddy. My Daddy and me love you. You have to be our friend now, okay?" Buddy's fear-maddened father yanked him above the surface. Jesus stayed in Buddy's bloodstream. Buddy prayed about twenty times a day. Sometimes he prayed for the ability to remember anything other than Bible verses and Beatle lyrics. Other times he prayed for good TV to come on.

"Looks like it might be a thunder-boomer," Buddy observed.

"I wouldn't doubt it," Mr. Holcomb agreed. "Kinda feels all clingy and sharp outside, dudnit."

"Yessir, it sure does."

"You best get movin' 'fore you get drenched. I think I 'bout gotcha fixed up here, Buddy. You have a good day now, awright?"

"Can't help but have a good day, Mr. Holcomb. It's the only kind the Lord makes." Mr. Holcomb patted Buddy on the shoulder affectionately and watched as he pedaled slowly up Providence Avenue. He remembered the day Buddy told him, "Jesus sure has given me a wonderful life, Mr. Holcomb." It was true. Buddy Sims had friends all over town. The good people of Sugar Roses, much like Jesus himself, would always embrace a simple heart.

Buddy had two good-sized bundles to deliver. The lesser

went to middle-class single family residences between Broadway and Anderson Parkway, but first he'd deliver the biggest bag of papers to Saving Grace. The corporate headquarters were conspicuously designed in the shape of a Christian cross, which in turn was intelligently redesigned from the tau, the first initial of Tammuz, a Babylonian deity. And so it goes. An unimaginative architectural concept, to be sure, but solidly reassuring in the broad helicopter view hanging over the marble reception desk. The shot was taken facing east; it caught most of Sugar Roses but none of the Choctaws' tribal land. The most prominent buildings in sight were the Heartland Mall, the Standard Hotel, the hospital on Townsend, and the inevitable Super Wal-Mart, all clustered in the northeast corner of town.

"Hey, Buddy," grinned Bettina, the near-skeletal lead receptionist. Bettina had been answering phones for Saving Grace since it opened its doors in 1973. They were different doors then, simple wooden doors in a former two-bedroom apartment in Ada, forty minutes east of Sugar Roses. Now rain skittered against the bank of thick electronic plexi airlock doors, and beyond that, it dripped off the banana seat of Buddy's bicycle as it rested unchained against an ornamental redbud. "Looks like you're about to get soaked."

"Thunder-boomer," Buddy agreed affably. Bettina made sure he had his special pass card and unlocked the security door to the rest of the building.

"How's your daddy doin'?"

"My daddy's kickin' like chicken!"

"That's what I like to hear," Bettina smiled, wondering yet again what that expression meant and where Buddy learned it. "You be good now."

Buddy shuffled through the door, a bag full of unsurprising news draped ponderously over his shoulder. He looked like Barney Rubble playing Santa Claus. "Ain't no other way to be," Buddy grinned. "Have a good day. I love you."

"We love you, too, Buddy," she said, as the security door clicked behind him. The air conditioner sighed, saving Bettina the trouble. She went back to her sudoku. "Bless his heart," she added, a peculiarly Bible Belt gesundheit that made it okay to think patronizing, even insulting thoughts about anyone. He's just slow as molasses, Bettina thought. Bless his heart.

As Buddy made his way through the building, he greeted each employee with radiant affection. "You're my friend!" he'd cry. "I love you!" "Let's do lunch!" Unfortunately, he couldn't remember most customers' names, so he referred to them as Pardner or Sweetheart. Yet there was nothing cynical or ironic about Sugar Roses' adoration of Buddy Sims, nor any restraint in his love for everyone and everything in it. The Lord blessed Buddy with that time-honored decoupage objective, serenity.

Shay Veracruz, thirty, short, and lushly feminine in the way of attractive Hispanic women, watched Buddy work the office and vice versa. Shay worked in customer service, answering phones eight hours a day and counting the minutes until each successive break. Sometimes she played math games in her head: *I've completed an hour. There are seven more to go, not counting lunch. Twelve point five percent of my day. Only eighty-seven point five percent left.* She imagined the time ticking off a bar like an Internet download: *Now I'm enjoying my coffee break. I timed it so I'm exactly a third of the way through my day. Now I have only three and three quarter hours to go, almost exactly the same length as* Gone With the Wind. *Now Scarlett goes to a party at Twelve Oaks. Now the assault on Atlanta. Where shall I go? What shall I do? Frankly, my dear, I don't give a damn. I mean darn. Can't cuss at work, even in my head, or I'll slip around one of the customers.* And so it went.

Over Shay's desk was a poster of a raccoon named Spike. Spike was the allegedly "edgy" Li'l Warrior who often sided with Saint Peter in Biblical disputes. Once, in a musical time warp accident, Spike helped Peter by gnawing off the ear of a Roman centurion. In this particular poster, a supposed perquisite of employment at Saving Grace, Inc., Spike rode a skateboard, and a speech bubble emerged from his sardonic muzzle. The bubble advised passersby to "GIVE UR PROPZ 2 JESUS!!!" At the request of Shay's supervisor Travis, a deacon in the Church of Christ, this replaced a quasi-inspirational poster with a self-hugging Happy Bunny and the aphorism, "Hating you makes me all warm inside." Her daughter Lacey liked both posters. The Lord never offered His opinion. The Lord, in point of fact, had been too busy to give Shay

7

a moment of His time for several years now, and she was starting to resent it.

"Hey, Buddy," she said, after putting a lonely Methodist on hold, you want some candy?"

"Packed with peanuts, Snickers really satisfies."

"I know, I totally agree with you. Here," she smiled, handing him a trial size Mounds bar. "These Snickers have coconut inside them."

"Thank you, sweetheart. I love you. You're the apple of my eye."

She watched him shuffle on his way and resumed a polite telephonic disagreement about the cost of illuminated stationery. "Ma'am, I know, I understand what you're saying, but the flyer clearly stated the special on God's Divine Word Post-Its would expire in February....Did he really?...Yes, I know. Have you seen our new special on Little Good Book phone organizers?" *Only five and a half hours to go, not counting lunch. Another freakin' Fiesta Salad from Taco Bell. Some fiesta.*

Maybe a drink with Judy after work. Another episode of *Survivor.* Maybe Zack would come over, a twelve-pack of Michelobs in tow. Better yet, maybe he wouldn't, and she'd get six hours of uninterrupted sleep.

Buddy turned a corner into the executive wing. Here cubicles evolved into actual offices, each with a snazzy glass name plaque. Reproductions of Christian paintings from the Italian Renaissance adorned the walls. Buddy admired them as he passed: *Mary looks at baby Jesus sleeping. A pretty lady angel holds Jesus, his cross, and a cup. A man angel in hospital pajamas and a sheet flies up into the sky and points at the Lord.*

Intimidated, Buddy kept conversations in this wing to a minimum, but he still liked to put the *Sentinel* directly into each executive's hand. Near the end of the hall, he padded into the office suite of Chuck Pettigrew, Senior V.P. of International Marketing. Mr. Pettigrew (or, as Buddy knew him, Mr. Pardner) was usually on the phone, so Buddy had to settle for leaving the *Sentinel* with his young assistant Paul. Buddy looked forward to seeing Paul, a nice black-haired man with interesting glasses who told him indecipherable knock-knock jokes, so he was surprised and disappointed to find both men missing. Buddy wandered in and listened for voices. Sure enough, he heard Mr. Pettigrew agreeing with someone nearby. "Yes," Mr. Pettigrew sighed. "Ah, yes."

It sounded like Mr. Pettigrew was inside a door in the back. It looked like a closet. Buddy opened the door. It was really a bathroom. Buddy forgot you could have an office with a bathroom inside it.

Mr. Pettigrew was sitting on the floor. Paul leaned over him but turned away quickly, grabbing his crotch. Mr. Pettigrew was sweaty and red now. "You should never come in here!" he yelled.

Careful! He was yelling! Was Paul getting ready to pee on Mr. Pardner? Standing, yelling! Mr. Pardner was ready to fight!

Buddy fled in a panic.

"I don't do that!" Pettigrew protested lamely, his body a taut exclamation point of fear.

Buddy left papers behind. He couldn't go back to that office. He didn't know what to do, so he went to Bettina and asked for help. When he told Bettina what happened, Bettina turned white and made some very confusing phone calls. Then things got weird and excited and somebody called Buddy's boss, Mr. Holcomb, to sort it all out. Mr. Holcomb sent Buddy home early that day, with pay and a soda, and he finished Buddy's deliveries himself.

Buddy didn't understand the *Sentinel* headline the next day, but he did recognize Mr. Pardner's picture on the front.

TRANSCRIPTS: AG360

Reprinted by permission of GlobalNewsNet.com; posted 12 March 20—

Aired March 11, 20-- - 22:00 ET

THIS IS A RUSH TRANSCRIPT. THIS COPY MAY NOT BE IN ITS FINAL FORM AND MAY BE UPDATED.

ARGYLE GREENWOOD, GNN ANCHOR: Good evening, everyone. Tonight, we'll take a look at an ongoing ecological catastrophe. Coral reefs are dying all over the planet, and the reason why may come as a surprise. GNN's Lauren Couey reports.

(BEGIN VIDEOTAPE)

LAUREN COUEY, GNN CORRESPONDENT: They are among the most beautiful ecosystems on earth. Home to countless species of aquatic wildlife, they're the undersea jewels of equatorial oceans. And they are dying. Experts say ten percent of them are already gone, with another sixty percent at risk. It's hard to say what the long-term impact of their disappearance will be, but no one doubts the loss to local fishermen – and fish eaters – will be devastating.

TOM SYNAR, DIRECTOR, THE NATURE CONSERVANCY:

We have programs in place to protect the Great Barrier Reef and other key areas, but we can't say for sure yet how well they're working. Maybe in twenty or thirty years we'll know. But for right now, we can't even keep up with human influence, let alone anything else. Humans are the number one threat facing these environments. We overfish. We pollute. Global warming takes its toll. Coral reefs can only survive within a narrow range of environmental conditions, and I'm sorry to say, we affect every one of them every day we go near them.

COUEY (ON-CAMERA): Right now, coral reefs in human areas are threatened by an unexpected culprit: herpes, the same virus that causes cold sores and sexually transmitted infections in people.

SYNAR: It seems counterintuitive, I know, but we've analyzed these areas for viral and microbial diseases, and herpes is the biggest factor in every location we studied. It's knocking the chemical balance out of kilter everywhere we look. The simple fact is, if a coral reef is anywhere near human beings, that coral reef will get sick and start to die. We can't afford to lose seventy percent of the world's coral reefs. We can't afford to lose seventy percent of anything.

COUEY: Unfortunately, the solution to this ecological nightmare scenario remains elusive. Here in Australia, marine biologists are struggling to find a way to avert an apocalypse in paradise. Lauren Couey, GNN, Melbourne.

(END VIDEOTAPE)

GREENWOOD: Serious stuff. For more on this subject, visit GlobalNewsNet.com/coral and submit your ideas on how to save a priceless, irreplaceable resource. You can also answer today's poll question, "Is coral necessary, or is plastic just as good?" Still to come, presidential elections: Do they really make a difference in the lives of ordinary Americans? And coming up after the break, you won't believe what Lindsay Lohan had to say about the North American Free Trade Agreement. We'll have that story when *AG360* continues.

(COMMERCIAL BREAK)

TO ORDER A VIDEO OF THIS TRANSCRIPT, PLEASE CALL 800-GNET-NEWS OR USE OUR SECURE ONLINE ORDER FORM LOCATED AT www.GlobalNewsNet.com.

B

Amanda Quinlan kicked a step roller down the aisle desultorily, then trudged after it toward 700.755, religious art. Concentrating on her library job was pathetically far beyond her today. Life was sucking for bus change. The last five text messages she received were all angry abbreviations from Tyler, culminating in the comprehensive, "u suk ur a bitch." True enough, she decided. A bitch who could do a lot better. Who needed Tyler, with his stringy green hair and his stupid Boba Fett tattoo and his weird collection of tentacle porn and his inexplicable fondness for Funyuns? Who needed Tyler's ridonkulous scooter and his smelly old T-shirts from Hot Topic and that weird habit he had of scratching his ear 'til it bled? It's not like she couldn't stand to be away from him for five minutes. Five hours, even. Maybe fifteen hours.

Fuck!

On top of which, she was probably coming down with SARS or avian flu—the back of her throat tasted like day-old Albanian puke—and she still had two hours left on her shift. Her boss Claudia was being a total rag hag. Amanda was out of cigarettes except for two limp GPCs she found deep in her backpack. She kept getting creepy emails from pervos at work. After harsh semesters in Music Theory and Algebra, retaining a three-point GPA seemed like a pipe dream. She had some weed left, but her neo-fascist mom had decided not to pay for her cable so she couldn't veg out in front of three hours of *Law and Order* reruns. Her new tragus piercing itched like a man-eating bitch.

Amanda leafed through the next book in her return stack, a collection of woodcuts by Albrecht Dürer. Very cool. She skimmed the biographical intro. Dürer was famous by the time he was thirty, known throughout Europe for his Biblical illustrations. Must be nice, she thought, to make a living creating art. Amanda painted, mostly faceless nude portraits of herself. She told people the model was her sister in Little Rock. Hence Amanda spent a fair amount of time sitting nude and cross-legged in front of a full-length mirror. By her own estimation she augmented herself by a full cup size in every painting. The skinny white Amanda bodies waited cryptically, each visage a blurry void of expectation, an orifice aching to be fed.

Then there was the serpentine Chihuahua coiled around an apple. She liked that painting best, even though it made her mom think she was psychotic. She had mixed feelings about the crying baby with a human heart rattle. She sketched that one after an intensely vivid nightmare. In the dream the baby smeared blood all over her face, clothes, and stroller, then cried Amanda's name until she woke doubled over from cramps.

She was now two days late. Which was probably stress, she thought. How could she not be fucking stressed with all this shit in her life? It'd be just like Tyler, wouldn't it? She'd probably wind up living alone with a baby in a damn mini-storage or something. Two days late. Except she couldn't be pregnant, could she? They'd been careful. She made Tyler wear a condom every time. Well, okay, maybe not every time, but it wasn't like she didn't know where she was in her cycle. Shit!

She turned another page to reveal Dürer's illumination of Revelation chapter twelve, "The Dragon with Seven Heads." One of the heads looked like a goat. Another, more apelike extremity vomited fire. The beast's naked tail lashed a third of the stars from heaven. Above the creature and its escort, the sneering whore of Babylon, a male figure crouched in the clouds. The figure looked down condescendingly, his right hand curled in an oddly Hindu two-fingered blessing. The figure, whoever he or He was, looked like Jerry Garcia.

The Apocalypse, Amanda thought. The Unveiling at the End of the World. Amanda didn't believe in God anymore, only three years after losing her virginity to a golden-skinned counselor at Falls Creek Christian Summer Camp, but she thought there might be something to all this spiritual truth stuff. Beasts were indeed roaming the earth. She knew them, by email address if not by name. She closed the book and slid it into place on a high shelf.

"Cool tatt," a voice said from behind her.

She whipped around. Look at this douchebag. Thirty-five if he was a day, hair that wasn't so much thinning as evaporating, thirty pounds overweight, and buttoned inside a wrinkled blue shirt from, like, 1985. "What?"

"I said I like your tattoo. Where'd you get it? I thought ink

14

was illegal here."

Ink. Jesus Christ. "Tattoos were legalized a few years ago, but I got most of mine from a guy named Tiger in the City before the ban lifted. Can I help you find something?"

"What's it mean, your tattoo?" the guy persisted, pointing at a character on her back. Which was ugh. Another pervo. She must have revealed the tattoo when she stretched to file the Dürer book.

"Oh. It means strength, in Japanese."

"I like it," the guy repeated. "I've got a Marvin the Martian on my arm." He pointed excitedly at his left upper sleeve.

"Cool," she admitted.

"Yeah, I used to have a buddy in Hollywood who was a tattoo artist. But seriously, embarrassing cliché aside, do I know you from somewhere?"

She froze, still perched on the wobbly step roller like some 1950s TV housewife fleeing a mouse. "I don't know. I work here."

"I used to live here, in Sugar Roses. Went to college at SOSU. You been working here long?"

"Just a few months."

"Do you go to SOSU?"

"I do now."

"Huh. Maybe I met you before I left for California."

"That was how many years ago?"

"Over a dozen."

"I was a kid then," she said, stepping down to floor level. "I didn't know anybody." Pervo. God, it sucked being five-four sometimes. He loomed eight inches over her now, still beaming the crookedly optimistic grin of the brain-damaged.

"No, I…yeah, I guess not. I don't know. You just look really familiar to me. Maybe you look like you belong in California. Well, anyway. Hi. I'm Scott Glass. I'm in town for a couple of

15

weeks doing some work for Excelsior."

"Excelsior? Like, Excelsior movies?"

"The studio, yeah. I'm a writer."

"Really." Could he be any more chock full of shit? "You write movies," she added, in the same flat tone she might use to comment, for example, *I hear you wear a utility belt and fight crime.*

"Lucky me," Scott said, laughing. "And you are?"

She found herself unable to muster the energy she'd need to buck protocol and ignore him. "I'm Amanda. Like...what does Excelsior want with Sugar Roses?"

"Fair question. You know the Turow book, you work in a library."

"*Court of Law.* We've been checked out for months."

"That's the one. Excelsior's optioned it for a movie. I've been hired to write a draft of the screenplay. Two other guys are writing one, too. If the studio likes my version better than theirs, then I get hired to write the next draft. At which point," he laughed, "they'll probably bring in Akiva Goldsman or Susannah Grant or somebody to polish it off and take all the credit."

"I don't know who they are."

"Nor should you, in fact. They're the masterminds behind *Batman & Robin* and *Pocahontas.*"

"Oh. Well, that doesn't sound good, then."

"Yeah, well," Scott admitted, "they also wrote *A Beautiful Mind* and *Erin Brockovich.*"

"Oh."

"So they've done some good stuff. It's all...delicate, y'know? One false move can turn a good script into a bad movie. Never the other way around, unfortunately."

"Right."

An awkward half-second passed. "So. I uh...didn't mean

16

to bother you. Just…you looked familiar. I don't know a lot of people in this town anymore."

"Right."

"I'll let you work. Sorry. I uh…right. Good to meet you." He bowed stiffly and turned to walk away.

She cocked a hip and wondered why she might be interested in stopping him. "Hey, wait," she said.

He turned back. "Yeah?"

"You don't really work for Excelsior, do you?"

"Yeah, I really do."

"And you live in, like, Hollywood."

"Nine double-oh two eight." His ZIP code.

"California."

"That's the one."

She wanted to believe him. "How does anybody go from Sugar Roses to Hollywood? Is that even possible?"

"Well," he said, scratching his neck, "I can only speak for myself, but…I drove my car there, so…yeah. It is possible."

"It seems like, I don't know, going to Jupiter or something."

"My friend, you have no idea. It wasn't easy. I miss…I don't know…" He indicated the library around them and, perhaps, the town beyond. "Sanity."

"*This* is sanity?"

"Yeah, this is normalcy. Hollywood is Movieland. Plastic. One big special effect."

"I just want to get out of Sugar Roses."

"I did, too. And you can. I swear, it can be done."

She gazed at him and wondered at the strange turns a world and a Wednesday might take. This fuckhat made it to California.

17

He stared back. "The thing is," he said finally, "it isn't what you think it's going to be. It's easier and harder and...I don't know, God, it'll kill you. It'll make you feel like shit until you feel like The God of All You Survey. Then it'll make you feel like even shittier shit, 'cause you know in the long run it's just...product. The guys I work for, they don't care about movies. They could be selling shoes or McDonald's or feminine hygiene products, they don't care. Right now I'm writing for Excelsior Upgrade, their so-called 'indie' division? But of course I'm really working for Excelsior, which in turn works for Argent Zurich, which in turn works for a vast nameless body of shareholders."

"Argent Zurich?"

"The global investment firm. They buy money. Then they sell it to people who want more money. So you can see where the artistry comes in."

"You don't sound happy to be there. It sounds like a hell of a life to me. Better than here."

"I know. I worked so many years to get where I am. And now...it's driving me crazy. Be careful what you wish for."

"Didn't I hear something about Argent Zurich in the news?"

"Yeah, some joker wrote letters to the paper claiming he's gonna commit some kinda terrorist act against the corporation."

The letters, written in red longhand on loose leaf paper, were signed "A.Q.U.S.A." "Hundreds will die," the letters insisted. "We are the barbarians at your gate. You cannot stop us."

"Scary."

"I worked at Disney for a while," Scott said, shrugging. "For a coupla years after 9/11, even Mauschwitz was rattled. They installed metal detectors at Disneyland."

"Mauschwitz?"

"Yeah, that's what they call Disney in L.A. It's not always the most fun place to work."

"All those animated rodents."

"Exactly. But they whistle while they work. Or Snow White beats them."

Amanda laughed, glad to be distracted from her crapathon morning. Unfortunately, she could see Claudia glaring at her from Circulation. *Nod at Claudia, Amanda. Make the scary bitch put her talons away.* "I gotta get to work. My boss is, you know, kind of a she-harpy."

"Are there he-harpies?"

"Man," she sighed, "don't even get me started."

Scott drifted off toward a bank of Web-connected computers. There he checked his Hotmail, Ain't It Cool News, GNN, and the *Sugar Roses Sentinel* website. He shouldn't have been flirting with Amanda, if that's what he was doing. Even Scott wasn't sure. He imagined poor Jessica stuck at work—missing him, he hoped—and felt a cramp of remorse.

Oh, look. Some knuckle-dragging ex-Marine on the *Sentinel* message board was decrying "Unholywood's" interest in a *Court of Law* film adaptation. "They don't know anything about Sugar Roses," the jarhead insisted. "All they know how to do is snort cocaine and spit in Christians' faces and make porno hookers out of our poor little girls." Maybe so, Scott agreed, but at least we can get a decent latte.

Then it hit him: Porno hookers. He didn't dare check his guess—the site was probably filtered here anyway—but he knew exactly where he'd seen Amanda and her kanji tattoo. Strength indeed. Was there a cool way to ask her? His mind raced through a dozen scenarios, two ending in sweaty library restroom fornication, most in tragic humiliation.

Amanda, he felt certain, was a model on RiotGrrlz.com, the beloved alternative softcore site that functioned as a kind of naughty Facebook for chubby or otherwise imperfect girls with piercings, tattoos, and sundry eclectic adornments. Her contradictory affection for *Aqua Teen Hunger Force* and Nabokov caught his eye on a Friday night wank surf. He'd seen her naked long before he met her. Stranger yet, that wasn't an odd experience for people working in the Hollywood film industry.

So she made a few bucks on the website, probably spent it on drugs or DVDs or some guy, all while drifting through undemanding classes at Southeastern Oklahoma State. Then, when Riot Grrlz failed to deliver on the glamour it promised, she went back to the real world of overdue books and a livelihood that didn't arrive care of PayPal. Across the library floor, she straightened VHS tapes and magazines. He smiled as she wiped a crimson blade of hair from her eye, tucking it back into her otherwise jet-black coiffure.

SUGAR ROSES SENTINEL

Serving Sugar Roses Since 1924

Forums > Headlines: Sugar Roses, OK > Religion

truthseeker (Old Pro) – Posted March 12, 20-- 01:44

> Hey, have any of you seen a pastor named Melissa Scott on TV? I saw her last night and couldn't get her out of my head. She has hair down to her waist and speaks in many different languages. I did some Google research on her and found out she used to be married to another pastor named Dr. Gene Scott. I know this is wrong to say, but she is incredibly hot! What's the story there?

Posts: 372 | Location: Oklahoma | Registered: January 07, 20—

SugarRosesNeedsChange (Old Pro) – Posted March 12, 20-- 09:13

> Truthseeker, whatever her qualifications for running the Gene Scott empire, Pastor Melissa Pastore Scott is indeed, to put it in the vernacular, hot. In fact, she has proof: In 1994, she won the title Miss Nude Can-Am Exotic. This was around the time she performed in adult videos ("Picture Perfect," for example) under the name Barbi Bridges. There's evidence that her father, Frank Peroff, was a Canadian Mafioso. She first appeared on Dr. Gene's "University Network" as a cheesy bikini dancer, but soon she was the only woman on the show. She apparently studied theology with Scott for about ten years before he died of cancer at age 75. She was only 36—You go, Pastor Gene!

> This was all available on Wikipedia for a while, but now the entry is gone, supposedly because it was vandalized by users. I have fond memories of getting high back in the 1980s—I would never stoop to such behavior in the present,

21

of course—and watching Gene berate heathens and sinners for hours on end. If his viewers didn't cough up enough cash, he'd scream at them as well. Mostly he just smoked his cigars, pontificated about esoteric Bible translation issues, and stared into space. Sometimes he'd sing, a habit Melissa has taken up with what may be described, in delicacy, as limited success. My favorite hymn was a catchy little ditty called "Kill a Pissant for Jesus." When Pastor Gene grew tired of talking about Jesus in Greek and Aramaic, he'd sermonize about UFOs and the Pyramids. I called his show once, claiming my sister was hooked on drugs and her behavior seemed similar to his, and he insulted me right on the air. "Listen, you little smartmouth!" he bellowed. "Let me tell you something! You're no damn good in the eyes of the Lord! You can't see holy when it's sittin' in front of you, so repent or get your sinning ass the hell out of my way!" My companion and I laughed for days.

I miss the old coot. I'm surprised Pastor Melissa isn't preaching in a bikini. It's probably what dirty old Pastor Gene would have wanted.

Posts: 1478 | Location: Oklahoma | Registered: October 22, 1999

Γ

Verle Hibberd pulled into the Standard Hotel parking lot and finished his cigarette. The bar was hopping, partly thanks to Wednesday Karaoke Nite. Some young socialite inside was caterwauling to "Jesus Take the Wheel"—probably Staci, shaming her ex-husband again by crooning at every buck-ass cowboy in town. She'd embarrassed Verle once by starting to give him a lapdance. He got up and stormed outside, angry for a reason he didn't fully understand.

Yep, there was Danny Murcheson's old truck, with Calvin pissing on a Ford emblem in the back window. Verle didn't know much about *Calvin and Hobbes*, but he sure didn't remember the kid having any kind of urinary streak in the Sunday paper. Some damn fool redrew the character to appeal to redneck idiots, and damned if Danny Murcheson wasn't redneck idiot enough to enjoy it. Verle would happily bet his life's savings there was at least an old pop can in the back of that truck, and probably half a dozen Busch cans as well.

When Danny wasn't out working some construction site, he holed up in his rickety old house on the edge of town. He devoted most of the house's wall space to cheesecake posters, gun racks and shelves full of ammo. There might even be army surplus munitions in there, shit he bought off the Internet black market. Danny's favorite song was a jaunty number from Cross Canadian Ragweed called "Them Oklahoma Boys," in which Ragweed claimed them Oklahoma boys rolled their joints all wrong. Verle had seen Danny Murcheson outsmarted by furniture on at least two occasions. He was a small man with a smaller life, even smaller than Verle's in too many ways, but he'd been in Verle's life too long to worry about it now.

Ah, well. Verle crushed the remains of his cigarette into the gravel and climbed the front stoop, where Fred Tibbs took his ten dollar bill and waved him in without a word. Sure enough, Staci was finishing her moment in the spotlight by pleading for Jesus to save her from this road she was on as she gazed into the eyes of some poor woman's husband. No doubt Tom Stokes was still paying for them titties of hers. Her little black dress was so tight

Verle could tell what kind of underwear she was wearing. Her bra was too tight. Was thirty-eight too old to wear a thong? Apparently Danny Murcheson didn't think so. His eyes were glued to Staci's backside like a hungry dog watching a man tear into a ribeye.

"I'd tell you to take a picture," Verle said, punching Danny's arm, "but you can probably find one on your computer somewhere."

"Oh, son, would I hit that like I mean it," Danny agreed. "Ol' Tom's a good fella, but his wife gets me harder'n Chinese algebra."

"Ex-wife."

"'Zactly. Dang, I gotta get my pecker wet, Verle. I got balls the color a blackberries."

"Size, too, I bet."

"Shi-i-it," Danny drawled.

The two men sucked Bud longnecks for a few minutes as a soppingly drunk college kid warbled his way through four minutes of heavy metal bullshit. His friends egged him on with encouragements like "Asshole!" and "You suck suck SUUUUCK!" If Verle had friends like that, he'd never stop smackin' 'em.

A familiar quartet took up residence for the night at a booth in the corner. Verle and Danny played weekend flag football with one of the four, a big guy named Rick Orzabal who sat with one arm draped casually over his hot Japanese-American wife. The other two Verle knew by reputation: The fella worked as a pharmacist at Walgreen's, while his wife stayed home to raise a six-year-old daughter from a previous marriage. Nice people, give or take a few drinks, but alcoholism wasn't what brought them out to the Standard three nights a week. No, these were what folks used to call "swingers." Nowadays, swingers liked to say they were "in the lifestyle," as if they'd taken up windsurfing.

Verle made the mistake one inebriated night of letting Danny in on the secret. Now it came up almost every damn Wednesday. Sure enough, Danny's eyes zeroed in on Mrs. Orzabal. "Lemme ask you something," Danny began.

"No."

"No, lemme ask you something; or no to what I was gonna ask?"

"Good question. Both."

Danny scratched the patchy stubble on his pockmarked chin. "You mean to tell me you wouldn't crawl over Rick to get to that?"

Verle shuddered. "Not unless they invented a penicillin that knows gol-damn karate."

"You been single too long."

"Maybe not long enough." Verle's ex, April, up and left two years ago in a fit of postpartum depression. Now Verle got to see his kids two weekends a month. Apparently April, class act that she was, once told his teenage daughter, "Your daddy's all right; the Good Lord just cursed him with a dick like a thumb in a rubber." Which was true, gol-damn it, but nobody else ever complained. You didn't hear him bitching when her idea of sexual wildfire was to take off her Hello Kitty nightshirt.

"What you need," Danny insisted, "is somethin' like that over there." He pointed across the bar to the pool tables, where, often as not, the unskilled won money from the un-sober.

"Which one?"

"There, in the back, with her fat friend."

Yeah, Verle had to admit, Danny'd pegged his type. He sat next to the girl—Shay something—one night, but he'd been too chicken to talk to her. That story he kept to himself. There was something about Shay that dissuaded any man with a GED in or a Skoal ring on his pocket. Besides, Verle heard she worked at Saving Grace, which probably meant she was too refined and Christian to put up with a smelly old cuss like him.

Shay text messaged someone on her cell phone. Her fat friend, who looked like H. R. Pufnstuf in a pair of Tony Lamas, kidded her about it in braying screeches. Judy something. There's always a fat friend, Verle thought sadly. It's like pretty girl border patrol. Get within arm's reach of a pair of ladies' jeans under size twelve, and Couch Ass starts wailing like a car alarm.

These were not the sort of thoughts, Verle decided, true gentlemen concerned themselves with.

Still. It had been a long time. Set aside how long it had been since he'd lured some embittered divorcée into his untidy bedroom; at his age, pushing fifty, he could go days without trouser timber. But there were nights, and there were days, when he dreamed of the soft, fragrant touch of the feminine. Women liked him. They did. And he damn sure liked 'em back. Problem was, they liked him when he fixed their cars, or they wanted to fix him dinner, or they drank all his beer. They didn't like to be *girls* anymore. Maybe that was it. Verle missed the way women acted when they had the time and inclination to be nothing but feminine. How long had that been? His early twenties? Verle wondered sometimes if he knew how to love a woman his own age. He felt cornered by women somehow. They made him feel like he owed 'em something before he ever said a word.

That Shay, though—What was she, maybe thirty at the most? It was hard to tell with señoritas, but there was a woman ripe as summer watermelon. Black shoulder-length hair, thick as a tar pit. Curves all the way down and around. Verle even liked her sweater. Underneath, he imagined, not bare skin—why be greedy—but silk. Sliding silk. Whisper silk.

"That is one sweet piece of ass," Danny sighed.

"…Y'know, Danny…"

"I'm jus' sayin'."

"Remind me never to take you to the ballet," Verle sighed, hoisting his beer.

"That's a deal," Danny agreed. "What, are you sayin' I ain't got a shot at a bitch like that?"

"Not if you're gonna call her a bitch, Danny. Maybe that ain't the best place for you to start."

"You don't know," Danny snapped. "You don't know nothin', Verle. Do you? You don't know what I can get."

"Yeah, if you say so."

"Oh, you callin' me a liar now, too?"

Danny got like this sometimes. "Jesus wept, Danny, no, I ain't callin' you a liar. Shit. I'm just tryin' to keep ya humble, a'right? Around these parts, it's not a bad idea to lower them expectations a yours."

"Yeah, go on, make that face at me. Go on. Laugh it up, cheese dick."

Verle chuckled, as quickly regretting it. "Settle down, hombre. Okay? Have another beer."

"Keep on talkin'."

Verle sighed heavily and drained half his longneck. Another fine night at the Standard Hotel. Yee-haw. The conversation lapsed as the two men went back to watching women drift past their feeble combined gravity, their trajectories completely unaltered.

Across the bar, Shay's purse vibrated. She dug for her cell phone, her face turning red.

"Him again?" Judy smirked.

"Let's find out," Shay answered. It was him again. Zack.

You coming over?

I can't. You come here.

And put on pants? Who has the time?

"Oh my God," Shay laughed.

"What?"

"He doesn't want to come here because he isn't dressed. Up," she added quickly.

"Who dresses up in Sugar Roses?"

"Hey! These are my best jeans."

"Oh," Judy managed, unsure for the billionth time whether Shay was kidding. "They look real pretty."

"Thank you," Shay said quietly.

27

"You want to go over there, don't you?"

"No. I wouldn't mind if he came here, but no."

"I'd go over there. Hell, yeah. He's good-lookin'. He's kinda got that…sexy dad thing going."

"No kids, though."

"No problem."

Shay smiled. "He kind of *is* like a dad. I don't think of him that way. He's kinda like…I don't know how to explain it. We hang out together. He laughs at my jokes. I don't know."

"And he never makes a move?"

"He used to," Shay lied.

"I'd let him in there so fast his zipper'd spark."

"Judy!"

It usually happened on Saturday nights. Shay got scared sometimes on Saturday night, scared it would always be like this, one disappointment after another. She put Lacey to bed and asked him in sometimes on Saturday nights. The sex was awkward at best; she allowed noises only when Lacey was over at her aunt's place. But he held her close, her fingers touched the muscles in his back, and when he left a few hours later she slept okay. Those nights she didn't dream of long, empty futures. Those nights she didn't wake up lost in the quiet. Those nights.

She wanted to trust him, but thus far, the only reassurance he ever offered her was physical. And sometimes, she caught him staring into the dark as if watching someone go.

The swingers bought each other drinks. Karaoke Nite soldiered on.

Verle slumped at the bar. *All the usual bullshit*, he thought. The usual parade of mediocre beer bottles. The usual dumbass jokes from Danny. The usual hypnosis in the presence of women. Even the same old songs; these new songs sounded just like the old ones. Staci found some cowboy to fall on. The four swingers grew bored with each other and drove home in pairs, the same pairs blessed in the Sugar Roses First Baptist Church. Verle figured "the lifestyle" must be kinda like running a fancy French restaurant: It only worked if you had a wide enough patron base.

It occurred to him he might be too drunk to drive, but that thought seemed downright un-American. Besides, he wasn't really drunk if he could walk. Even cops knew that. He rolled out of the parking lot, gravel crunching under his tires. He headed east on Highway 19, carefully watching his speed and staying between the yellow lines. He rolled down his window and listened to Sugar Roses as he left it behind.

He lit a cigarette and thought about Shay, the tumble of her hair, the curve of her shoulders, the ways he'd have to change to get a woman like her. He wondered if a woman so young and desirable could ever understand loneliness as deep, full and heavy as his.

Five miles out of town, Highway 133 broke off north. Verle was alone on the road, headed to his trailer on County Road 1510. Only a few dim stars of porch light broke the darkness. This late on a work night, most folks were sensible enough to be asleep. Most folks had families to protect, warm bodies to curl up against. Most sensible folks had better things to do than hold down a bar stool and trade lame jokes with noodle bait like Danny Murcheson—

The deer flew sideways out of the dark. Its hooves barely clicked asphalt before the truck slammed into it at forty miles an hour.

He felt the collision in his hands. A spray of blood misted in the headlights. The deer slid down the highway as silent and stiff as a carousel horse. A stab of pain, piercing hot—The cigarette lay in Verle's lap. He chucked it out the window and parked beside the road. Slowly breaching from a thick sea of shock, he rummaged for a flashlight and staggered from the truck.

He listened. No sound. He walked slowly down the highway, looking for the deer. A burst of movement exploded in the ditch to his right. He aimed the flashlight instantly, startled from his skin. The deer kicked weeds and ran in place, its left flank concave. Verle smelled bloody copper and wondered how to put the deer out of its misery.

The deer leapt to its feet. Verle fell on his ass.

The flashlight clattered to the highway, its beam a sweeping radar as it spun out of arm's reach. He and the deer stared at each other, stunned in the moonlight. The deer took two steps toward him. Its eyes were liquid black beneath Disney lashes. It steadied its footing, drew in a shuddering breath that reinflated its wounded side, ambled forward, and leaned in to butt Verle's leg gently. *Be careful, will ya? There are animals trying to live lives out here.*

"I'm sorry," Verle heard himself saying.

The deer stared at him in open chastisement, then raced into the Campbells' back pasture and the black woods beyond.

Verle woke in his trailer the next morning and wondered if he dreamt the whole thing. There was blood and fur in his grille, but no animal carcass by the side of the road as he drove in to work. He prayed for the first time in months, and he didn't take a drink for two whole weeks. By then, of course, the End Times had come.

He played no role in the ensuing events, as he himself could have easily predicted. And Verle would've sworn on a stack of Bibles his old drinkin' buddy Danny Murcheson was fated for similarly conspicuous insignificance—but in that, as in so many things, Verle could not have been more wrong.

Thursday, March 13, 20—
Into the Ocean, End It All

On the news today I saw a story about the Carteret Islands in the Pacific, the first inhabited land area disappearing from the world thanks to global warming. It's sinking right into the ocean. The people are suffering horribly. The Carteret Islands are coral atolls, and the highest point of land there is only about as high above sea level as a doorknob. There used to be tress around the islands that kept the ocean away, but the islanders chopped them all down and cut them up for firewood. They had to. Their natural resources are sinking under the waves. Places that used to be beautiful beaches are now slimy trash fields when the tide is out, and several feet underwater when it's in. Sharks and stingrays swim around in people's front yards.

The kids are starving. You can see their pot bellies, so cute and so sad all at the same time. The people have nothing to feed them but fish and coconuts. They don't even have fresh water, so the kids drink mostly coconut milk. A big wave could come at any time and wash their whole world away. Even if a tidal wave doesn't kill them all, the island will keep sinking under the ocean In less than ten years, it'll be gone, and if we don't do anything about it, these poor people will go with it. The nevarest island that isn't in trouble from global warming is 75 miles away. Some of the people tried moving there once, but even the safer islands are wrapped up in Papua New Guinea's civil war so the people got scared and came back. Talk about screwed.

I think we all have days when it feels like our whole world is sinking into the ocean. I watched that Spike Lee thing about Hurricane Katrina and cried and cried. I couldn't sleep for days after that. Just because people were black or brown, we didn't care if they got swept away or their children lived in filth or their women were raped. Imagine how little we'll care when the tide comes in and covers New Orleans for good, because the Carteret Islands aren't the only inhabited place close to sea level. If the ocean doesn't get us, trash or disease or terrorists will. And people still have children and send them into this shit?

Because this is our Apocalypse. Tell me you can't feel it coming. I know the ocean is rising. Before it was sucking at my toes like a relaxing beach. Then it climbed my legs and went under my skirt. Now it's at my chin. Soon it'll be in my mouth and nose and the whole world will go blue and far away. Does anyone hear me out here calling for help? Does my family understand? Does Tyler hear the ocean coming for both of us? Can he put down his Xbox controller long enough to see the tidal wave rising?

△

It would not be stretching the truth overmuch to describe Sugar Roses as the lone intellectual oasis in the vast semiliterate desert between Norman and Dallas. It would not be gilding the lily to characterize Bayeux Entertainment (formerly Bayeux Books and Video) as a beacon of hope for the literarily inclined in small town Oklahoma. And it would not be an act of hysterical hyperbole to nominate Phillip Mars as the gatekeeper to all that is smart in Sugar Roses. Some compared him, most often derisively, to Truman Capote. Others dismissed his circle of confederates as the Heartland Mall Round Table. Zack Heath described him as a cross between John Waters and Lex Luthor. He saw himself merely as an island fortress, defending all that is exquisite against a bloated invasion of Bedazzled barbarians.

Phillip Mars, Book Department Manager, straightened his pocket square as he strode through nonfiction. Other Bayeux employees wondered how he could afford such immaculate clothing. He had a different suit for every day of the week. He wore those suits all year, from the subzero ice storms of February to the rain forest heat and humidity of August in the former Dust Bowl. Few had seen him sweat, though he did have a tendency to blush in duress. His thin mustache seemed drawn on with a Sharpie. His bald dome never showed a trace of stubble, despite the fact that Phillip was only forty-five. He wore the same pair of Hugo Boss shoes every day, yet they never seemed to pick up any scuffs or discoloration. He favored plaid patterns that seemed more suited to 1970s London than twenty-first century America. But while college students who frequented the store assumed he was exclusively homosexual, no one had ever seen him out on a date. No one had been propositioned, not even Sugar Roses' few openly gay students. Furthermore, no one had heard or seen Phillip do or say anything sexual at all.

The truth, while prosaic, would not have accommodated community standards. Phillip had been in a relationship with Matt Lumley, the closeted high school music teacher, for over a decade. Matt also went to movies sometimes with Karen, a quiet accountant at Saving Grace. The accountant was utterly baffled by Matt's disinterest in physical matters. Never did she suspect he had the fellatio skills of a heavy metal groupie, yet their sham of a romance served to pacify the phobic on the Sugar Roses school board.

This was the first year SOSU hosted a Gay/Lesbian Student Alliance. Phillip and Matt regarded the new openness warily. These kids had no idea how bad things could get. There was always the risk of homicidal atrocity. The word "faggot" appeared in restroom graffiti all over town. Violence against gay and lesbian students excited little interest from campus or city police. Poor Chuck Pettigrew had been practically run out of town on a rail of sniggering hatred. Up in eternally hierarchical Heaven, the Christian God was still resolutely opposed to any sexual contact that didn't result in a family, so down below, the ground hosted millions of people who lived their whole lives as undercover agents in the heterosexual majority. Phillip and Matt considered themselves the luckiest couple in town, simply for knowing each other's orientation and interest. Their parents either had no idea or kept their ideas to themselves. Phillip wore a silver chain with a letter M pendant, and he told anyone who asked that it stood for Mars. Matt made his feelings for Phillip clear in other, less cerebral ways.

Phillip roamed through Periodicals, straightening the racks with pianist's fingers. He often had to cover gaps between gay porn titles, as the magazines were the most commonly shoplifted items in the store. To give the impression of equal time and attention, he also spent an unnecessary number of minutes straightening the *Playboy*s and *Maxim*s, sales for which dwindled when Sugar Roses went online. Phillip spotted Zack Heath and a young female companion coming into the store. "Well," he drawled, "if it isn't Sugar Roses' very own answer to P. G. Wodehouse."

"Come on, Phillip," Zack smiled. "You know I'm all about Nick Hornby and Richard Russo. I'm a man of the people."

"That's not the impression I get, Dr. Heath. The natives are restless."

"Restless? About what, the book?"

"*Mais bien sur.*"

Zack chewed his lip. Black-haired at forty-seven, lanky, once

34

an NCAA pitching sensation, he carried himself with an athlete's poise. "Is it selling any better, at least?"

"See for yourself," Phillip answered, indicating a display table still covered in Zack's debut novel, *Commedia dell'Heartland*. "Most people don't even know how to pronounce it."

"It'll sell," Zack's blonde companion announced. "It's so awesome. People just need to give it a chance."

Zack seemed startled to recall she was next to him. "Phillip! Do you know Laura? She's a student of mine."

"You bought the new Palahniuk," Phillip told her. It was something of a lucky guess.

"I buy every Palahniuk."

"Of course," Phillip smiled. Laura looked miffed but didn't know how to respond.

"Laura's in my Intermediate Acting class." Zack taught theatre at the college, directed a play a year, and thought about his second novel on weekends. Then a game would come on, or he'd receive an especially inviting text message, or his backyard Jacuzzi would look lonely. He hadn't written a word of new fiction in over a year, but at least he wasn't hurting for company.

"Do you fancy yourself a disciple of Uta Hagen?" Phillip asked Laura.

"Who?"

"Uta Hagen, dear. Sensei of the stage. Zachary, Doctor, what are you teaching our young people?"

"Laura's not so much about…She's really just mastering theory at this point."

"I see."

"It's become a kind of therapy for me," Laura said.

"You were fortunate," Phillip told her, "to have earned your way into the inner circle of our resident theatrical guru."

"That's what I keep telling her," Zack sighed. Laura

35

considered her response, suspected she was the butt of the joke, and decided maturely to wander off into Music.

"You kids be good," she said, waving over her shoulder.

"She's a darling," Phillip drawled.

"With champagne wishes and caviar dreams," Zack said wryly.

"Hollywood beckons?"

"That's its job. Oh, don't look at me like that."

"Far be it from me to stand in the way of an artistic libertine."

"Cram it. So how many books have I sold this week?"

"Four or five. The library bought another two."

"*God*, I can't believe the beating I'm taking on this thing." After two years of searching in vain for an agent or publisher, Zack finally bit the bullet and self-published through a company he found on the Internet. James Joyce self-published, he thought. So did William Blake, Whitman and Woolf. So that counted, right? "I was hoping to sell a few hundred copies in town, a couple thousand on Amazon. It's a good book. You read it, right?"

"I've skimmed it. Some local literature critics were kind enough to show me a photocopy."

"A photocopy? What? Are you shitting me?"

"No, not at all."

"I can't have people copying *Commedia* for free! This is bullshit!"

"I know, I was outraged. The local cognoscenti were particularly enthralled by the scene in the Paradise Motel." Zack grew up in Sugar Roses and, like all lifelong residents, knew exactly what went on in the Paradise Motel off I-35. The place was famous for miles around, and it wasn't for the continental breakfast, nor was it for cleanliness. No, the Paradise featured a service that wouldn't earn it a mention in Zagat. That service, which employed let's-say-eighteen-year-old girls in cutoff jeans and translucent T-shirts, was a favorite of lowlife truckers and, rumor had it, cops.

In the scene, which was probably dog-eared in every copy of *Commedia dell'Heartland* in existence, college freshman Gus Herod attends a kegger at the Paradise. Around two in the morning, long after sobriety dwindles in the collective rear view mirror, there comes a knock on the motel room door. Assuming it's the manager complaining about the noise, Gus opens the door sheepishly. Instead, it's a nubile young girl, asking if Gus wants to party. "I love to party," Gus replies. "Come on in." Completely oblivious to the purpose of the girl's visit, Gus offers her a taco from a takeout bag he brought to the party. The bemused girl eventually gives up on Gus's naïve ass and trudges down the hall, silently wishing she'd taken the taco. Gus's friends rib him mercilessly. Later that night, another guy drives home from the party, only to fly through the windshield after wrapping his car around a tree. The scene, like most of *Commedia dell'Heartland*, was taken directly from Zack's college years.

"I don't see how they can complain about the scene," he insisted. "It's not like what goes on at the Paradise Motel is a secret."

"It's *their* open secret," Phillip said.

"Unbelievable."

"You might have at least renamed the hotel. There were also some parental concerns about the scene at Brady Point."

The scene at Brady Point begins with an excess of Jack Daniels and ends in what can only be described as an underage orgy. This was also based on a cherished high school memory, and Zack could name at least half a dozen prominent locals who were willing participants in the depravity. All six were now parents, one a Sunday School teacher.

"Parental concerns."

"Concerns from people who happen to be parents, allegedly because their little pitchers have such big eyes. The better to read you with, my dear."

"You've got to be kidding."

37

"We mustn't defile the young."

"Have they talked to their kids? Have they had one conversation? I coached Little League for a season. Those kids could give Sting sex tips. And that's just the boys. The girls…Let's just say Brooke Shields and her Calvins had nothing on these girls."

"I know that and so do you, but apparently a teacher at Sugar Roses' blessed academy of learning found a copy of your roman à clef in the gentlemen's room."

"Lemme guess, they were using it as stroke fodder."

"What an artistic turn of phrase. It's no wonder you're our very own Balzac."

"Ay ay ay. So have they scheduled the book burning? Do I need to stock up on fire extinguishers? Or are they jumping straight ahead to the crucifixion?"

"Propriety forbids me from offering an opinion, Professor, especially on such a sacred matter as crucifixion. After all, the good employees of Saving Grace are our most profligate customers." Phillip indicated a display of Saving Grace T-shirts and various Christian paraphernalia. The Sugar Roses Bayeux did steady business in Christian-themed merchandise, especially "positive pop" CDs and *Li'l Warriors* video collections.

"'Profligate' has two meanings, y'know."

"Does it? I had no idea," drawled Phillip, having an idea.

"It's not like I set the book in Sugar Roses."

"You could have set the book in Lower Manhattan. It wouldn't have mattered. The good people of Sugar Roses know who you are, Zack. They know what you know. They know *who* you know. Or is it whom?"

"Beats me. Look…The bastards made photocopies?"

"I gather the book has been scanned and emailed around town like a *Harry Potter* novel."

"Difference is, Jo Rowling has a billion dollars. I want to pay off my student loans."

"Doesn't it thrill you at all, being a local cause célèbre?"

"People tell stories about me to scare their kids, Phillip. Last week Dan Taylor at First Baptist prayed for the souls of local atheists, starting with 'local authors.' I've never said a word about him or his church, but now I'm the Antichrist of Garvin County. These people need to get lives."

"They have lives, Professor. Dismal lives. Tedious, stultifying lives. Moreover, they—One moment, *s'il te plaît*." A hirsute man with a Caterpillar cap and a pot belly tumbling over capacious urban jean shorts wandered toward them. "Yes, sir, how may I help you?"

"Y'all got any books about NASCAR?" the man asked.

"Case in point," Phillip muttered. "Yes, they're over in Sports…for some reason. I'll walk you over."

Left alone, Zack looked around the store. Only about a dozen people populated the book section, most drinking coffee and reading magazines in Periodicals. The bulk of Bayeux's business came from DVD sales and rentals, but the store also sold hundreds of music CDs a week. This week's featured artists, the Flaming Lips, droned away on overhead speakers. The Flaming Lips hailed from Norman. It was possible to break out. It was possible to do artistic work in this state. It was even possible to sell artistic work, so long as no one thought they or their faith were being mocked.

But they were. Zack had to admit they were. He could call *Commedia dell'Heartland* a tribute or an affectionate satire or a damn Chinese pillow book, it didn't matter; the people of Sugar Roses were sharp enough to recognize themselves in its pages. Was it possible to parody with love? He realized his dwindling output had less to do with publishing difficulties than with the simple fact that he was getting too old to be angry. And without rage, without that caffeine jolt of indignation, he no longer felt the imperialist drive to colonize every blank page. All he felt was hopeless, and hopelessness didn't make art. Besides, his ideal audience was gone. His future held nothing but teaching, bad plays, Sugar Roses, and long gloomy mornings after dark nights before.

He watched Laura talking to her friends, her nineteen-year-old friends. What the fuck was he doing? One soft touch on his arm, and he was back into his old pattern, the same pattern that cost him so much happiness already. *I wonder if we could run lines, Dr. Heath. You give excellent advice, Dr. Heath. I love your house, Dr. Heath. It's so late, Dr. Heath. I can keep it a secret, Dr. Heath.*

The last time the whole thing came too damn close to exploding in his face. He swore he'd never do that again. At least Shay was out of school. But every next morning—no matter how smoothly he got away with whatever he did—he felt the same disappointments, the same dull despair because it was Laura, or Shay, or some sophomore to be named later, not the woman he really wanted. It wasn't Alyssa's body. It wasn't her touch. It wasn't her voice. It wasn't Alyssa, with her world-weary wit and her Black Sabbath T-shirts and her long legs and short fingernails. It wasn't *her*, damn it, gone to Shawnee with that stupid-happy grudge fuck she glorified into the role of a mediocre husband. It wasn't her. The absence of Alyssa bored into him, a miner extracting everything precious and leaving only stone.

Last night he dreamed Alyssa told him a joke. Knock, knock. Who's there? *I miss you.* He woke up to Laura's cold hips and Cabernet breath. It was a very mean joke.

Published: Thursday, March 13, 20— 09:54 a.m.

They Were Naked, But Not Ashamed

Print   Email   Discuss

By Jacob Arnett

Lifestyles Editor

LAKE KONAWA – Before anyone asks, I decided I would not participate. You're welcome.

I've been asked to keep the exact location of Camp Eden secret, so let's just say it's tucked away in a corner of scenic Lake Konawa. There are stands of blackberry, black willow, and even grapevines around beautiful blue fishing holes, but that wasn't the scenery that caught my eye first. That's because Camp Eden is one of Oklahoma's three nudist colonies. (Enthusiasts refer to them as "naturist parks.") Depew hosts Oaklake Trails, and Tulsans avert their eyes from Willow Beach. The folks in Camp Eden look almost exactly like the jaybirds in the other two camps, but they're different in one confusing respect: They identify themselves as Christian nudists.

I spent Friday night and most of Saturday in the camp. For two days I saw more skin than a tattoo artist. Going in I imagined I'd get used to it in no time. I didn't. When I arrived, I was wearing shorts and a T-shirt. After hours in the company of people who wore only SPF 30, I felt the urge to put clothes on rather than take them off. I left in jeans and a windbreaker. I'm surprised I wasn't wearing a parka. Remind me to invest in a gym membership.

41

If the reader has ever harbored fantasies of nudist colonies as tanned and fit as the grotto at Hugh Hefner's crib, it's time to relinquish those daydreams now. These weren't Playboy bodies, they were Wal-Mart bodies. Never had the phrase "naked as God made us" left one in such theological doubt. At the risk of offending or nauseating the reader, gravity works in Konawa pretty much the same way it works everywhere. Over time, the human body goes the way of Newton's apple. In the verified opinion of this writer, modern underwear is an amazing and necessary invention.

But enough about the nakedness. I could have hung out at Night Trips for that, and with happier (if costlier) results. I wanted to know more about the God of this Garden. It turns out the Edenites are as Christian as Easter Sunday, despite their unconventional dress code. Pastor John Humphries leads services every morning, shouting God's greatness to the open blue sky in an outdoor cathedral. Pastor Humphries likes to say God Himself is their Decorator. I offer God a prayer of thanks for the beach towels I noticed on every pew.

Like many in Oklahoma, I was raised Baptist on Sunday, heckbound heathen Monday through Saturday. I'm okay with a little flexibility in my Biblical interpretation, but I couldn't help asking how purity and Christian meditation could be maintained in this Konawa flesh pit. I was especially confused by the dance on Friday night. Granted, the worst sin I observed was a fondness for ABBA, but even with gyrating bodies discreetly far apart, I imagined sensuality flourishing in every RV and cabin.

"These are mostly married couples," Pastor Humphries explained. "Occasionally we'll get somebody in here who isn't pure of heart, but either we change their minds in a hurry or they get bored and leave." Camp Eden does have a hot tub, but singles are seated apart, separated by married Edenites. Mostly the hot tub functions as a place to relax and meditate. Some even come here to pray.

"The swingers can stay at Willow Beach. I wish them well," Pastor Humphries sighs. "As for me and my household, we will worship the Lord." Indeed, Camp Eden is a family affair. I met Pastor Humphries' wife, son, and daughter. Pastor Humphries noticed me keeping a respectful distance from all three.

"It's okay, don't be shy. They won't bite," he assured me. I asked him if he worried about the possibility of infiltration by pedophiles or other human predators. I told him most people are uncomfortable in the presence of naked children, and the danger of sending them bare-bottomed into the world would scare me if I were a naturist parent.

"Part of being a Christian is having faith," he explained, "and faith is just a stronger word for trust. I trust these people implicitly. They're my brothers and sisters. The Africans say it takes a village to raise a child. Politicians are always going on about family values. Well, we have family values. We have a village. Greater love hath no man than this, that a man lay down his life for his friends. I know any of these dear Christians would give his or her life for my children. I know it. And I would do the same for them. It's like Peter said, seeing you have purified your souls in obedience, love one another from the heart fervently. That's how we live. I come here for a vacation from sin and the world every weekend. This is our paradise. And anyone who thinks there isn't love here, or that love isn't Christian, well—I think they might need to reread all those red words in their family Bibles."

Fair enough, Pastor, I said, but I spent a fair amount of time in Sunday school, too. Weren't Adam and Eve clothed by God? If the Lord saw fit to cover the First Couple in fig leaves, who are we to disagree? Pastor Humphries answered with the obvious weariness of a man who's had to answer that question about a million times before. "The Bible says Adam and Eve ate of the Tree of Knowledge of Good and Bad, then became ashamed and sewed themselves aprons out of fig leaves. God the Father had nothing to do with it. He asked them how they knew they were naked, then reproved them for the sin of second-guessing Him. We know the Garden was perfect, and Adam and Eve were naked within it. Clearly, that was part of God's will. We're adhering to God's plan, not defying it. We're sanctifying our bodies to Christ. The way I see it, Christianity has two choices, greater openness and trust, or closed-mindedness and fear. We all got to make a decision. I don't judge other Christians for theirs, but I can't say they extend us the same courtesy."

I bumped into a resident of Sugar Roses – not literally, thank goodness - who asked me to keep her identity secret. I will happily comply. She met me wrapped only in a beach towel depicting Jedediah Bear from *Li'l Warriors*. Bear, bare – surely that can't be a coincidence? To clarify (and hopefully avoid any chance of a lawsuit), the camper doesn't work at Saving Grace. She was, however, well established in one of Sugar Roses' more mainstream churches. I'll call her Eve.

"I went every Sunday for years," Eve said. "To tell you the truth, I really miss it. I miss all the people. But you know, along the way, I ran into this, and it just felt right. I started coming here more and more. I knew this was where the Lord wanted me to be. I tried going to both, but after a while it felt like I was living a lie. I can't be lukewarm in my life as a Christian, I have to be on fire for Jesus. The Bible says Jesus washed his disciples' feet by wiping them with his own lower garment. Now you tell me what he had on when he took that off. He lowered himself like a slave to show us the meaning of love and devotion, to each other, to him, and to God. People say, 'What Would Jesus Do,' but they draw the line at dropping their drawers in his presence. And make no mistake, we are always in the presence of Jesus. The Bible says we're part of the bride class. So why should I be ashamed to get naked in the presence and love of my husband?"

I can think of worse explanations, and I don't have any steamy sex tales to relate about the sincere Christian soldiers I met at Camp Eden. But if it's all the same to my own personal Lord and Savior, I don't believe we have that kind of marriage. I thank him mostly for natural fibers and a little miracle I like to call "Deep Woods Off."

• **Click to discuss this story with other readers on our forums.**

E

"In the beginning was the Word." Saint John, or the ghost writer who authored the gospel in his name, opened with a pun. *Bereshith*, a Hebrew word that means "in the beginning," is also the first word of the Torah. First-century Greek-influenced Jews believed the Logos, or Word of God, had the power to create. They believed the First Moment—indeed, the Cosmos itself—was an act of imagination. In the beginning was the Word, and the Word was with God. Then that Word was fleshed into existence, the imagination of God become matter, and the world was newborn.

FADE IN, Scott wrote, scribbling in a notepad. EXT. SUGAR ROSES, OKLAHOMA – NIGHT. Establishing.

In the beginning was the word. Paradoxically, the Oklahoma City bombing incited the modest success Scott enjoyed in Los Angeles. "I touch the remains of a family. An agony unzips in my heart." This phrase, written in tears, launched his career. The email that followed, an internal missive from Joel Adamov, Senior Vice President of Production at Excelsior Studios, blasted pure liquid joy through Scott's bloodstream. In the beginning was the word, and the word was with the Hollywood gods, and the word was finally, thrillingly *Yes*.

He'd been scratching out stories for years. A child prodigy from nearby Ardmore, he wrote his first sentence at age four. Then the rest of the world gradually caught up with his brain, and by the time he was thirty, he was shaping up to be a major disappointment. He wrote movie reviews for the *SOSU Advance* but never managed to land another steady writing gig after graduation. He sold poems to *Common Ground*, *Pulsar*, a couple of ezines. He wrote freelance for various websites and fed short stories to his desk drawer. Each tale seemed to him ingenious, a Christmas gift of wonders all wrapped in white paper, but only on first reading. Then they decayed. Over time, the phrases turned artless. His characters sagged into types.

In 1995, Scott was living in Oklahoma City, saving money for grad school or a move west, whichever happened first. Less than a year out of college, his future seemed intergalactic in scope. He was headed for B. Dalton, as always a few minutes late for work, when he heard a blunt concussion.

What followed that first telegram of sound was a chaos of smoke and spilled blood. As he ran toward the remains of the Alfred P. Murrah Building, he noticed the power steering assembly from a Ryder truck embedded in a van across the street from the wreckage. He looked up at what used to be a mundane office building, now chopped cruelly into bookends. Time went by in awful jolts. He sat in an unfamiliar church to mourn a hundred and sixty-eight dead. He wept tears of heartbreak and rage when he saw a photo of fireman Chris Fields carrying one-year-old Bailey Almon to an ambulance. The child died shortly thereafter, broken by the hate of a stranger. Scott still couldn't look at the iconic image without crying. It encapsulated some of the history of his heart. He moved to L.A. and played the role of "Unsold Screenwriter" in the waitstaff at Wolfgang Puck Café.

He temped for a year at an agency that specialized in studio work, mostly Disney. Some days he woke at four to do grunt labor on movie and television sets. He met celebs and fetched them coffee. Anne Hathaway hugged him and called him a sweetie. David Caruso called him Fucknuts and invited him to enjoy a lovely snack on his balls. Scott found he preferred office work, and for the next few months he cycled through executive suites. The morning of September 11, 2001, he heard the awful news in a taqueria on Gower and raced home. He turned to GNN in time to watch a near-million pounds of jetliner pierce the South Tower. The horror felt all too familiar.

In the wake of that awful morning, he felt compelled to remind the world of Oklahoma's agony. He wrote about the day, a week after the Oklahoma City bombing, when he and his sister visited the tragic epicenter. They gazed at the ruins through a chain link fence stuffed with photos, cards, and toys left behind by families in the memory of their murdered children. He brushed his fingers through a teddy bear's fur and sobbed blindly for an hour. His sister cried out, "Babies! They were babies." He wrote his long essay in a single run, not even pausing to correct typos, and when it was finished he fell asleep weeping all over again. The article was published in *LA Weekly* ("In Grief Undiminished," 14 April 20—) and caught the eyes of Excelsior execs. He picked up work writing for TV, mostly jokes for a sketch show and a pilot that never made the network schedule. But Joel Adamov remembered him—Scott Turow, Scott Glass, it only made sense—and when Excelsior optioned *Court of Law*, he offered Scott the chance to write a paid first draft. If that draft worked, he'd be offered the next draft, and so on, and so on, in what the industry referred to as a step contract. He took the opportunity to return to Oklahoma for a month and reimmerse himself in the world of his childhood. He felt like an alien being.

A soft rain had fallen all night and morning. The white noise helped Scott think, and he pounded through a scene in a matter of minutes. Then he listened to Miles Davis while transferring notes to Final Draft on his laptop. The Standard Hotel was mostly empty. He'd negotiated a rate of thirty a night for the month. It was cheaper than his apartment off Sunset, and the hotel paid his cable and made his bed every morning. He rented a car for a week when his plane arrived in Oklahoma City but took it back after only four days. Everything in town was within walking distance, and most of it wasn't worth the walk. He'd either rent another car in three weeks or cadge a ride. This was Oklahoma: In less than a month, he could make a new friend who would drive him to the airport. He could also make enemies for life, merely by describing Sugar Roses in a less than adoring manner.

He spent his first week in Sugar Roses rereading *Court of Law* while sitting under trees at its locations. No one asked what he wanted there. Some people asked who he was, but they accepted his usual answer: I'm a fan of Scott Turow's. He hadn't told anyone his real business until the girl in the library--Amanda. He wasn't sure why, unless it was pure self-indulgent paranoia. He was afraid to out himself as a Hollywood spy.

He imagined being interviewed by the *Sugar Roses Sentinel*: Local Boy Makes Good, Paints Us as Rubes. "'I hope to bring authenticity to this story,' said amoral Hollywood liberal Glass, winking. 'These are my friends, my people. Say, Jim Bob, can you point me in the direction of the nearest Starbucks? My drugs just kicked in, and I'm jonesing for a venti mocha latte.'" If anyone remembered him from his college years, they neglected to mention it.

He was stuck between scenes, distracted by daydreams. He

stood, stretched his back, and retrieved a takeout carton of pork fried rice from the mini-fridge. He should've sprung for a room with a kitchenette. Instead, he'd become a recurring bit player in various local restaurants—Qun's Happy Reunion on Main, the TGI Friday's on Townsend, Abilene Sam's Country Steakhouse just east of the highway on Anderson Parkway. Different nights, different waitresses, the same lonely experience, hunched over Turow's book shoving indifferently prepared food in his face. He'd never met Turow; probably never would. No relation, he'd tell reporters.

Traffic cruised by on the parkway with a sound like tearing paper. Locals often griped about the congestion near Highway 19. They blamed it on the expansion of Heartland Mall and the newer stores and restaurants surrounding it. Some were even bold enough to blame it on Saving Grace. No one blamed it on good old-fashioned sexual intercourse, but that was the truth. Enrollment at the college was scarcely higher than when Scott was an undergrad. No, the locals just kept right on having babies and raising them to adulthood. There was nothing unusual about that. It was humanity's favorite hobby. Over the last twenty years, the population of Sugar Roses doubled, and new folks meant new checkbooks, wallets and purses. New businesses. Traffic. The towns and cities blended into one, a chain mall ingesting America.

Someday, Scott thought, someday soon, I won't even recognize this place.

The rain slowly pattered into silence. A gust of wind sang through the open window. It carried a slam of arctic sting. That was odd. Scott could almost feel invisible isobars slicing through the room.

"Do you feel that?" someone asked outside, a college kid talking to his friend.

Scott moved to shut the window. The temperature plunged like an out-of-control DC-10. It shouldn't be this cold in March. It shouldn't be this cold this *fast*. The glass in the window ticked sharply, and snow began to fall.

There was a sound in the air now, a low tone, a thrumming, a squeezing in his ears.

Outside, another guest and his wife emerged to watch the falling snow. "I can't believe it's snowing so late in the year."

"It's cold, honey. Let's go inside."

"Did it snow in spring last year?"

"I don't remember, honey, honestly."

"Was it cold like this all morning?"

"No, I thought it was supposed to be up in the fifties."

"It feels like twenty or thirty degrees."

Scott had a pretty good internal temperature gauge. It was twenty degrees, maybe less. The mercury had fallen thirty degrees in a matter of minutes. The monotone increased, not only in volume but intensity of pressure against his head.

"Do you hear that, honey? What is that?"

"It sounds like a transformer."

"You should come inside," Scott heard himself say to the couple. "Hurry! Something's coming." He set down his carton of rice. He almost missed the table. His hands quivered.

The guy opened his mouth to reply. The low tone suddenly spiked into all-sound. Scott heard voices in the air. *Jesus*, the woman's mouth said.

The tone lasted seven more seconds. It retained all its power when Scott clamped both hands over his ears. It drowned his sudden yelp of confusion. Then it vanished for the length of an eye blink, only to be replaced by a CRACK of expended electricity. A tang of ozone flooded his nostrils. The power went out in the room. Scott fell to his knees. He trembled. The hair stood up on his arms. Even the cheap hotel carpet waved like a tropical sea floor.

Earthquake weather, he thought.

Silence. The press of invisible hosts teemed in the air, then slowly dissipated.

What the hell is going on?

51

Scott stood and rushed to the window. Traffic outside skidded to a standstill, with several cars kissed against each other. No one was hurt as far as he could see. People glanced at the dents in their fenders, then immediately stared back at the sky.

Snow fell another two hours but never stuck. The sun returned to the world around five. A new thing was happening. A Word had been spoken.

The following is a 911 audio transcript, an excerpt of which appeared in the Sugar Roses Sentinel. *The call began at 2:47 on the afternoon of Friday, 14 March 20—.*

911 Operator #1: Sugar Roses 911, what is your emergency?

Shirley Zeigler: My daughter, my daughter!

911 Operator #1: What's the problem, ma'am?

Shirley Zeigler: She can't stop! She's scared! Please help her!

911 Operator #1: Can't stop what?

Shirley Zeigler: She can't breathe!

911 Operator #1: Is she choking?

Shirley Zeigler: No, she's...

Background Voice: ...(*unintelligible*)...

Shirley Zeigler: Honey, stop it! Please!

911 Operator #1: Ma'am, what is she doing?

Shirley Zeigler: Please just get here! Honey, no... (*unintelligible*)...

911 Operator #1: Ma'am, you have to tell me what's wrong.

Background Voice: ...(*unintelligible*)...

911 Operator #1: Ma'am?

Background Voice: ...(*unintelligible*)...

Shirley Zeigler: ...(*unintelligible*)... I don't know what to do!

911 Operator #1: She isn't choking?

Shirley Zeigler: No, she's just yelling all this stuff!

911 Operator #1: I don't understand. She's yelling at you?

Shirley Zeigler: She's scared, oh God, she's turning blue!

911 Operator #1: Verifying your address, ma'am...

Background Voice: ...(*unintelligible*)...

911 Operator #1: ...are you at 830 East D Street?

Background Voice: ...(*unintelligible*)...

Shirley Zeigler: Just stop, honey! Stop!...What'd you say?

911 Operator #1: 830 East D Street?

Shirley Zeigler: Yes, just get here! Oh God...

Background Voice: ...(*unintelligible*)...

Shirley Zeigler: She's rolling on the floor!

911 Operator #1: Try to get her to relax, ma'am. I'm sending someone out to you now.

Shirley Zeigler: Honey, please stop! ...(*unintelligible*)...

RADIO: ...(*unintelligible*)... Clear.

911 Operator #1: Medical emergency at 830 East David Street. Possible domestic disturbance.

RADIO: Responding... (*unintelligible*)...

Shirley Zeigler: Hurry, she can't breathe!

911 Operator #1: Someone is on their way out to you now, ma'am.

Background Voice: ...(*unintelligible*)...

911 Operator #1: How old is your daughter, ma'am?

Shirley Zeigler: Ten, she's ten years old!

RADIO: ...(*unintelligible*)...

Background Voice: ...(*unintelligible*)...

RADIO: ...(*siren*)...

911 Operator #1: Can you get her to lie down?

Shirley Zeigler: She's on the floor. God, she's freaking out!

911 Operator #1:	Does she have a clear airway?
Shirley Zeigler:	Airway? No! She's yelling all this stuff! I need help!
911 Operator #1:	What is she yelling, ma'am?
Background Voice:	...(*unintelligible*)...
Shirley Zeigler:	Can you hear her?
RADIO:	...(*tone – signal broadcast*)...
Shirley Zeigler:	She's freaking out! I don't know if she's breathing!
911 Operator #1:	Attention 901, unknown medical emergency at 830 East David. Cross street 8th and 9th. Attention 901 medical emergency...
Shirley Zeigler:	Breathe!
Background Voice:	...(*unintelligible*)...
911 Operator #2:	...like Tourette's, maybe?
911 Operator #1:	I don't know. I hear something. I can't make out what she's saying.
Background Voice:	...(*unintelligible*)...
Shirley Zeigler:	I don't know what she's saying!
RADIO:	...(*unintelligible*)...
911 Operator #1:	She says her child is yelling and she won't breathe.
Shirley Zeigler:	She can't!
RADIO:	...(*unintelligible*)...
911 Operator #1:	Unable to ascertain...
RADIO:	...(*unintelligible*)... en route code...
Shirley Zeigler:	Help me!
911 Operator #1:	They're almost there, ma'am.

Background Voice: ...(*unintelligible*)...

911 Operator #1: Code... (*unintelligible*)... Are you getting this?

911 Operator #2: I don't know what she's saying.

Background Voice: ...(*unintelligible*)...

911 Operator #1: Ma'am, how long ago did this start?

Shirley Zeigler: Oh my God. About five, ten minutes ago. I don't know. It was just after that weird noise. She started yelling all this stuff and

I don't know what it means and now she can't get any air to breathe!

RADIO: ...(*unintelligible*)...

911 Operator #2: The ambulance is almost there, ma'am.

911 Operator #1: Is she yelling at you?

Shirley Zeigler: No, she's... (*unintelligible*)...

911 Operator #1: Is she swearing?

Shirley Zeigler: No, she's just... (*unintelligible*)... Listen!

Background Voice: ...(*unintelligible* [*14 seconds—see below*])

The following is an expert transcription of the fourteen seconds of audio attributed to "Background Voice" above, alleged to be Carrie Zeigler age 10, as heard and testified to by Dr. Marion Kalatzis of Oklahoma State University. The language spoken in the audio sample has been identified as "Koine" or "common" Greek as spoken from the third century B.C. to the third century A.D. The words are a quotation from Revelation, chapter 6, verse 8. Neither Miss Zeigler nor any of her family or peers have any training in or experience with Koine Greek.

Background Voice: ...(*unintelligible*)... Idou hippos chloros kai ho kathemai epano autos onoma autos ho Thanatos kai ho Hades akoloutheo meta autos.

Kai didomi autos exousia epi ho tetartos ho ge apokteino en rhomphaia kai en limos kai en thanatos... (*unintelligible*)

Shirley Zeigler: [*English*] She's crying, my baby is crying!

The Greek passage translates as follows:

Background Voice: ...Behold, a pale horse, and his name that sat on him was Death, and Hell followed with him. And power was given unto them over the fourth part of the earth, to kill with sword, and with hunger, and with death...

Z

"Oh my God," Shay murmured, leaning against a cabinet. "What just happened?" It was 2:39 Friday afternoon. She was in the Saving Grace break room with two other employees, a junior accountant and Alice, a fellow customer service rep.

"Was it a tornado?" Alice asked, somewhere in the darkness.

"Where are the flashlights?" the accountant asked.

"I don't think we have any," Shay replied. "Do we have a generator?"

"Hang on a second," the accountant said, and suddenly the blue waving eye of his cell phone opened in the darkness. "No bars. I'm not getting a signal. I hope the towers aren't down."

The phrase resonated awfully in the room.

Alice withdrew a cigarette lighter and started poking around in break room drawers. She found leftover candles from an office birthday party and stabbed them into dishwashing sponges. She lit them on party plates and handed them out. "I need to call my little grandbabies," she fretted.

"Oh, Lacey must be totally freaking out," Shay agreed. Lacey was in preschool with only minutes to go before Aunt Linda picked her up.

"Somebody said it was snowing just before it happened," the accountant said, then trotted off to his office. The customer service floor was crawling back from chaos. A few people withdrew flashlights from drawers and purses. Others stabbed away at cell phones. The land lines were dead, every extension.

Travis, the customer service lead, raised his arms in the gloom. "Okay, listen up, people," he announced. "As I'm sure y'all have noticed, we have suffered a loss of power. Okay, now, Saving Grace does have a generator, which I'm pretty sure they're hooking up now. They're mostly workin' on the phones, so y'all can take calls again. The private branch exchange is down—the switchboard. We'll prolly have lots of incoming calls, an' I know

59

y'all want to call your families but let's hold off on that for now, okay?"

The lights and phones came on within seconds of each other. Of course, Sugar Roses' most highly-paid customer service team ignored the request from middle management and checked in with family members immediately. One woman ran toward the door, not even bothering to log out before racing home to her injured mother. "Who was that?" Travis hollered in vain.

Lacey was fine. Power was still out at the school, but they were firing up the buses and sending kids home early. Lacey's teacher would stay with her until Linda arrived. She also talked to Linda, who vented her usual concerns that her neighbor might use the blackout as a chance to steal items from Linda's "proppety." Linda was an adequate babysitter, but she had an unconscious craving for melodrama. She saw every accidental slight as part of a grand campaign to wreck her whole existence. It was all Shay could do to get her off the phone. The cable was out, even both local radio stations were silent, and Linda was convinced The Terrorists were on their way.

"I told you we needed to get Osama bin Laden," Linda insisted, as if others were recommending the president buy him a timeshare in Cabo. "Now it's on, honey, it is on. Think about it. We been cut off from the rest of the world. What better time for Osama to, you know, make his move? We could be up to our ass in Al Qaeda and no one would even know it."

"Al Qaeda?" Shay exclaimed, and immediately coworkers on either side of her yanked off their headsets. *What? Al Qaeda? Shay's saying it's al Qaeda!* "No, it's not al Qaeda."

"They hate our way of life," Linda insisted. "They're jealous of our freedom."

"They live in caves!" Shay said. "I'd be jealous of our freedom, too! Linda, what would al Qaeda want with Sugar Roses? What's their target, the Olive Garden?"

"Remember when that bridge fell in? That was I-35. Shay, *we're* on I-35! If they could shut that down—They're watching us, honey! They know!"

"Oh my God, Linda. Are you cooking meth again?" Shay demanded.

"No," was the grumpy reply.

"Is she saying it's al Qaeda?" someone asked.

"No. Listen, Linda, I gotta go. Just keep an eye on Lacey, okay? She gets scared in the dark."

"Darryl's lightin' candles. Darryl, don't use the good ones! Those are for your momma's sixtieth birthday."

"That's in four years!" Darryl yelled in the background.

"I don't care. You think we're made outta money?"

"They were from the Dollar General!"

"They got frogs on 'em! Your momma likes frogs!" Linda sighed raspily. Apparently she was smoking again. "You see what I go through?"

"Linda, please don't blow cigarette smoke on my daughter."

"You know I don't smoke around her. 'Less I just have to."

"I gotta go."

"Be careful on your way here," Linda said, deflated. "They's cars and shit all over the road."

"I know there are cars on the road, Linda."

"You know what I mean! And watch out for...you know, whatever."

"I will." Travis glowered at her. "I know!" she yelled back at him. "I'll call you later, Linda. Just hang on to her 'til I get there at six. I'll run by and see if I can buy us some groceries. I'll stock up."

"Get them spicy Tater Tots. Darryl likes those."

"'Bye." Shay hung up and took a deep breath. "Good *night*!" she euphemized, and punched the ready button on her phone. It rang and lit up instantly. "Saving Grace, giving Jesus the praise, this is Shay. How may I help you?"

"It's about toe-eem!" a New Jersey accent exclaimed. "I been on the phone for two hou-uhs!" Shay glanced at the call time board. The most the woman could have waited was seventeen minutes.

"We're a bit stacked up here, ma'am. We just got repaired after a blackout. How may I provide you with excellent customer service today?" Shay winced. The rote customer service phrases infiltrated her brain, like those disgusting slimy worm creatures in the Amazon. Or was it *Star Wars*? She couldn't remember. Zack would know.

"This is Juliet Farquhar in Ah-ringe, New Jersey. We just had a power outage hee-uh, too. I heard a loud noise and the powuh blacked out and I got awl kinds uh dizzy. Now the TV won't come back awn and my neighbuhs uh freakin' out."

"You say you're in Orange, New Jersey?"

"Yeah, and my kids uh both at Princeton. I can't reach neithuh one of 'em. Their cell phones ain't workin'."

"I'm sorry, ma'am. I'm sure they'll be fine."

"Izzat all you have to say about it? Jesus, I cawled you fuh counseling!"

"Ohhhhh," Shay said, rubbing her forehead. Now she understood. Saving Grace employed a few dozen semi-trained counselors to field calls from Christians around the world and talk them through spiritual crises, most of which were the result of enthusiastic substance abuse and/or fornication and/or adultery. The phone lines were swamped, and the overspill was routed to customer service. That's why Travis was so desperate to get everyone back on the phones. Super duper.

"Ma'am, can you see street lights or anything like that around you? How far around you is the blackout?"

"I dunno. Somebody tole me it was all ovuh the East Coast. Where uh you?"

"I'm in southern Oklahoma."

"Oklahoma! And there ain't no powuh theh, neithuh?"

"No, ma'am, we're running off a generator."

"Oh, fuh Pete's sake. I hope it's not one uh them Ay-rab sons uh bitches." Shay found constant paradoxical amazement in the number of people who swore at her on Christian customer service calls. One guy called her "a fucking Catholic."

"I don't think so, ma'am. Do you want me to pray with you?" The inspiration came to her in mid-sentence.

"Would you, honey? I'm a single lady, a widow ya know, and it gets a little scary hee-uh sometoe-eems."

"I'd be happy to, ma'am." Problem was, Shay had developed a rather slapdash internal prayer monologue over the years: *Dear God, please don't let this check bounce. Jesus, help me get Lacey's shoes on her before I hit her in the face. Please don't let the cops catch me drunk-driving, amen.* She suspected this day would require a more formal protocol. "Uh, dear Lord, Heavenly Father, we uh, ask You now for help and comfort for this woman, Miz Fark, uh, Fark-yu-har."
"It's Farquhar, sweetie."

"Farquhar. God, we uh, we ask that You comfort her in the valley of the shadow of duhhh…darkness. Lord, we know that Miz Farquhar has a good heart and a Christian soul. She asks for Your protection in the face of…of difficult times."

"And my kids."

"Yes, her kids, Lord. They require Your protection as well. They're good students and uh…God loved the world so much He gave his only-begotten Son, amen."

"In Jesus' name."

"In Jesus' name we ask this, amen."

"Thank you, sweetie," Ms. Farquhar said, catching her breath. "It helps, it really does. Things'uh been crazy around hee-uh."

"I know, ma'am. It's been crazy around here, too."

"Oh, the lights just come back awn!" Farquhar bleated. "I can watch my *Judge Judy*!"

"Okay, ma'am, glad we could help."

"You have a good day, now, sweetie. Thank Gawd fuh you people."

"We appreciate that, ma'am, thank you. Have a blessed day, and remember, 'if God is for us who can be against us?'" She uttered that rote farewell so many times each day she once heard herself go halfway through it after unsuccessful phone sex with Zack. He hung up laughing. Her face burned for an hour.

"This is crazy," another rep said. "I just got a call from Sarasota, Florida. Bernice got one from some place called Yreka, California. This blackout is everywhere. Most people don't have TV yet. Some of the radio stations came back on, but the DJs don't know anything, either. Nobody knows what's going on."

"How do you lose electric power all over the country?" another rep asked.

"It was that Sound," the first rep said, "the humming sound. Y'all heard that, too, didn't ya? Crazy," she repeated.

"It felt like electricity," Shay agreed.

"The lady in Sarasota heard the same exact sound."

"We need to turn on a radio," Shay said, and accepted another call. "Saving Grace, giving Jesus the praise, this is Shay. How may I help you?"

A child was crying on the other end of the line. A mother herself, Shay knew the sound of a girl in abject panic. Something was horribly wrong. Ice water flooded her veins. "What is it, honey, how may I help you?" Shay repeated.

"My mommy fell down. She hit her head!"

"Is she okay?"

"She's all bleeding!"

"Have you called 911?"

"Yes," the child answered. "They came over. She's got blood all around her. I'm scared!"

64

"The paramedics are there now?"

"Yes."

"Honey, do what they tell you. You did the right thing. You called 911, and now they're there to help. You were very grown-up."

"My mommy's still sleeping." It sounded like the girl was only a year or two older than Lacey.

"She's getting better, honey. That's why the paramedics are there, to help her."

"I called you because I'm scared."

"I don't blame you, honey; really, I'd be scared, too. But y'know what? You did exactly the right thing. She's gonna be fine."

"Okay."

"What's your name?"

"My name is Dina."

"Mine's Shay."

"Shay?"

"Uh-huh."

"Um, Shay, I heard a 'splosion."

"You mean the lightning sound?"

"Yes."

"I did, too, honey. Are the lights on where you are?"

"No," Dina answered. "It's daytime."

"I know, honey. What I mea—"

"The TV is on."

"It is? What's it showing?"

"*Finding Nemo.*"

Oh, so power but no cable. They were watching a DVD.

"Honey, maybe you should—"

"My mommy's okay now," Dina blurted. "Buh-bye."

"Okay, honey, thank you for ca—" Click. The child abruptly hung up. Shay's heart jogged in her chest. She didn't sign up to be an emergency dispatcher.

"Okay, listen up, people," Travis began again, more frantically this time. "As I'm sure you've noticed by now, we're starting to get lap-over calls from Counseling. Now, don't you worry about that. Some a you veterans'll remember it used to happen a lot before we got the new phone system put in. You know what to do, people. Just handle 'em like any other call."

"But Travis," Shay called out, "I *don't* know what to do. I got a call from a little girl whose mother was bleeding to death on the floor. I'm not qualified for this."

"That's a good question," Travis replied, his voice quavering. *It wasn't a question,* Shay thought, *it was a statement.* "People, we're not emergency services. Just tell 'em to call 911, stay positive, and say a little prayer for 'em if they need it."

"They need help, Travis! Real help! I'm not ready for this."

"Hang on, Shay. I'll be right there, okay?" Travis rolled his eyes. Shay slumped in her desk chair, arms crossed over her chest. She wanted to be home with her daughter. "Relax, people. We're gonna get through this. Y'all are Saving Grace associates. If God is for us, who can be against us? Rock on, man. Cool." The whole customer service floor seemed to grumble indecipherably in response.

Associates, Shay thought for the hundredth time. Not employees, and certainly not friends. Just people they're willing to be seen with. Travis trudged over to her cubicle.

"I'm sorry, Travis, I'm just freaking out."

"I know, Shay. It's a stressful day. I feel ya on that. I don't even have Internet in my office. The servers are down. I can't tell *what's* goin' on."

"I'm worried about Lacey. She gets scared in the dark."

"Lacey's your cat?"

"*No*, Travis, Lacey's my daughter. She's the same age as yours, remember?" Shay pointed at Lacey's photo on the desk.

"Oh, right. Pretty girl. Look, I don't blame ya, okay, but I need ya right here, Shay. I need everyone on the floor. We're in real bad shape. We're prolly gonna call the night shift in early."

"I know, I just…That little girl upset me so badly. I'm not qualified to handle emergency calls."

"None of us are, Shay," Travis sighed. "Y'know? Just…care for 'em, okay? That's all you can do. Just be someone who cares. I know you can do that. Take a deep breath, say a personal prayer, get your stuff together and get on the phone and help some a these people out. Okay?"

"Are you gonna take calls?"

"Uhh, yeah," Travis drawled, "I'm headed that way now. How 'bout you manage your own work, okay? Let me worry about the big picture. Sheez Almighty." Shay knew he'd rather get crabs from a convict than take incoming calls, so why did she bother asking? Now they were both pissed.

"Thanks, Travis," she said, meaning exactly none of it.

"You can do this," he finished lamely. "Okay? Get a grip." When he left, she took part of his advice and indulged in a long, deep breath. Inhale, exhale. *That poor girl.* Inhale, exhale. *Just get these people to call 911.*

Her cell phone sat quietly in the corner of her desk, tucked behind a dark computer monitor. As per company rules, she kept the phone off at work except during her break and lunch periods. This was different. She had her own emergencies to contend with. She reached out suddenly, tucked the phone under her desk, and keyed the power button. Thankfully, she remembered to leave it on vibrate, so the phone provider logo didn't make any noise. No bars. One message. She looked around to make sure no one was watching, then rang her voicemail.

Three tones. "Thank you for calling. The message you have selected failed to record properly," an alto computer voice

67

complained. "We are experiencing system difficulties. Please try again later on. We apologize for any inconvenience. Repeating. We are experiencing—" She disconnected the call and turned her phone off in a rage. What the hell was going on? She reached to take another incoming call, but the light started blinking before she hit the ready button. The light meant an incoming call directly to her extension.

"Hello?"

"Shay, I'm sorry to bother you at work. You gotta get over here now. Pick up Lacey and come to the house."

"I can't, Zack, I'm stuck here at work."

"You don't get it. I picked up a station out of Dallas, a radio station. Did you hear that loud noise before the crack, the humming noise?"

"Yeah," she said, shaking.

"Well, they heard it, too. In Dallas, Texas. The world is going nuts. My lights are still off, but at least I have food and water saved."

"I can't come over, at least not 'til later. They've got us answering counselor calls. I'll probably be here late. They're coming in from all over the country. They heard the Sound, too."

"They heard it everywhere, Shay. The power went out everywhere, cars on the freeway, planes for all we know."

Shay said nothing. The news was too much for her to process. She needed to get home to her daughter. Saving Grace could suck eggs.

"Just get Lacey and come by the house when you get off work tonight."

"I will, Zack. I promise. It was sweet of you to call."

He seemed uncomfortable. "I try to check up on you."

"I know."

He paused awkwardly. "This is something. I don't know

what it is. But it's gonna get worse before it gets better. Call me as soon as you can."

"I will, Zack." Another long pause.

"I…" The silence went jagged, a rush of surf crashing against deep winter coastline. "Just be careful."

"I will."

"Goodbye, kiddo."

She hung up and stared at the phone. "Kiddo." That's exactly how he treated her—like a kid, like an obligation. She didn't know where they were going or how things would be when they got there. But she did feel some comfort in his presence, and now was when she needed it most.

She thought about the noise on the line as she accepted an outside call. Something magic was happening. An energy was loose in the world.

Shortwave radio enthusiasts are familiar with so-called "numbers stations," which broadcast strings of digits in various languages. The sources are often unclear, though U.S. experts believe the stations may be used to send coded messages between spies and/or drug dealers. The following is a transcript of a message sent Friday, 14 March 20--. It was broadcast in a monotonous, possibly computer-generated child's voice at 8719 kHz. The message has been translated from the Tōhoku dialect of Japanese. To date, the numbers portion of the message has never been decrypted.

VOICE: Attention, attention. Good morning. 11111 74397 09265 26504 68813 77811 23427 96451 18416 78118 48742 02157 01319 31714 02486 98102 28048 20413 36478 12484 82865 47112 28545 11111. End transmission.

This message is known to have repeated at least 237 times that morning.

However, at exactly 1946 Zulu (Coordinated Universal Time), the following message was broadcast instead:

VOICE: Attention, attention. Good morning. 11111 74397 09265 26504 68813 77811 23427 96451 18416 78118 48742 02157 013 [*Screeching tone.*] Attention,

attention.   Interrupt.   11111, breaking 11111. **Attention. Attention 666.** Repeat. **Attention 666.** End transmission. Confirm.

The voice was the same, a monotonous child's voice speaking Tōhoku —ben Japanese. No further messages have been heard on this frequency.

H

Scott was thankful for a number of things as he marched through light snow. Among the simplest of these was his carton of leftover rice. Who knew how long he'd be stuck in that tiny hotel room? Every last calorie helped; hence his current shopping trip. Another break was the proximity of his hotel to a certain Arkansas-based retail superstore. He was far less thankful for the heaving mob that beat him to its doors.

The question of where he directed his thanks would perhaps be relevant soon. He was raised Baptist, but much like the soft flakes drifting through the air, it didn't stick. He found it difficult to accept the idea of an invisible Jewish superhero in the sky, but even harder to believe a Big Bang could produce a Bigger Something out of nothing. Maybe these Intelligent Design folks were on the right track. Either way, he was glad his cosmological confusion left room for him to sleep in on Sunday mornings.

"Everything happens for a reason." That was his mother's favorite credo, back before she crossed the wrong street and got hit by a police car. Apparently the reason that happened was she was wearing a hooded raincoat, and some jackass held up an Arby's half a mile away. *Go figure.*

His mind returned to *Court of Law*, the reason he was back in Sugar Roses in the first place. He knew almost nothing about law. That was the first problem. He read Turow's book more carefully and discovered he wasn't a fan. That was the second problem. And while Turow did a fair job representing Sugar Roses—both he and a research assistant visited the town several times—there was nothing inherently cinematic about the book. It wasn't as if Poke Duncan, the de facto protagonist of the account, were any kind of hero. On the contrary, he admitted to the attempted date rape of a minor for no better reason than he liked her Tater Tots. Good luck convincing Ryan Gosling to take that role.

Scott schlepped through the stately parking lot full of snow-dusty cars and hustled past impatient drivers to enter the store. Bedlam. Pure bedlam. The power was back on, but disconnection from the Internet meant credit and debit card purchases couldn't be processed. Local checks were okay, but ATMs were down so no one could withdraw any cash. And as Choctaws and many other low-income locals were seemingly allergic to checking accounts, the clerks were, as his dad liked to say, up to their asses in alligators.

"I'm sorry, ma'am. I'm sorry, ma'am!" the nearest clerk yelled. The poor kid looked to be about five minutes away from a murder-suicide.

"You're sorry? Well, sorry ain't gonna feed my kids!"

At least Scott had cash in his pockets. That was another thing he was thankful for. When the power went out in Hollywood, the same riotous behavior broke out, except in colorful Spanglish. Here at least, you could understand every four-letter word.

Scott grabbed a cart and chuckled to himself as he pressed deeper into the store. Well, you had to laugh, didn't you? Once you got the joke, that is. The punch line is it never really matters. These people were acting like the Apocalypse was upon them.

A fellow writer once told him the best comedy derives from overreaction to un-tragic circumstances. "Take it even farther than that," the writer explained, "and bang, you've got Elizabethan tragedy. *Hamlet. Othello.* 'Are you kidding? They all *died?* That's just crazy!' Now, instead of bumping all those people off, wound them instead, and there you go: You're right back in slapstick country."

Scott looked around the store. *Yep. High comedy, all right.* A minor skirmish broke out in aisle five, where an angry clerk refused to make change for a hundred. The even angrier customer, a septuagenarian black lady, threw a basket full of roast chicken directly at the clerk's head. The outraged clerk sputtered incoherently. "You do not throw a chicken!" he huffed.

As Scott worked his way deeper into the grocery aisles looking for canned goods and other non-perishables, he employed a relaxation trick he developed at Excelsior: Watch the world like a movie. Turn off the sound in your head and write music. Score the scene, in other words. He tried to imagine this fracas as if it were directed by Stanley Kubrick. Kubrick would've used classical, he thought. In his head now he heard the Blue Danube Waltz. It was giddily sublime. Then he tried circus music. *Too on-the-nose,* as

72

his screenwriter acquaintance would say. *Too dead on.*

Scott passed a display of *Li'l Warriors* coloring books. A chipmunk and a beaver stood on a grassy knoll and watched David square off against Goliath. On another cover, a retarded-looking squirrel peeked out from a patriarch's beard. The patriarch waved a stick and declaimed something important, probably "Thou shalt not kill" or "Be kind; rewind!" This was the religious training of America in the twenty-first century. This was what passed for theosophical insight: time-traveling, fundamentalist squirrels. No wonder people were freaking out. They probably thought angry Muslim bears were coming.

To Scott, God was a fuzzy but reassuring place in his consciousness, a philosophical shortcut that eliminated many of life's most general concerns. What'd happen to him when he died, for example? No idea, but whatever it was, it'd be better, more noble, than mere putrefaction. God could fix that. Was there an absolute moral code, an elemental right and wrong? Scott wasn't sure, but God would keep the ship on course until it reached its destination. *Everything happened for a reason*, and hopefully some of those reasons were good. He didn't hold the death of his mother against God, nor did he praise God for making the sun shine on the just and the unjust. He gave God His share of credit for the fact that good usually held its own against evil. That was something. In fact, it was plenty. God, to Scott Glass, was the Thing That Makes It All Work Out, the grand universal equivalent to movies he liked to watch when he was sick with the flu: *Ah, The Princess Bride. Maybe things will get better after all.*

Oklahoma was founded on a land rush—that and the forced migration of Native Americans—and a rush to acquire, Scott reflected, was a part of human nature in any case. It was certainly alive here today. Boomer Sooner! Docile housewives shoved each other for family-size packages of chicken thighs. Seniors in motorized wheelchairs duked it out *Murderball*-style over tubes of hamburger meat.

It took Scott a moment to identify a weird emptiness in the store: There wasn't any music playing on the speakers, not even in-store advertisements. He was so used to the inoffensive croon of soft pop-rock and country overhead that he'd taken it for granted.

73

Without it, the store felt hangarlike, oppressive. He saw it for what it was, a giant box full of mediocre food, half-stitched clothing, and other shoddy items made in China and priced to leap directly into carts. Jessica had been to Europe once and regaled him with wild tales of how everything was different there. "In Europe," she said, "people make things by hand, as well as they can, and other people are happy to pay them what those items are worth." Scott very much doubted this was true. Surely Europe had just as many people with no taste, or at least no money to act on good taste if they had it. Surely Europe sold crap in abundance just like America. By the end of her story, she made it sound like Ricardo Montalbán and Hervé Villechaize greeted you when you got off the plane at Charles de Gaulle.

Without music, the air seemed too close around his neck. He inhaled raggedy and struggled to relax.

This is it, Scott realized. This is America. In America, quantity over quality is king. Why sell fine cuisine, even simple handmade delicacies, when you can crush a cow's entrails into hamburger and slap it in a bun? ("100% USDA Inspected!" the ads bragged pathetically.) Why bake potatoes when you can fry them in minutes? Why drink wine when fountain soda costs eighty cents a tanker? And it wasn't just fast food, it was fast everything. Clothes made by Taiwanese children in less than an hour. Furniture that comes in a box. People slap the shit together with hammers and hope it doesn't break before they move it across the room.

Even art, so-called fine art, was made at breakneck speed by no-talent slackers who never learned anything about technique or art history. Classical music requires dozens of musicians, each a trained virtuoso. Opera requires weaponized voices. Even mariachis know what they're doing. But American music, country, rock and roll, rap music, none of that requires any actual knowledge. There are glorified garage bands all over America, some of whom have major record deals, who can't explain the difference between 3/4 and common time. Most rappers don't know poetry. How could anyone rap without knowing meter, alliteration, or metaphor? Thanks to Photoshop, visual artists don't have to learn how to paint. Writers devolve into bloggers, and the panoply of human expression withers into "ROFLMAO" and "☺." People "writing as James Patterson" sell books, for Chrissakes. At times like these,

Scott considered himself a wine connoisseur in a Grape Kool-Aid nation.

But y'know what? That was okay, too. He could work around that. He worked around it every day. If only he could work around this fat animal in canned goods. If you can't move your ass without a motorized wheelchair, lady, then lose some fucking tonnage! Jesus, how much of a clue do you need?

"I'm sorry," the lady said, a model of mildness. "It's just so crowded in here today."

"Hey, no problem," Scott said automatically. "I'm in no hurry." Which was true. So why was he furious? That wasn't like him. His temper was spiking out of nowhere.

He looked around the store again, and jolted into focus with a snap. Everywhere he looked, people were arguing over items they didn't need.

One guy yelled at his wife, "I ain't buyin' that! Them kids need a vitamin, damn it!"

"Don't tell me I don't know how to be a mother to my own kids!"

The kids punched each other.

Clerks yelled and pointed.

Even the checkout scanners beeped accusatory tones. Scott's jaw fell open. Viewed clearly, the store seemed to teeter on the edge of violence, a retail Beirut.

Well, why *shouldn't* they smack each other around, the white trash troglodytes? They were all wrestling fans; they'd probably make it entertaining, hit each other with folding chairs and the like. Trot their wives around in bikinis. Vince McMahon could officiate: Welcome to BlubberMania! Jesus, look at this chromosome surplus over here. Those kids are so ugly David Lynch would run and hide. Not a *Wheel of Fortune* winner in the store. "Hi, Pat, I'm here with my wife-beating husband and my two failed abortions!"

Wow, Scott laughed. That was over the line. Who spiked my Post Toasties with gamma rays? On second thought, everything was over the line. What was wrong with him today? He looked down at his cart. A more random assortment of groceries would be hard to imagine. He didn't know how to cook any of this stuff. So why did he buy it? His fists were clenched. He had no memory of closing them. He wanted to throttle someone, anyone. *Jesus!*

He had to get out of there. He damn near ran for the checkout aisle. He was having a panic attack. Maybe something was in the air, released by the climate control ducts when the power came back on. He was probably losing lung capacity by the second. He'd sue these bastards from here to their evil corporate stronghold in Bentonville, just see if he didn't!

"Christ Almighty, just pick an aisle and stay in it!" he blurted. The woman in front of him wheeled around with murder in her eye.

"What'd you say to me?"

"I said people are trying to get through here!"

"You shut up!" her filthy offspring contributed.

"And you eat a vitamin!" Scott retorted.

"My kids can eat anything they want!"

"Yeah, *clearly*!"

"Are you *tryin'* to make me kick your ass?"

"Hey, at least I can lug mine around without a wheelbarrow! Shit!"

"Mommmmm!" the kids screamed. "He cussed!" And they screamed. And they screamed! A common yammer rose in the store, a crescendo of outrage and hatred. There were two dozen infants in the store; all their minuscule faces were open, screaming, crimson with fury. Every child wailed in fear. Each adult burned to fight. The screaming didn't stop, merely leapt up in volume.

Somehow, at the last possible second, Scott noticed what was happening and refused to join in. He wasn't sure people knew what they were doing. Screeches, cursing, and incoherent battle cries blended into a complex chord of rage. Scott stood there, paralyzed by wonder, yet aching to contribute to the chorus. He was desperate to submit. He left his cart behind, ran for the door, and escaped into cold air. Even then he wasn't free. He threw his head back, his arms open wide, and SCREAMED! He fell to his knees for the second time that day, his body depleted, and waited for the madness to pass.

Meanwhile, back in America's favorite discount emporium, the atmosphere trembled in hot waves of Lorelei war song.

NEWS DEPARTMENT

DETROIT FREE PRESS

600 W. FORE

DETROIT, MI 48226

DEAR EDITOR.

THIS IS TO INFORM THE EMPLOYEES OF ARGENT ZURICH THAT THEY HAVE VERY LITTLE TIME TO SEVER THEIR ASSOCIATION WITH AN AMORAL MONOLITH. WE ARE ONTO YOU. WE KNOW WHAT YOU DO. NO LONGER WILL YOU BE PERMITTED TO USURP DEMOCRACY FOR YOUR OWN GREEDY ENDS. EVEN AS THE SAND SLIDES FATALLY DOWN THROUGH THE HOURGLASS, KNOW THIS: YOUR DESTINY WILL BE SEPARATE. YOUR DESTINY WILL COME FORTH AT HUMAN HANDS. IT IS TIME FOR RIGHT-THINKING CITIZENS TO RISE UP AGAINST YOU AND TAKE WHAT IS THEIRS. NO LONGER WILL THE DISPARITY BETWEEN THE WORKER AND HIS AVARICIOUS MASTER BE ALLOWED TO WIDEN. NO LONGER WILL THE VOTE OF A CORPORATE ENTITY MATTER MORE THAN THE VOTE OF A CITIZEN. "THE FIRST ONE NOW WILL LATER BE LAST." YOU HAVE BEEN WARNED.

A.Q.U.S.A.

⊖

Buddy sat on the porch of the Mackenzies' house and wept uncontrollably. He finished his newspaper deliveries a few minutes late today and couldn't find the words to explain why to Mr. Holcomb. Mr. Holcomb seemed to understand anyway. *Scary noises in the sky!* The snow made it harder to see when he rode his bike, and sometimes the wheels wanted to slip. It was a very unusual day today. A very unusual day, and you could take that to the bank!

He rented a room upstairs from the Mackenzies, but he didn't feel like being up there today. The TV wasn't working right. Even the radio went off and on with lots of loud hissing and squealing noises in between. "Trying to," the DJ said. "Not even sure why.... Nickel difficulties." He knew the radio man, a nice fella named Righteous Mike who worked at the radio station out on Anderson Parkway. Buddy even got to be on the radio once when Righteous Mike did his radio show from Scooter's Stop 'n' Git. Buddy told Righteous Mike how good the soda pop was at Scooter's and how sometimes they gave him free egg rolls.

"You can't beat that with a stick," Righteous Mike prompted him.

Buddy agreed wholeheartedly. "I don't even want to!" he added.

Buddy liked Righteous Mike's station. It played all kinda Beatles songs and Jesus songs on Sundays. They even played Pastor Dan's sermons from the Baptist Church, they just played 'em a week late. That was fine with Buddy. He liked to hear 'em again.

He shouldn't oughta be crying out here on the street. He'd probably make people sad, that's for sure. Wasn't nothin' to be scared of, anyway. So he heard some funny noises. Maybe they was airplanes or somethin'. Except he didn't think so, 'cause it was kinda like he heard 'em in his whole body. What was really scary was how the last one made him hateful. It was like he wanted to fight people with his hands, and that wasn't how Jesus wanted him to be. That wasn't a mild spirit, no way, José. Then he got the shakes somethin' fierce. He got a feeling like he was stuck in an elevator, even though he wasn't.

Police cars and ambulances went back and forth like crazy. They was sirens all over town. People was really hurtin' today. He wished he knew what he could do about it.

Dear Jesus, he prayed, bowing his head. *I want all the people to be okay, and as much as you love all the people, I bet you do, too. So if they's somethin' you want me to do about it, then please help me to understand how I can help all the people. Someday I'm gonna go to Heaven and live with you and you'll be like my real friend. I'm gonna tell you how much I love you, Jesus. I love you so much. I think you and me is maybe gonna go fishin' and then you can tell me all the stuff I don't understand, 'cause you'll be like my favorite friend an' everything. But maybe they's some way I can help you with all these sirens, and I want you to be proud of me, so you gotta tell me what needs to get done. In Jesus' name, I love you. Amen.*

He listened with his ears and he looked with his eyes. He sang a Jesus song to himself: "I will enter His gates with Thanksgiving in my heart. I will enter His horse with praise. I will say this is the day that the Lord has made; I'm Willie Joyce, for He has made me glad." His breathing got slower and he started to feel okay. "He has made me glad, He has made me glad. I'm Willie Joyce, for He has made me glad."

Buddy wasn't crying anymore. "Thank you for making me glad, Jesus!"

You're welcome, a voice said.

This had happened before. Jesus talked to Buddy sometimes when he prayed. Buddy tried to be extra polite around Jesus, so he nodded and waited humbly for Jesus to talk.

You and me sure is good friends, Buddy, Jesus continued.

"We sure is, Jesus." Buddy looked around for Jesus but didn't see him this time. "You and me is best friends."

So how come you cryin'?

"I heard a funny noise or somethin'. It was all crazy like."

Kate Mackenzie stood on tippy-toes to watch through the window. "Mommy," she said, "ol' Buddy's talkin' to hisself again."

"Leave him alone, honey. He's prayin'."

"Does Jesus talk to Buddy sometimes?"

"Oh," her mommy answered from the next room, "Jesus talks to everybody, honey. You just gotta know how to listen."

"I want to see if I can hear him."

"Okay, honey. Just don't go pickin' on Buddy when he's tryin' to pray, okay?"

"I won't." Silly Buddy. He was funny sometimes. "Come and watch!"

"Let Mommy rest, okay?"

"Okay."

Buddy, Jesus said. *What you got to be scared about? Don't you trust me, or what?*

"You know I trust you, Jesus. You cain't tell no lies or nothin'."

That's right. I love you so much. You're my special friend.

Tears welled up in Buddy's eyes again.

Don't go cryin', now, Buddy. They ain't nothin' to cry about.

"They ain't?"

No. Why you cryin'?

"I heard all them sirens, Jesus. I don't know what's goin' on. I heard noises in my heart."

They's some things you just cain't understand, Buddy. It's like your daddy said: 'You ain't a big fella, you's small in stature and just as small in learnin'.' He wadn't tryin' to be mean to you when he said that, Buddy. He just knew somethin' different about you. Ain't nothin' wrong with bein' simple.

"I know it." Wadn't no reason for Jesus to get all personal about it.

I want to tell you what's goin' on, but it's kindly over your head, okay? They's lotsa things happenin'. It's real complicated.

"So is that why it's snowing?"

Kindly sorta. Not really. They's some stuff gonna happen most people won't know nothin' about. It'll be like spirit things. I don't know how it's all gonna work out.

"*You* don't know? Holy smokes!" Buddy laughed. If Jesus didn't know what was going on, who did? You can tell that to the Marines!

I got a pretty good ideal, Jesus answered. *You done heard a lot about this in church, but you prob'ly didn't understand it all. Funny part is, they didn't, either. Don't nobody understand. They don't know. The Bible says it comes like a thief in the night, but it don't tell you what the thief is gonna look like or how he's gonna act. Truth is, them folks was just makin' stuff up all the time the best they knew how.*

"They was makin' it up?" Buddy asked. "No way, Jesus. Pastor Dan says them folks was inspired. They got the Holy Spirit an' whatnot."

You know where the Holy Spirit comes from? Jesus asked. *It comes from inside your heart, Buddy. That's a good thing. You need what you got inside there to come out. But they ain't nothin' in there you didn't already have. I done already put it in there. Ain't no special kinda truth in there you don't already know. An' they ain't no secrets in there you ain't been keepin' from yourself the whole time.*

"I don't understand," Buddy admitted.

Them people had questions, Jesus explained. *They didn't know who to ask all that stuff. So they listened inside their hearts and sang songs and prayed prayers and waited for me to tell 'em what was goin' on. Now, you tell me, Buddy: How'm I gonna tell 'em something like that? Ain't nobody tellin' me nothin', neither. They's secrets in the world ain't been told yet. Cain't be told! People can tell you they know what's gonna happen, but that ain't nothin' but talk, Buddy. You cain't look into the future like it was TV or nothin'. You and me is both stuck in our times, Buddy. We make plans and we hope we know what we're doin', but it ain't always true. We don't always know everything.*

"So you don't know if I'm goin' to Heaven?" Buddy realized.

Kate turned away from the window, startled. "Buddy's crying, Mommy."

"He's just upset, honey. He'll be okay." Kate listened closer.

I know you got a good heart, Buddy. Ain't no badness in you. But even good folks can have bad stuff happen to 'em sometimes. You know that.

"I don't want to go to Hell, Jesus."

"You ain't goin' to Hell, Buddy," Kate promised.

Hell? Is that what you're worried about?

"Yes."

Oh, Buddy, come on now. They ain't no Hell like they told you.

"They ain't?"

You look around, Buddy. Ain't folks sad enough as it is?

"Yessir. They shore are."

I don't know everything they is to know about Daddy, but I'll tell you this for dang sure: He don't got no bidness makin' Hell for no people to live in forever. Burnin' 'em up like they was hot dogs. What kinda foolishness is that?

"I don't know."

Now, you listen to me, Buddy. All you got when you die is the gladness in your heart. That's the truth. I ain't even gonna try to tell you what happens after that, 'cause ain't no way to tell you somethin' like that. Ain't no words could even talk about it. But if you was to get kilt tomorrow, you gonna tell me you afraid of some craziness like Hellfire? You afraid the Lord gonna do somethin' hateful to you?

"No," Buddy said. "That don't make no sense. *I* don't think."

And you right. You dang sure are. But they's a hate in this world even good people cain't do nothin' about. And I'm tellin' you sure as I'm standin' here that it's gonna make some terrible things happen for a while. You gonna hear some things make you shake in your sleep!

"Are all my friends gonna be okay?"

You know somethin', Buddy? A good fella like you got more friends than he know what to do with. Ain't no speakin' for all them people. You got friends all over town.

"I love you, Jesus."

I love you, too, Buddy. You be strong, now. You keep singin' them songs, okay? They gonna cheer you up when nothin' else will. You keep singin' an' believin' in your heart.

"I love God with all my heart," Buddy sang, "and with all my soul. He is the one I love so much…"

"I love the Lord with all my heart and every part of my soul," Kate sang along.

There, Jesus said. *You hear that little girl singin' inside?*

"That's Kate," Buddy said. "She's my friend."

She sure is. Now you get in there and tell her everything's gonna be okay.

Buddy nodded, then remembered something important. "I thought you said you didn't know if things was gonna be okay."

Dudn't matter what I know, Buddy, Jesus said. *Dudn't matter what you know. This ain't about what people know. It's about what you think when you're scared and you don't know nothin'. You can think things is gonna be terrible, and then you get crazy and do terrible things. Or you can think things is gonna be good, and you do good things. You see what I mean?*

"I think so," Buddy said. "You talkin' 'bout faith an' whatnot."

I sure am, Buddy. I'm talkin' 'bout believin' in your heart, 'cause that's where everything that's really you comes from. I'm talkin' about doin' good things 'cause you know they ain't no other way you can be and still be friends with Daddy and me. If you friends with us, you friends with everyone else. You reckon?

"I sure do."

Okay, now. You get in there and you hug that little girl.

"Ain't gonna be *nothin'* wrong," Buddy said.

You sure?

"'Course I am, Jesus. You ain't gonna let things turn out wrong. I may be simple, but even I know that. Shoot."

Thank you, Buddy, Jesus said. Buddy thought he heard a smile in Jesus's voice. *That's exactly what I needed to hear. You a good friend,*

Buddy. You an' me gone be okay.

"I love you, Jesus. I'm gonna talk to you later, okay?"

Every day, Buddy. I love you, too. I'll talk to you later.

Buddy sat on the porch and took a few minutes to get his head on straight. He didn't want little Kate to see him cryin', no, sir.

In the house, Kate went into the next room, where Mommy was layin' on a couch. Mommy got a headache earlier and was tryin' to get better.

"I saw Jesus hugging Buddy outside, Mommy."

Mommy laughed. "Sure you did, honey. Let Mommy have some quiet time, okay?"

"Okay." Kate went into the living room and rolled her cars around. "I saw Jesus hugging Buddy," she insisted.

Friday March 14, 20—

Affiliated Press: Breaking News

Latest Headlines

National

- Rare Identical Sextuplets Born
- World's Oldest Woman Now 117
- Texas Execution Delayed By Blackout
- Massive Fire Rages in St. Louis
- Archbishops Convene in Crisis
- Psychic Channels Saint Peter
- Obituaries in the News
- Clear Channel Network Restored
- Fox News "Rapture Watch"
- 747 Crash in Scottsdale, AZ
- Catherine Coulter: "Told You So"
- Suicide Hotline Overloaded
- Pat Robertson: "The Day Is at Hand"
- Traffic Stalls for Hours on LA's 405
- Riots in New Orleans Kill Dozens
- President, VP in Secret Location
- Slashdot: UUNET Repairs Underway
- NBA Postpones Weekend Games
- Comcast Offline Nationwide
- NY Governor: "We're On It"
- Volcanic Tremors in Alaska
- Idaho Army Nat'l Guard in Revolt

- DC on Highest Security Alert
- DJ Buzz Da Ramfunkshus Plans Benefit
- Jetliners Collide Over Newark
- Saving Grace CEO Calls Larry King
- Hundreds Killed in Disney World Riot
- CDC Investigation Continues
- Newspapers Plan Saturday Edition
- Mail Bomb Scare at GNN
- Detroit Imposes Martial Law
- DirecTV Service Restored
- Clooney Gives Boy CPR, Saves Life
- FAA Grounds All Domestic Flights
- FedEx CEO: "What the [Expletive]?"
- Threat Level Elevated to Red

I

Amanda pulled over to cry after less than five blocks. It was all too much for her. The streets of Sugar Roses were a nightmare, cars abandoned, windows drawn. The air was thick with sirens, raised voices, and ozone. She sat in her beat-up Accord and tried to pull herself together. She'd call Tyler to come pick her up, but his fucking Jeep was up on blocks in the yard, and she'd be damned if she'd perch on the back of his scooter again. *Useless!* Claudia should've let her go home hours ago. Now she had to contend with all this shit, and for what? To keep a library open? Jesus, it's not like anyone was in a mood to read. She had to pull two old guys out of a fistfight. One of 'em looked like the kinda guy who might break a bottle and wave it at people. The other guy looked like Woody Allen. It woulda been entertaining if she hadn't been directly between them. She screamed her ass off the whole time. Way to keep it together, Amanda. Way to boost your street cred. Not that screaming didn't feel good sometimes, but it wasn't exactly an approved work time activity at the Althea T. Vandyke Municipal Library. Get a grip, girl, *shit!*

Well, it was The Day After Fucking Tomorrow, after all, so it's not like she wasn't entitled to a PMS moment. Everyone was acting all psycho today. Claudia kept praying under her breath, Kathleen started biting her nails, and she was pretty sure Dustin was jerking off in the men's room. Why else would she catch him coming out of there with an issue of *Allure*? That guy gave her the creeps anyway. If he ever found out about Riot Grrlz, oh my God, she'd have to kill herself with extreme prejudice. That'd be it. Death before dishonor, compadres.

"I wish we had more information to give you about what's going on here locally," Righteous Mike said on the radio. "Obviously, what we're getting off the news feed is just...I mean, you can't even imagine it'd all be happening on the same day. I sure hope everyone out there is safe and sound and...Y'know, now's the kinda time when you just...you want to be with the ones you love, maybe gather your family around you and keep your head down. We're gonna do the best we can to keep you informed here and bring you all the news as it comes into the station. I just...Y'know, our prayers are out there with all of you, our listeners and our friends in Sugar Roses and all over Garvin County. I just got a call from my daughter, and boy, did that put my heart at ease."

She couldn't remember Righteous Mike ever acting all family guy before. Usually he just introduced Vanessa Carlton records and tried not to sound like a fucking middle-aged douchebag. She didn't even know he had a daughter. She wondered what Righteous Mike's last name was. She wondered if he was old enough that she might've gone to school with Spawn of Righteous Mike. She wondered if Righteous Mike was a fellow alumnus of Sugar Roses High School. He probably sat in algebra class back in the day and sketched Van Halen and Def Leppard logos on his Trapper Keeper and dreamed of being a rock star. He probably had a mullet. He probably got his rocks off fantasizing about puddles of ecstatic groupies. At the very least, he must've dreamed of spinning records for some big station in Dallas or California or someplace. No one ever daydreamed about life in Sugar Roses, no matter how big a local star they might turn out to be.

No one imagined life being like this. Now her boyfriend was a dork and her clothes were all stupid and her tits ached and her period wouldn't start. No one ever saw the diminishment coming. Life got small, the world got small, people got small, it all sank into meaningless bullshit. She cried so hard it felt like it might cause permanent damage, a piercing of her heart.

The sun was out just in time to sink toward the horizon. Righteous Mike played a series of commercials. No sense putting business on hold, now, was there? It was only the end of the fucking world, so why not make a few bucks on your way to the grand finale? His voice in the commercials seemed incongruously upbeat after his stammering news report. She imagined Righteous Mike coming into the station at five in the morning or whenever, pouring a fat cup of coffee, and reading ad copy with a fake-ass smile on his face. "Come into Scooter's Stop-n-Git, where you're not just a customer, you're family!" What a bunch of shit.

She wondered if Righteous Mike and his daughter hung out on weekends. She wondered if Righteous Mike went to parent-teacher conferences and used his cheesy commercial voice. "Little Jennifer's not just our daughter, she's family!" he'd say, beaming like a fucking moron. Amanda and her dad used to be tight. They used to go fishing together and window shop at the mall and all kinds of wholesome shit like that. He used to go to her art exhibits and grin like he got paid by the tooth. Things were different now. Now he slumped when he looked at her, like she was an art project gone horribly wrong. He didn't introduce her to his friends anymore. He didn't ask her to go to church with Mom and Jeff and the kids. It was like she'd become the family secret. He never called her Amanda Bear anymore. And while he was always polite to Tyler, he also made sarcastic remarks he knew would fly right over Tyler's head. It never failed to embarrass her when they did. Or maybe Tyler just knew how to blow the guy off, him and his sarcasm. She wished he'd teach her how to do it.

She called her mom everyday. Sometimes dear old Mom even picked up the phone. More often she let it go to voicemail. It's like they were putting her in isolation, or quarantine. Sacrifices had to be made. The good of the family demanded distance. What was that shit her mom said to her once? "Honey, your father and I will always love you. But people grow apart sometimes, and you can't keep on testing our limits and expect us to approve." Whatever happened to unconditional love? Oh, wait, it was their friendship that had conditions. She'd trade their love for their time in a moment. She needed their friendship more.

She couldn't be pregnant. She couldn't. That was …No. She couldn't get her head around it. It reminded her of angry customers: "That is simply unacceptable." But sometimes the world took a dump on your head whether you accepted it or not. Shoulda remembered to bring your umbrella.

Her cell phone started working around four. It was buzzing now. She picked it up out of her car's drink well. It was Tyler, text messaging her again: *plz let me know ur ok im freaking out*. She wiped her eyes and took pity on him.

I'm okay, she typed. *I'm on my way home.*

Her phone vibrated again mere seconds later: *be super carful and get home safe i love u.*

Was the world *trying* to fuck her up? She shuddered and sobbed all over again. That was Tyler in a nutshell. One minute he's calling her a bitch, the next he loves her and it's like she's supposed to take those crazy spins without so much as a complaint. And all the while he has no idea the nuclear bomb she was probably gonna have to drop on him soon. *NO.* She was late because she was stressed. That's all it was. She couldn't be pregnant. They'd been careful. Sorry: *carful.*

She was attracted to Tyler the second she met him, but it was starting to dawn on her that sometimes she had a tough time telling attraction and pity apart. She felt like a better, stronger person when she was with him, but maybe that was because he made her feel she was constantly rescuing him. And sometimes he'd brush the green hair from his green eyes and she'd explode into a supernova of love for him. She'd lay awake at night and watch him sleep, try to live his dreams with him by watching his eyes jitter under his eyelids.

He could barely make it through a conversation. He had like a thirty-second attention span. He never got around to enrolling in college, though it was definitely on his To Do list. But when he played video games, or guitar, it was like divine powers took him over. He couldn't even sing. He barely tried. Amanda just watched his agile fingers dance, and her breath jammed up crossways in her throat. Once, one time only, she talked him into playing "guitar" on her arm. She shut her eyes and savored the music on her skin.

A vision of Tyler's hands holding their child hit her like a meteor. The force of it should've left a crater ten feet wide. She couldn't take it.

And yet...people dealt with stuff like this. Somehow they did. What she was going through was nothing compared to the shit Righteous Mike talked about on the news. Somehow people turned into grown-ups and dealt with ugly divorces and Sudden Infant Death Syndrome and breast cancer and Great Depressions and God, it was like they were made out of something bulletproof. How many planes crashed today, not to mention all the murders and fires and car accidents? She didn't understand how people could deal with shit like that and not go crazy, how they could still be identified as sane human beings. It didn't seem humanly possible to lose a family, as so many people probably had all over the world today, and still get out of bed tomorrow. She couldn't understand the superhuman transformation that was supposedly about to happen to her that would make her an adult. In Tyler's stupid comic books, it was always radiation or genetic mutations or ancient Norse gods that turned ordinary kids into supermen. In real life, it was nothing but years that did the trick.

Righteous Mike came on the radio again. "We're getting reports that apparently not all those plane crashes were caused by the blackout. We think there have been, what was it, five plane crashes so far. Now, according to the FAA, it wasn't any kind of terrorist activity. They don't have any evidence of that. But apparently some of it was the blackout, apparently the pilots lost instruments and what have you, but some of it wasn't. On two of those flights, the pilots just deliberately crashed the aircraft. One pilot flew into another plane. Another just knifed into the ground. Can you believe that? It's insane. What would cause such a thing? The FAA says it has no idea. What's weird is, an hour ago people all over the country just started acting crazy. We felt it here at the station. Y'know, by the way, Tina—Tina's one of our interns here at the station—I want to apologize for what I said about your sister. That was completely uncalled for."

Amanda wondered if Righteous Mike used his cheesy commercial voice to insult Tina's sister. *Your sister's a whore, Tina, now with extra prostitution! Fellas, swing by and get yours today!*

Amanda didn't freak out as bad as everybody else did an hour ago, but maybe there was something to all this. Maybe she wasn't just upset, maybe she was going through some kind of group hallucination. Maybe one of those chemtrails her brother Jeff talked about had poisoned the air, and now everyone was on some kind of bad acid trip. That would certainly explain those two old guys in the library. It would also explain Claudia's sudden interest in prayer. Maybe it would even explain Dustin jerking off all day, though she suspected that was kind of a hobby for him. Oh God, he didn't think of her when he did it, did he? Oh, well. He might as well get some fun out of her. It's not like she was ever nice to him in person. Besides, in six months, she'd look so fat and disgusting no one would ever want to fuck her again.

God. Oh my *God.* "I'm pregnant," Amanda said, and the waterworks started all over again.

"We managed to get a hold of the Sugar Roses Police

93

Department," Righteous Mike said, "and man, those guys are working their tails off. Guys and gals. You can hear the sirens going back and forth from here at the station, and I tell ya, they are getting a real workout today. According to Officer Mark Fulton, they've responded to over a dozen car accidents and would you believe it, something like forty domestic disturbance calls. People are beating the snot out of each other today, and Officer Fulton asks you to kindly keep your mitts to yourself. He said a couple of officers had been assaulted while on duty, and there's just no call for that. So we want to take this opportunity to thank our local police officers for doing such a diligent job keeping on top of all this. It sure ain't an easy job, and our hearts go out to 'em. You can imagine the kind of violence they're seeing today. We also want to thank Emergency Services. The paramedics have been extremely busy, with everything from heart attacks to a drug overdose to some guy, and I'm not making this up, folks, waving a scythe in Ace Hardware. Apparently two people including a store employee were very badly injured in that particular incident. But things are finally calming down out there, and I hope that trend continues so these good people can finish cleaning up and get home to their families."

Family, family, *family*. Fine, she got it, Righteous Mike, holy shit. She picked up the phone again and called home. Her mom picked up on the fourth ring, a split second before the voicemail picked it up. "Honey?" she said. "Is that you?"

"You know it's me, Mom. You've got caller ID. Why haven't you called me?"

"I was busy, honey. I was trying to reach your father. He's out on a job site with Ray. The phone works both ways, y'know. You could've called me when things started going crazy. I didn't want to bother you at work. You told me not to call you there."

"Good excuse, Mom."

"Honey…Let's not do this right now, okay?"

"I'm not doing anything. I'm asking why you didn't call me. You called Jeff and Marcy, right?"

"They have babies in the house, Amanda. You know that. I wanted to make sure the grandbabies were okay." Actually, that was good news. If and when Amanda did drop her bundle of joy, maybe her parents would remember she was alive again.

"I bet you called Theresa." Her sister in Little Rock, God's gift to mothers everywhere.

"She called me, Amanda. She called me first thing."

"Oh, whatever. I'm fine, by the way."

"Are you out driving? It sounds like you're in the car."

"Yeah, Mom, I'm on my way home."

"To your little place? No, you should come here, honey, if you want to. I'm making pork chops for dinner."

"That sounds good. Can Tyler come?" The line went dead silent.

"Oh…honey," her mother finally stammered, "I thought we might just have a nice family dinner."

God, why even ask? "Tyler's nice. Tyler's family."

"He's your boyfriend, honey. There's a difference."

"For now."

That seemed to jolt the fear of God into her. "Jeff and Marcy wanted to drive over from Norman, but your father said absolutely not. He said the roads were too dangerous."

"I thought you said you couldn't get a hold of him."

"Who, your father?" Amanda heard a sudden note of panic in her mother's voice. Her mother, for all her gifts, was the worst liar in the history of the whole fucking planet.

"Yes, Mom. My father. You said he was out on a job and his cell phone wouldn't work."

"Oh. Well, it didn't. I just reached him, just now. That's why I was in the other room."

"Okay, Mom. Jesus, whatever."

"Honey, please don't use Jesus' name like that. It's not right.

You know how much it bothers me."

"That bothers you? Mom, have you been listening to the radio? The whole world's going crazy."

"I know, honey, I know. That's why it's more important than ever. I hope you've given some serious thought to this. We don't know what's happening out there. Maybe it's just... nothing. Maybe people are having a crazy day. But I heard those noises this afternoon just like everybody else. In fact..."

"Yes?" Amanda said after a long beat.

"Oh, you'll think I'm crazy. You already do, Amanda."

"I don't think you're crazy, Mom."

"You told me you thought I was losing it big time."

"That's because you couldn't remember where you put your keys, Mom. It wasn't a total psychiatric assessment. It was one stupid day."

"I know, I...Oh, I thought I heard voices."

"When, just now?"

"No, this afternoon."

"You heard voices?"

"I don't know. Maybe. I thought I did."

"You're not still hearing 'em, are you?"

"No, just for a second, after the humming noise. During the humming noise. I don't know. Things were all mixed up."

"I heard 'em, too."

"You did?"

"Yeah, for just, like, half a second."

"Are you making fun of me?"

"No, Mom, I'm not."

"You shouldn't make fun of me, Amanda. I'm the only

mother you're ever going to have." Amanda groaned. Her mom was full of old needlepoint tidbits like that. "Well, it's true. And you know your father and I worry about you. All those decisions you're making."

"Oh, here we go."

"Honey, listen. We don't know what's going on in the world today. What if this is…I mean, seriously, honey, think about it. It all has to come to an end sometime. That's just common sense. The Bible says the end times are upon us. Wars and rumors of wars. There'll be earthquakes in one place after another. Pestilence and suffering."

"Settle down, Mom."

"Don't make fun of me, Amanda! You know as well as I do the world can't get much worse without falling apart. Okay, so maybe it has. Maybe we're finally at that moment. Maybe the world has taken all it's gonna put up with. Maybe God has. I know you don't believe like we believe, Amanda, but even you can see things are falling apart. Everything ends eventually. There's always a last day. Shoot, there's airplanes falling out of the sky. What if those al Qaeda people start getting ideas? Honey, you need to take time and think seriously about the road you're on and the choices you're making. I don't want things to get any worse with you still out there floating. You're just floating, honey, you're looking for direction."

Amanda sighed, her voice drifting higher. "Mom, please don't lecture me."

"I'm not lecturing you, honey. I'm worried about you."

"I can't take it, Mom. I'm having a shitty enough day as it is."

"Honey, please. Language."

"Okay, mom, geez! God! I call you to make sure everyone's okay, and you turn it into an excuse to lecture me about my 'life choices.'"

"Oh, honey, I can't talk to you when you're like this."

"I am like this, Mom! I am exactly like this! This is totally how I am!" She burst into tears. "I need you to talk to me no matter what I'm like! Can't you fucking see that?"

Several seconds ticked by. "I'm hanging up now, Amanda. You don't have any business talking to your mother like that."

"Oh, God!" Amanda bawled and shut her phone off, then threw it into the junk on her passenger side floorboard. "Jesus, what a fucking—!" How could her mother take her there so fucking *fast?* How did she know all the right buttons to push exactly when? Now Amanda wanted to drive off a fucking bridge. Problem was, she lived in Oklahoma, where the nearest bridge was twenty miles away. "Fucking bitch!"

Through her tears, she noticed a tricycle under a nearby tree. She remembered a similar tricycle she used to ride around the neighborhood. Things were easier then, but she was too young to know it. Back then she could pedal her tricycle around the block all day and no one would say boo to her. Her parents didn't have to worry about some slobbering sexual predator carrying her off into the woods. Or who knows, maybe they did need to worry but nobody realized it. Maybe life was already fucked up under the surface and everyone was just living in a happy self-delusion. Back then, she didn't read newspapers, she didn't watch GNN, and she didn't know the whole human race was out on a pier that was rotting under its feet. Back then a skinned knee was the end of the world. Now she was about to have a baby of her own, a baby she could never afford to buy a tricycle or God, even food, and it was just one more thing happening to her on just another ordinary fucked-up day.

Today it was pilots flying airplanes into each other and nutbags with scythes in Ace Hardware and a weird overstuffed feeling in her breasts. Tomorrow it'd be hantavirus outbreaks and rigged presidential elections and the polar ice caps melting and goddamn afterbirth. Tomorrow it'd be a whole new Armageddon, and no matter what anyone told her, that's what it meant to be a grown-up: every day a new end of the world.

Published: Friday, March 14, 20— 08:16 a.m.

Bigfoot in Oklahoma?   Print   Email   Discuss

By Colleen Perry

News Reporter

ELMORE CITY – This looks like a case for TV's 'Mythbusters.' According to lifelong Elmore City resident Odell Taylor, a creature similar to the fabled Bigfoot roams the Oklahoma woods. Taylor claims to have seen the creature, known locally as Ole Red, on three different occasions. A member of the Choctaw tribe, Taylor says Ole Red is a Shampe, a forest monster that features prominently in Native American legends. He thinks the Sasquatch legends of the Pacific Northwest, and possibly even the Yeti stories of the Himalayas, describe the same creature or its close biological cousin.

"That's just science," he says. "It's common sense. If it walks like a duck, looks like a duck, and quacks like a duck, then by golly it's got to be a duck. I don't need no Ph.D. to tell me that." Taylor is an amateur scientist himself. He is a five-year member of the Bigfoot Field Researchers Organization, which has collected 62 local accounts of Bigfoot sightings since its inception in 1971. The group maintains a website at www.BFRO.net.

According to the BFRO database, most Oklahoma sightings take place in Le Flore County, where tracks were spotted near

Big Cedar only a few years ago. "[Shampes] like them forests out there," Taylor explains, "but we got our share out this-away, too. I seen tracks all over my property, and sometimes you can hear them like calling to each other out there." Taylor describes the call of the Shampe as a high-pitched scream, similar to wood going into a circular saw. "The noise will carry for miles," he says. "Man, it like to drive them dogs I got plumb out of their skins. They don't like hearing it."

Taylor, a dedicated coon hunter, thinks he shot a Shampe once but was unable to find the carcass on later inspection. "I did find some blood. Them dogs wouldn't go anywhere near it. You could still smell the Shampe out there even after he done run away. He got a stink about him, kind of like a cross between sewer and garbage. Once you smell it, you won't ever forget it."

Taylor describes Ole Red as an apelike creature, eight or nine feet tall, with clay-red fur covering most of its body. "He got a big eyebrow on him, you know, like a caveman, and his face is all wrinkled like. A lot of people, first time they see Ole Red, they think he's just some old boy rambling in the woods, but then they get a smell of him and they realize he ain't no person, you know. He's a Shampe." Often, Taylor says, eyewitnesses will experience a strong feeling of being watched for minutes or hours before the creature is finally sighted.

The word Sasquatch is a Coast Salish Indian word meaning "Old Man." The term "Bigfoot" was invented by newspaper reporters in northern California. Louisiana Choctaws refer to the creature as Nalusa Fayala, or "Long Monster," and they say it lives deep in the bayou. Some Oklahoma Choctaws believe the Shampe has a powerful sense of smell and is drawn to the smell of blood. They believe that's why the creature appears so often to hunters. Skeptics disagree. They claim the frequency of sightings has more to do with the quantity of beer consumed on hunting trips than the Shampe's keen nose.

Billy Rose is Taylor's neighbor. He's spent most of his life around the Oklahoma woods, but he doesn't believe in Ole Red or any other Bigfoot. "It does get scary out here at night sometimes. You start imagining all kinds of things. I heard people say Ole Red is like a missing link, but them folks is just ignorant. Ain't no such thing in the Bible. They need to get a better education." Rose discounts physical evidence he discovered on his property after he heard shuffling sounds outside one autumn night. "I found some fur out there. Yes, I sure did," Rose recalls. "It was smashed up against this tree out back of my property line. It was red all right, but for all I know, that was horse hair or maybe some old Irish boy or whatnot. I can't say what it was, exactly. I think people like to see what they want to see. Things ain't true just because you want them to be true."

Taylor remains undeterred by skeptics, though he admits he gets kidded about his interest in the Shampe. "Let them laugh," he says. "They ain't seen what I've seen. Last time I run up on Ole Red, we just looked at each other for a long time—a long time. It seemed like hours. He didn't make no noise or nothing, but I kindly heard his voice in my head like. I can't explain it. It's like he didn't know no words. He just talked to me in pictures. I kindly got the feeling he was trying to tell me something important. They was lots of people screaming in my head, like I remembered something bad but it ain't even happened yet. I don't know what it was. I wish I could figure it out, though. I tell you what, a thing like that can sure keep an old boy awake at night."

The day after that mysterious incident, Taylor photographed humanlike footprints in the mud by a nearby stream. It is difficult to determine print length from the close-up photographs taken that day, and some have accused Taylor of shooting regular human footprints. "The Bigfoot I seen was a young one. It wasn't Ole Red. It could've been a female. They don't get up as big as the male ones do." He insists the footprints were made by a Shampe. "I know what I saw. I'm a Christian. Why am I going to lie about a thing like that?"

Taylor asks Oklahomans who have stories about Ole Red to contact the BFRO through its website. "We want to get a real expedition to go into these woods and sort this thing out one way or the other," he says. "Until then, I think folks should keep an open mind and say, 'If people are so sure there ain't no creature out there, then how come they ain't been able to figure out what it is?'"

• **Click to discuss this story with other readers on our forums.**

K

Two hours before the first tone and blackout, Zack was all smiles. The next week was SOSU's spring break, and he looked forward to nine days of heavy drinking and poor behavior. He taught only one class on Fridays, a nine o'clock, then grabbed a long lunch at the Olive Garden. Lunch consisted of soup, salad, and two or three beers. And why not? All he had left to do on campus was grade thirty pop quizzes, and that wouldn't take more than a few minutes. For the last three years, the first four answers on any Zack Heath multiple choice exam were A, B, B, and A. So far as he knew, no one had ever paid close enough attention to notice this mnemonic tribute to everyone's favorite Swedish pop quartet. These were theatre students; they could barely find their way to school in the morning. Not one of them would be working in theatre ten years down the road, so why pretend anything he taught them even mattered?

He was finishing the last few exams when Laura knocked on the inside of his door frame.

"Heyyy," he said, immediately displeased to see her. "How's it going?"

"Pretty good. You doing anything tonight?"

"I hadn't decided. Why?"

"I was thinking…There's this play at OU tonight. One of the Greek ones. I can never keep 'em straight. My friend Becca's in it. I thought you might want to go."

Not so much. "The Greeks don't want no freaks, Laura."

"What does that mean?"

"I don't know. I'm not a big fan of tragedy, Greek or otherwise."

"I thought it might be fun for us, y'know. Maybe grab some dinner, get an early start on Spring Break."

"Yeah, I don't think so. You should go hang out with Becca."

"You never want to do anything."

"You always overgeneralize," he replied, sneering.

She snorted. "Yeah, I get it. Ooh, you're so smart."

"Smart enough to avoid an hour-long drive to watch undergrads wail in cheap togas."

"Well, *I'm* going," she said, petulantly enough to make her point. "And I'm probably gonna hang around there tonight, so."

"Okay, have fun."

"I mean," she said, glancing behind herself to make sure the hall was empty, "I'm not coming back over to your place."

"Ever?"

"Tonight."

"That's unfortunate."

"It certainly is," she said, cocking her hip. "There's a party after the show. Who knows what might happen. I thought it might be a fun date."

He looked her up and down, digging the journey. Laura was the third-hottest female student in the department. He'd spent a fair amount of time over the last few months determining this. The hottest was a musical comedy major named Jill Sexton, but Jill was so deeply in love with Jesus she probably inscribed their names together in her yearbook. Ordinarily he found Christianity an ineffectual sexual deterrent, but she also had a boyfriend in the Fellowship of Christian Athletes. Poor bastard. She probably kept him one degree away from Kevin Bacon, so to speak, every night they were together. Tough break, farm boy. The second was Rhonda Mulcahey, whose ass was so perfectly heart-shaped it ought to be granted recognition as a national landmark. Unfortunately, Rhonda Mulcahey was also what his male students referred to as a butterface—that is, everything on her looked good but her face. Cruel world, Rhonda. No movie stardom for you. Still, Zack wouldn't mind a few hours of playful hot tub time with her, and he intended to pursue that if she stayed in town for the summer semester.

Which left Laura, whom he kept around largely because the alternatives were lonely nights moping about Alyssa or frustrating nights wishing Shay never reproduced. Little Lacey was single-handedly ruining his sex life. Was there any sexual buzzkill on earth to compete with the anti-erectile shock waves of a four-year-old girl in the house? As much as he enjoyed having Shay around, naked or not, there was always the kid to contend with. Zack had taken the extreme measure of getting a vasectomy in his early thirties to ensure his eternal freedom. He considered it a small price to pay for security; he'd slam a car door on his situation if that's what it took. But every third or fourth night it was "I want to watch *Dora the Explorer*" and "Mommy, I gotta go potty" and uncovered sneezes and God help him, once even Chuck E. Cheese, what the *fuck*, Chuck E. Cheese, he'd rather be pelted with rocks.

Look, it was okay in this country to say you enjoyed masturbating to porn on the Internet. You could even compare wish lists of celebrity sex tapes. (His first-round draft pick was Faith Hill, followed closely by Amy Grant and Carrie Underwood, just because. Rachael Ray was number four with a bullet.) You could walk around Target with a tattoo that said "I FUCKING HATE YOU" and all anyone would do is clear a path. You could express revulsion for the president or capitalism or *American Idol* or the work of Maya Angelou, and the most violent reaction you'd get would be an angry comment on your Facebook page. But you say one less-than-sycophantic phoneme about children, and suddenly you're the Antichrist and should be burned at the stake before you infect anyone else with your life-crushing hatred.

"Are you even listening?"

"Y'know," Zack said, tossing a baseball, "I don't really think of us as dating, per se."

"You don't. Well, what do you call it?"

"I thought we were just…having some fun."

"Oh, is that right?" She stared at him, her hip cocked, her mouth a freckled hyphen. "Happy fun time, eh?"

"Right. Two consenting adults, who keep it between them. The first rule of Fight Club, et cetera."

"I don't know what the fuck you're even talking about."

"Exactly," he said, shooting her the gun finger.

One of these days, he reflected, Shay would expect him to teach Lacey how to swim. Then it'd be riding a bike. Before he knew it, he'd be asked to help buy her first tampon or training bra, an errand he'd unhesitatingly poison himself with boric acid milkshakes to avoid. Laura might not be the sharpest spork in the KFC, but at least she kept her ovulation to herself. So those were the thoughts in his head when the tone sounded and the lights went out. He spent the next hour in faculty parking, skipping between radio stations as they slowly returned to the air. He called Shay and practically begged her to stay at his house that night. She didn't seem thrilled by the suggestion, maybe because she had her hands full at work. But she'd come over, sure enough, and if the gods were smiling maybe little Lacey would even be at her meth-addled aunt's for the weekend.

Hours passed. The world stayed confused. He forgot about his conversation with Laura until she rapped on his car door. The clock on his dash read 3:46 P.M.

"Oh my God," Laura gasped.

"So much for tragedy in Norman, huh?" he said, indicating the radio. "We got all the tragedy you could ask for, right here in River City." Indeed, sirens pierced the air.

She slid into the car, shivering. "It's kinda freaking me out."

"I can see why it would."

"Zack...would you mind if I came over tonight?"

"Oh," Zack said, startled. Not with Shay coming over, she couldn't. "When you said you were—You know, the Greek thing. I made other plans."

"Other plans?"

"Yeah, I've got...family coming over," Zack stammered.

"Family?"

"My brother's coming by with his kids."

106

"I wouldn't mind meeting him."

Zack froze. "That's not gonna happen," he said, already bristling.

"Oh, excuse the living fuck outta me."

"Don't even start this shit, Laura. I got stuff to deal with that doesn't concern you."

"Oh, I'm so sorry, *Professor.*"

"Professor? Are you...Really? That's how you want to do this? That's what you want to discuss? Now, in the middle of God knows what? That's just perfect, Laura. Perfect fucking timing."

"I don't *have* perfect timing, Zack, okay, I don't *know* perfect timing. All I know is, the power went out all over the country, including half the cars, and it's probably gonna happen again. I don't want to go back to my apartment, okay? Is that so insane you just can't understand it?"

"Of course I understand it."

"You can't understand how I might be scared at a time like this?"

"I understand it, Laura, I just have my hands full at the moment."

"Am I being some, like, crazy *girl?*"

"Knock it off!" he exploded. "No, you're not being crazy. It has nothing to do with that. I just have other obligations right now."

"Obligations. Is that what I am to you, an obligation?"

"Oh, for fuck's sake..."

"No, so what am I, Zack, seriously? What is 'fun' to you? Am I just, like, your little fuck toy?"

"No! You're not anything to me!" he said, instantly regretting it.

Her mouth hung open for a beat. *"Fuck you!"*

107

"I didn't mean—"

"Oh, wait, I already did."

"And you should've known then! This is not a relationship!" Laura gaped. "Whatever it is, little girl, it isn't that. I'm not your family, and I'm certainly not your—You should be with them, your family. I'm not your boyfriend. I never will be. Deal with it."

That's why Laura was already crying when the air seemed to waver and her self-control vanished. She launched herself at him. *"Fuck you!"* she screamed again, slapping him over and over. He pushed her back furiously; she came at him with what must have been car keys. His left cheek ignited. He bashed her in the mouth. She fell against the door, stunned, and touched her lips. Her fingers came away bloody. She kicked the car door open and tumbled outside, then crawled away panting, her blood spraying over the snow-wet asphalt. There was crimson on the inside of his windshield. He staggered outside and vomited, his heart racing. When he turned to help, she was already gone. The die had been cast.

It took him a while to figure out every professor and student on campus lost his or her ever-loving mind that afternoon, primarily because he was holed up in the theatre men's room mopping blood from an inch-long gash in his cheek. Hopefully no one noticed the outraged cries of "You crazy bitch!" he emitted every few seconds for the half-hour he was in there. He decided to get stitches at the hospital, but wasn't even halfway back to the car when he realized Sugar Roses was in total traffic meltdown. Never mind; he didn't want to explain the cut to emergency room staff anyway. He slapped three Band-Aids on the wound, locked his office, and raced over to his place on Old Dominion Road. What he heard on the radio...It didn't feel true. He was halfway convinced it was an elaborate prank, a modern Orson Welles *War of the Worlds*. It wouldn't be long before rednecks were out shooting water towers again, whether this was a true calamity or not.

Zack had satellite TV; what he saw on it when he got home was damn near impossible to process. There were already five messages stored on his land line phone, but he was too mesmerized by news reports to listen. Instead he answered his cell phone when it rang in his hand. "Hello."

"Zack." It was Jimmy Napolitano, tech director extraordinaire and Zack's buddy in the department. "I've been trying to get hold of you for an hour."

"Are you seeing this?"

"I don't have to."

"I'm at home, Jim. I'm watching the news. This is crazy. It's 9/11 all over again."

"I'm in my office with the radio on. The students are freaking out."

"I don't blame 'em."

Some of 'em are hours away ing and asking if they're okay. hel has her hands full with the

em here. I've got room for vhat to think. I'm watching

s in Newark?"

nn plane into the next one le to do it. Three hundred

ne," Jim agreed. "Zack, start sending 'em over. I yself. The streets on the le are out fighting in the just gone crazy."

middle of a lecture on Russian Constructivism."

"Nice. That's exactly what the tenure committee'll be looking for."

"Oh, I can't wait to tell my children how I handled the

109

situation with quiet heroism. You okay?"

Zack rubbed his forehead. "No, Jim, I'm not. I….Fuck, I hit a student."

"Are you serious?"

"Yeah, she tagged me first, but I popped her clean in the mouth."

"Jesus, Zack. Which one?"

"Laura Reese."

"Laura Reese…" Jim let the name hang on the line. "Isn't she a friend of yours?"

"They're all friends of mine, Jimmy." Silence. "I shouldn't have hit her. I don't know what came over me."

"Yeah, well…Listen, man, you sure this is okay, me bringing these kids over?"

"They gotta go somewhere, Jim. It'll be fine. We'll fire up the grill, make a party of it. I've got hamburger patties for days."

"I sure do appreciate this."

"Ah, it's gotta be done," Zack sighed. "All part of the job of enriching young minds. We'll get high and watch *SpongeBob.*"

"I'm inspired, Zack."

"I know."

"You've inspired me."

"Don't bring Laura."

"I won't. I haven't seen her," Jim said.

"And don't tell anyone what I did."

"I won't. Just…deal with it when you get the chance."

"I will."

"I believe you," Jim said, though he probably didn't.

"I appreciate it. I'll see you in a bit."

"Okay. Expect the worst, Zack. These kids are barely hanging on."

"I'm watching live coverage of a riot in Downtown Disney. I think Mickey just set a kid on fire. I'm right there with 'em, my friend."

MELODY CARSON, GNN ANCHOR:

One quick programming note: We want to thank our sponsors for their generosity in allowing us to bring you complete coverage tonight with no commercial interruption. We're hoping to continue that as long as possible. We're especially grateful to McDonald's, home of everyone's favorite double-beef hamburger, the Big Mac sandwich. I'm lovin' it. We now return to GNN correspondent Ken Uematsu in Tokyo, where Aum Shinrikyo cultists have shot and killed about forty civilians in the Ginza shopping district.

Λ

Scott wandered around for what felt like hours, but it was snowing and he was cold so it probably wasn't that long after all. After a while the sirens got farther away and he heard them less often. People found ways to get their cars started and drove past him in snits of surly humiliation. Their radios played news, always news, always voices. The voices sounded anguished or terrified or gloomily resigned, never joyful or mercenary. The only music he heard was from Oklahoma City or Dallas advertising jingles. He missed the reassuring hookiness of radio that didn't matter.

Once he stopped to pet a cat. He didn't care for cats, particularly, but the cat didn't seem to know anything had gone crazy; and Scott enjoyed the diversion.

He bought a Coke from a machine outside a gas station. A disheveled man sitting on a curb there asked him if he 'prayed regular.' Scott stretched the truth and said yes. The disheveled man scratched his stomach and said, "Jesus is Lord, King of Kings." Scott wondered why Americans are so nostalgic for monarchy, but kept that to himself.

He saw a pay phone and thought about calling Jessica, but she was at work at Argent Zurich and he knew he couldn't reach her cell phone. Besides, this was one of those months they weren't seeing each other much. They'd date until they ran out of small talk, take a break, then drift back together a few weeks later in unstated angst. The sex was okay, not great but okay, and they enjoyed professional baseball on TV or at Dodger Stadium. Argent Zurich had a box there. She had freckles. He liked freckles. She smoked menthol cigarettes. He wasn't so crazy about that. She knew how to knit. The whole relationship was starting to feel like a balked pitch, an unfinished statement, a crossword with most of the clues left unsolved.

His footsteps took him back toward Anderson Parkway, but he didn't want to return to his hotel and he sure didn't want to brave the insanity of Wally World again. He watched the cars a while and tried to imagine where the citizens of Sugar Roses would unite in times of crisis. High school and college students would eventually congregate at Cuppa Joe's over by the college. The old folks would find a bar, probably the club at the Standard. Everyone else would be drawn toward warmth and...*food*. They'd want food. The lights were back on starting less than an hour after the tone, but the wave of aggression scared many small restaurant owners into closing for the night.

Scott followed a line of cars east toward the highway underpass. He suddenly realized where they were going. Only one restaurant in town had a fireplace: Abilene Sam's Country Steakhouse. The afternoon was warming, but the fire would draw people in anyway. Fire meant safety. It meant conviviality and comfort food and torches should the urgent necessity arise. Abilene Sam's was also blessed with a liquor license, a decided advantage any day of the week, but an absolute godsend right now. Scott just hoped their credit and debit card readers worked off a dialup connection. They didn't, as it turned out, but the restaurant agreed to run a tab until the system rebooted that night.

He wound up sitting at the bar for hours. He liked this place, Ponderosa gear and all. He liked the jukebox and wished he had quarters in his pocket so he could play Steve Earle and Roy Orbison and KT Tunstall. Instead he nursed rum and Cokes and a plate of barbecue nachos while bobbing along with the locals' musical selections, mostly Brad Paisley and Rascal Flatts and other country artists he didn't know much about. *When in Rome*, he thought, especially if Rome was burning.

There was a small TV over the bar, but the cable was out, so the bartender saw fit to keep it off a while. Sometimes people would come in and describe things they heard on the radio. Their voices when they did this were timid and low, as if speaking ill of the dead. Occasionally Scott would order a beer, bartender's choice, and forget to take it away from the bartender. The bartender, a quiet guy the regulars called Doyle, appreciated this oversight and neglected to stint on the rum in Scott's drinks.

Doyle was able to process Scott's credit card around seven. Scott added an order of barbecue ribs, which Doyle boxed up for his walk back to his hotel. The streets were quiet, and Scott's tennis shoes scuffed against gravel and asphalt as he walked a drunken sine wave home.

He heard frantic TV noise inside a few rooms as he meandered down the Standard Hotel second floor hallway, but when he keyed into his own room, he simply collapsed onto the king bed and shut his eyes. TV and its funeral dirges could wait. The room wavered around him like a heat mirage. His cell phone rang a few minutes later.

"Hello."

"Hey, Scott. It's me." Her voice on the line seemed extra far away, brittle and drained.

"Hey, Jessica. I meant to call you."

"Are you okay? You sound weird."

"Yeah. I've been drinking."

"Oh. It's later there. I forget. I'm sorry, baby. I just got out of the office."

"Are you at home?"

"Are you kidding? I've barely made it out of Argent Zurich's garage. I'm sitting in a parking lot that extends from here to the damn horizon. I don't know if I'll ever get home. I'll just sit here forever like a mastodon in a tar pit."

"Tell me things are calmer in L.A. than here for a change."

"Do you imagine there's any chance that might be true?"

"No."

"Then you'd be right about being wrong. My day started with FBI agents and speed-slalomed downhill from there."

"FBI?"

"The F, it turns out, stands for federal case."

"There's also a bureau in there somewhere, but I forgot where."

"The middle, I think." The line hissed for a moment. "We got another threat letter, Scott. It passed right through my hot little hands." Jessica was one of three executive assistants for Roger

Lutz, the general partner assigned to the West Coast.

"What'd it say?"

"Nothing good. Death threats. Anticorporate terrorist statements. A Dylan quote, which at least added some hippie cred."

"Dylan Thomas?"

"The other one. The Dylan who makes my dad drink whiskey."

"Right."

"I'm scared, Scott. If nothing else happened today, that alone would have pushed me onto Prozac. And then things got *really* disturbing."

"Yeah, we had a blackout here. Among other things."

"I don't know if you heard, drunky bunny, but your blackout was pretty much everywhere. The entire civilized world took a field trip to the nineteenth century for a day."

"Did it learn anything?"

"What, the civilized world? No, it mostly just played grab-ass in the back of the bus."

"We should never have signed its permission slip."

"You kid," Jessica laughed wearily. "I'm glad you can. You're not staring at the nether end of every SUV in California, wondering if the radio decided to put Stephen King in charge of the news for a while."

"I'm drunk because I'm freaked out myself," Scott admitted. "I recommend it. It helps."

"I had to leave my desk for half an hour because I was sobbing my face off. Roger kept punching the walls. The FBI stayed in the building all day, and one of the agents kept biting his nails. I think he drew blood. Today was not a banner day in my world."

"I miss you," Scott said.

"Aww," she answered automatically. "Are you okay? What's to do in the hinterland when the lanterns are off and the cows are a-lowin' in the fields?"

"No lanterns. Some cows. No lowing. They're mostly in their delicious barbecue phase." He stretched. The world was settling into place again. "It didn't last long, the blackout. People got crazy for a while and then…I dunno, I guess they just went back to work. People work here. They have real jobs, most of 'em. Not too many screenwriters or executive assistants or, you know, porn star baristas. I did meet a girl I'm pretty sure was on Riot Grrlz."

"And what, pray tell, is Riot Grrlz?"

"Oh, some website. Naked Goth girls. Rock and roll hoochie-coo."

"Hmm. Remind me to go through your Internet Favorites."

"All research, ma'am, I assure you."

They could trade banter like this for days. She had a great mind. She often made him use his. Yet he never seemed to pull her in deep. We're not in love, he thought. Not really. We're like some couple on TV. How Los Angeles of us.

The line went quiet while Jessica lit a cigarette. She exhaled into his ear. "Scott."

"Yeah."

"What do you think the end of the world will look like, if it happens?"

He curled more tightly into an understuffed Standard Hotel pillow. "I dunno. I guess I never really thought about it much."

"I never did, either, even after 9/11. I was there, y'know, in New York."

"I didn't know that."

"My MA is from Columbia."

"Oh, yeah," he said. "I guess I never put it together."

"For a year after that, it seemed like all the bad guys turned into supervillains. Jet planes into major American landmarks. Anthrax in the mail. Chechnyan terrorists in snow camo rappelled into some theater in Moscow. It was silly. It wasn't real crime, it was movie crime. It was special effects an evil genius might throw at Superman."

"Timothy McVeigh," he added, remembering.

"At least that's a real name! Osama bin Laden? Osama *bin Laden*? I mean, wasn't that one of Batman's arch-nemeses?"

"I think that was Ra's al Ghul."

"Oh my God, you actually know that."

"I'm a writer. Gimme a break."

"I'm never having sex with you again."

"I bet you say that to all the boys."

"How droll. My point is, today reminded me of that. Which means it's happening more often. We have Lex Luthor but no Superman."

"Narnia but no Aslan."

"Exactly. We're helpless."

"I guess."

"God, you're not even gonna try to cheer me up, are you?"

"I'm fuckhammered, Jessi. Whaddya want from me?"

"I want you to tell me the Man of Steel is streaking in from planet Krypton."

"I think it's just one more disaster," he said. "I mean yesterday it was bees vanishing and stock market crashes and poison in Chinese toys. I've been reading all these stories about the end of the world, everything from coral with herpes to prophecies from Sasquatch. This shit's on GNN every hour on the hour. Okay, so what else is new? Tomorrow it'll be killer nanobots or Pepsi with AIDS. And we'll all know about it twenty-four hours a day, 'cause it'll be on *Larry King*, between puppies who can roller skate and the next movie project from Jessica Biel. And we'll instantly forget it any time anyone has the balls to tell us the world is going south. We'll get way more upset about Nicole Richie's heroin baby than we do about global warming. It's the way people are. The world has always been damaged. It just has to slap us in the face sometimes to remind us."

"Maybe," she said, "but what about all this weird 'voices in the air' business?"

"Voices in the air?"

"Yeah, a lot of people say they heard voices during the tone."

"I didn't hear 'em," Scott lied. "Did you?"

"No," she said, after a beat. "But Celia in the next office did. She said it sounded like another language."

"I've met Celia. Everything she says sounds like another language."

"She's Libyan. Or lesbian. Or something. I don't remember. She wears a funny belt."

Scott laughed. "Yes, she does."

"She said it sounded like Latin."

"Oh, whatever, Jessi. Next she'll be saying it was the Hallelujah Chorus. What, is Celia a Latin scholar now?" All Scott had heard was gibberish.

"She's a Catholic."

"She's as Catholic as anyone else who ever read *The Da Vinci Code*."

"No, seriously, Scott. Her family went to Christmas Mass."

"So did Joel Adamov's. Okay, so maybe she's a Catholic in recovery who falls off the secular wagon sometimes. That's why she heard Latin. People hear what they want to hear."

"You think Muslims heard Arabic?"

"And Jews heard Hebrew, and Trekkies heard Klingon. I

dunno. Your buddy Brian probably heard Judy Garland."

"That's not fair, Scott. He's trying to be a Baptist again."

"In L.A.? Is that legal?"

"He put away his Celine Dion CDs and everything."

"He'll be back at Club 7969 in a week."

"Don't tell him that. He's trying to get right with Jesus."

"Last time I saw him, he was trying to get right with a Filipino in the parking lot outside the Mother Lode."

"Scott," she said, laughing.

"It's just another news day, Jessi. That's all it is. We'll be back to talking about Barry Bonds and the Olsen twins by this time tomorrow."

"Are the Olsen twins on steroids now, too?"

"I dunno. Are there calories in anabolic steroids?"

"I imagine."

"Then no."

She laughed again, sighing. "Many thanks, drunky bunny."

"Yeah? For what?"

"For cheering me up after all. I wasn't looking forward to two hours of road rage with nothing but the radio to keep me company."

"People like me 'cause I'm perky."

"Is that so?"

"I remind them of someone they wish they'd dated longer before they got caught cheating on him with dimwitted bartenders."

"I told you, Scott, it's pizza delivery boys or nothin'. That's a promise from me to you."

"I gotta go."

"Awww." That *aww* had the extra *w* of seeming sincerity.

"I mean it."

"You're not gonna keep me company any more in my hour of need?"

"I mean it, I really gotta go. I gotta vent all this liquor," he lied.

"Oh. Well, that does seem urgent. Call me tomorrow?"

"I will."

"Like you, baby." It was their standard, sans-pressure salutation and signoff.

"Like you too."

"Get some sleep."

"Seacrest out," he slurred, and turned off his phone. He tossed it onto a chair and gazed at the ceiling. He swept his eyes over its stucco surface and imagined himself a lunar lander. Oncoming sobriety dulled the illusion. "Houston," he slurred, "we have a problem."

Eventually he tried the TV, drawn to the news but turning first to Comedy Central. He watched a cartoon with the comic potential of crib death. Then curiosity got the better of him and he flipped over to GNN. Argyle Greenwood faced one of those oversize greenscreen panels ubiquitous on cable news. A child of the '70s, Scott always thought of it as the TroubAlert, the helpful computer monitor in the Hall of Justice on *SuperFriends*. Right now the TroubAlert was bisected to display two figures even Scott the Unchurched recognized. The first was Kenny Ray Thibodeau, the amiable Shreveport minister whose sermons sounded more like inspirational standup routines. Joel Osteen called him "the Seinfeld of contemporary Christianity," an offhand remark that caused five minutes of furor when some dope insisted it was anti-Semitic. The other was Thomas Jefferson Stonecipher—T. J. to his friends and loyal viewers—the dour millenarian fixture on Trinity Broadcast Network, whom GNN called when other networks rang up the decreasingly stable Pat Robertson. Joel Osteen never said anything publicly about T. J. Stonecipher—perhaps a mere oversight. An ex-

121

staffer alleged gambling and porn addictions, but the charges never stuck. This, of course, didn't discourage Bill Maher from calling him "Ol' Dirty Pastor" on a regular basis.

Greenwood's hair was as shiny and perfect as a neutron star, his voice unemotional, his cleft chin a double barrel shotgun. Maybe this is our superhero, Scott thought; all the superhero we're likely to get. Compared to the GNN anchorbot, Stonecipher looked as conically toadlike as Joseph McCarthy. "I realize we're still collecting information," Greenwood said silkily, "but it seems to me this crisis represents a paradigm shift, a broader catastrophe than we've seen before. Pastor Thibodeau, I'll begin with you. Is this the end of the world, or more of a hiccup?"

Thibodeau resembled a cherub with a hangover.

"Argahl, the last thing we wawnt is to make light of a tragic situation. These families are just...they're just goin' through so much pain an' suffering right nah, an' Lord, ar hearts an' ar prayers go out to 'em so much. It jus' grieves me so much Ah cain't tell ya. It pains m' hawrt. But Ah would be remiss in my duties as a pastor if Ah, you know, leaped to a conclusion on this. The fact is, the Bible says no man knows the day or the ah-wer of Christ's return. Ah'm sure there was people back in nineteen fo'teen who thawght the world was comin' to an end then, an' again in nineteen an' thuhty-six. We don' know what tomorruh's gonna bring. We jus' have to pray for strength an' peace in the Lord Jesus Christ to deal with the situation as it occuhs."

"Pastor Stonecipher, what do you think? Is this the beginning of the end?"

"Mr. Greenwood," Stonecipher rumbled in his seismic baritone, "at the risk of being at odds with my brother in Christ, the estimable Pastor Thibodeau, I do believe we have reached a significant milestone in the history of God's earthly creation."

"How so?"

"Mr. Greenwood, for the first time, all humanity has shared an experience that was purely internal. It was not an event of the physical world, but an echo of something far more momentous and climactic. Thus far, human science has been unable to explain

122

this event. In my opinion, no mundane physical mechanic will be able to reduce it to an atomic wavelength or a chemical reaction. I believe this is the physical manifestation of events in the spiritual realm."

"You mean in heaven?"

"I mean on Earth as it is in Heaven. I believe the Devil himself has been unleashed to do his worst against the forces of righteousness, both human and superhuman. I believe the battle of Har-Magedon has begun, the Apocalyptic conflict at the end of the world. Events will only degenerate from this point forward. The Bible warns of a great tribulation such as the world has never known. For many years Christian brethren have differed in their conception of when the tribulation would occur in relation to the prophesied Rapture. I maintain the Rapture will follow after it, and I believe, firmly and devoutly, that the great day of the Lord Almighty is at hand."

"Interesting. Pastor Thibodeau, you believe that assessment is premature?"

"Ah…Luh-listen," Thibodeau stammered, "Ah jus' think it's too early to tell. Nah, there ah many, many events that Revelation says must occuh befo' we can truly say we're in the time o' tribulation. Fo' one thing, Revelation makes it very cleah that a fawlse worl' religion will arahse, unda the leadaship of a global figya refuh'd to as the Antahchrist. In mah view, we have not yet seen such a figya."

"With all due respect to my dear colleague," Stonecipher thrummed, "I submit to you and your viewers that such a false world religion does exist. I submit to you that the overweening and damnable doctrine of this century is secularism and scientism itself, under the leadership of such antichristian figures as the so-called Professor Allan Sylvan. I believe reason, informed by faith and confirmed by the inescapable truth of God's word, has given way to a cynical attitude of disrespect for divine majesty. The glory of earthly and heavenly creation has been diminished and debased to a cosmic accident. Moral truth is now derided as inabsolute. Our schools and our legislative bodies ignore the will of perfect Almighty God in favor of pointless, irrational human debate. I believe the death knell is sounding for this sinful old world, and the tone we heard today is nothing more than its funeral bell."

"You may be right, Pastuh Stoneciphuh," Thibodeau admitted, "but Ah sure do hope an' pray the Lord God will see fit to make it cleah to awl the people, sinnuhs and saved awl at once, to know f' sure what this is and to have one las' chance to repent and be saved an' enjoy the blessings of Christ's perfec' kingdom."

"Humanity, in my opinion, has had its chance," Stonecipher insisted. "The Bible speaks of a time of great judgment. We are called into the courtroom of Almighty God. The people cry out for justice. At long last, Mr. Greenwood, the advent of perfect earthly justice is upon us. And in this cosmic courtroom, the Lord God Jehovah of Armies is absolute Judge, Jury, and eternal, ineluctable Executioner."

"Scary stuff," Greenwood replied. "When we come back, we'll have more on the reignited conflict between Protestants and the Catholic minority in Northern Ireland. And we'll talk to actress and comedienne Roseanne Barr about Hollywood's responsibility to the victims of sectarian violence. Be sure to go online and check out tonight's GNN poll, 'Was the unidentified tone we heard today a fulfillment of Biblical prophecy?' We want to know what you think, America."

"'Cause *we* know," Scott said, laughing. We Americans, we've got it all figured out.

"My sister moved to Brooklyn on the night of Sept. 10. On the morning of the 11th, she and her best friend coped the best way they knew how: They climbed to their roof with a bottle of tequila, watched the towers burn, and toasted the day with a black-humor contest. Whoever could think of the grimmest, ugliest, most horrifying joke would win. My sister called out, 'To an unobstructed view of lower Manhattan!' and tossed off her tequila. The winning toast turned out to be, 'To employment opportunities in the New York Fire Department!'"

"Being largely ignorant of which businesses were located in the WTC, I searched the Web with faint hope that any of my various credit card or student loan debt records might have been destroyed."

"My husband and I were playing Jenga afterward. When the Jenga collapsed, I shouted 'North Tower.' Then the second round of the game, we shouted, 'South Tower.' Now we don't call it Jenga anymore. We call it North Tower."

--reactions to 9/11, posted anonymously to Salon

M

"Who the fuck is that?" Danny Murcheson demanded, swiping thick fingers nervously through the lonely patch of oily hair on his forehead. He was sitting in his crusty pickup, parked outside the Standard Hotel, alone as far as he could see.

Like many in Sugar Roses and everywhere else, Danny Murcheson heard voices when the tone sounded that morning. Difference was, he kept hearing one. The voice sounded like that Darth Vader fella who played the Lion King. Verle told Danny that fella was colored, but obviously Verle was just yankin' his chain, 'cause Danny saw he was white in the last *Star Wars* movie, the one with the lava and shit. The voice he heard today talked in some kinda Chinese, then African talk for a while. Then it almost went away totally, then came back with a fury an hour later.

"Hey," Danny yelped. "Come on! Shut the fuck up."

"What do *you* want?" the voice demanded.

"I want to know who you are."

"I ain't talkin' to you." The voice sounded real pissed off.

"I know you ain't, but you're yellin' where I can hear you, so..."

"I can do whatever I want. Why don't you mind your own bidness?" the voice demanded.

"I said tell me who you are right now, or git on."

"Oh, git on, huh? You got some balls on you, boy."

"That's right," Danny said. "And I ain't no boy, neither. I ain't been a boy in a long damn time, so you can jus' come on out and make y'self known."

The voice done thought about it. "'Me tell you somethin'," it said.

"No, sir," Danny answered immediately. "That dog won't hunt. You git on out here and show y'self. I ain't playin'.'"

"Yeah, thass good," the voice admitted. "I know you ain't.

127

You some kinda tough sumbitch f' your size, ain't ya?" Danny stood five-six in his boots, a grizzled trash can with an overbite.

"Yessir, I am, tough enough to finish what I need to git done."

"And what *is* that?"

"What?"

"What do *you* need to git done?"

"Shit, you ain't even tole me who you was yet, I'm s'posed to tell you somethin' personal like that?"

"Well."

"What do I need to get done," Danny repeated. "Shit, you ain't got time to hear all the things I need to git done."

"Then why ain't you out there doin' none of 'em now?"

"Shit, you gonna talk to me like that? Holy shit. You ain't my daddy."

"I AM THE MEGATRON," the voice said all over the place.

Danny didn't know what to say to that.

"Oh, you deaf now, is that it?" the voice prodded.

"No sir."

"Then why you actin' like you ain't heard me?"

"I was thinkin'."

"Oh, you was thinkin', huh? My feelin' is you don't want to go too far down *that* road. You ain't built for it. I SAID, I AM THE MEGATRON."

"I heard ya the first time."

"Then what do you got to say about that?"

"I guess I ain't 'zactly sure what that is."

"I am the voice of all thunders. I am the voice of heaven's cries."

128

"Is that right?"

"I AM THE MEGATRON!"

"Okayyy…"

"Don't you take that tone with me, little man. I will flat kick your ass from here to Dallas, you sumbitch."

"You come on, then, you think you're big enough to try!"

The voice laughed in his head. "I like the gumption on you, boy!"

"I said don't call me boy!"

"Oh, you a man now, huh? Settle down, son—"

"Fuckin' A right I'm a man—"

"YOU AIN'T SHIT!" the voice exploded. "YOU AIN'T SHIT! BEST YOU FIGURE THAT OUT, I MEAN RIGHT FUCKIN' NOW! I tell you what, though, you can be *made* to be important."

"Izzat right?" Danny managed, though his lap was all hot so he probably pissed himself. It smelled like he did.

"You can be a mighty soldier for God."

"I ain't tryin' to be no soldier for God."

"You ain't been tryin' so far. But I tell you what, Danny Murcheson, an' you can take this shit straight to the bank: Ain't nobody gonna be between sides no more. We ain't havin' that bullshit from now on. You will put a gun in your right hand for God's army or so help me, you son of a bitch, I will fuck you up myself. I will throw you to the Got-damn dogs and let Satan use your asshole for a rubber. Are you hearin' me, shitheel?"

"Yessir."

"Am I gettin' through to you now?"

"Yessir. You are."

"Good. 'Cause I'm gettin' real fuckin' tarred o' repeatin' myself. Now, take notes if you have to, or scratch it on the inside

129

o' your fuckin' eyelids with a jackknife if that's the only way your wetheaded, retard fuckin' brain can hold onto it, but whatever you do, DO NOT MAKE ME SAY THIS SHIT AGAIN. Are you listening?"

"Yessir. I am."

"Okay. We let the Devil have his run o' this shit for too Got-damn long. I AM THE MEGATRON. AS HE SPEAKS, SO AM I. AS HE WILLS, I AM SENT. I go before the one who follows."

"Okay."

"Don't act like you don't know who I'm talkin' about."

"I uh. The one who…?"

"Follows. The one who follows. I am the cry before the battle, and he is the blade of God's anger. FOR GOD'S PATIENCE IS NOW AT AN END, HIS LAWS UNHEEDED, AND HIS RAGE BECOME THE END OF ALL THINGS."

"Holy shit," Danny said. A middle-aged couple staggered from the bar and eyed him as they passed. He flipped them off angrily and smacked at the windshield. They drove away cowed.

"You got that right, son. Now listen. From now on I'm gonna do a whole lotta talkin', an' for your part, you'll be doin' a whole lotta not sayin' *shit*. You hear me? You been drafted into God's angel army. You the blade. And if you really are as tough as you say you are, then the jobs I give you are gonna be a hell of a lot more important than anything you done in your whole sorry life."

"I can fight."

"Well, awright, then. An' if you do, son, the things I can do for you in return…"

"Oh yeah?"

"What goes around comes around."

"You mean like…money?"

"Money? I guess. If you want that. Ain't gonna do you no

good, though. What you want from me is bigger'n that."

"It is?"

"You tell me. You 'bout tired o' gittin' pushed around?"

"Yessir."

"You tired o' people makin' fun o' yer dumb country ass?"

"Yeah."

"You want 'em to bow an' kiss 'at ass instead?"

Was this a trick question? "Yeah, I do."

"You want pussy?"

"Oh, *hell*, yeah."

"Been a while for you, ain't it?"

"Shit, yeah."

"Uh-huh. You 'bout tired o' this truck?"

"What about it?"

"Brand new one more your speed? Fuckin' bass boat?"

"That sounds awright."

"Yeah, you want that, you need money. Yes sir, you want bitches, you can buy you some ass—but I'll tell you what that money ain't never gonna buy you."

"What's that?"

The voice took its time before answering. "MAGNIFICENCE."

"Magnificence." The word tasted awesome in Danny's mouth.

"MAJESTY.   GLORY.   Everlasting GRANDEUR. Dominion. Control. The power to do what you want, when you want. Listen up, son, you can buy you a piece of ass at any truck stop, but you can never make a real woman *beg you to touch her.* Only true magnificence will make her want you. Need you. Love you.

131

Desire you." The voice let that sink in real good.

"Shit."

"Why you think all them bitches been leavin' you alone so much, Danny? Hah? You think maybe it's 'cause you ain't a good person, 'cause you deserve to get treated like that? Aw, *hell*, no. That ain't how it works no ways. It ain't about no woman thinkin' you're good or you ain't, or you deserve it or you don't. It ain't about that. It's the power you have, because the power you have becomes the power you show. The power you show becomes the power they want to be around, Danny, 'cause they know they ain't never gonna get none for themselves. You hear me? You show power in God's army, and He will reward your show of power with a BOLT OF HIS HOLY MAGNIFICENCE FROM ON HIGH. You will be made GLORIOUS. You will rule as GOD'S FIST. The kings of nations shall bow weeping at your feet, Danny, and their daughters shall surrender their flesh to you at your very command."

Danny was overcome. "Boy, I *mean*," he finally whispered.

"That's what *I'm* sayin'," the Megatron agreed. "Now. You with us?"

"Hell yeah!"

"Then go home an' find a damn Bible. And start readin' it! Who am I?"

"Yer His voice," Danny said, his head bowed.

"You damn right I am, son. I AM THE MEGATRON."

"You are. Yer the Megatron."

"And you are God's fist."

"I am..." Danny trailed off. His head was still down, but a grin split his face like a razor. God's fist. It's about time, he thought. "I'm His *power*," he said quietly.

132

The following note was recovered from the home of Mrs. Phyllis Montgomery Hanczyk, 52, on the morning of Saturday, 15 March 20—. The Sugar Roses Police Department believes she committed suicide by poisoning the preceding day. The note was handwritten in ink. Spelling and other errors have been reproduced exactly as written. Grateful acknowledgement is extended to Charles Hanczyk, Mrs. Hanczyk's only son, for his permission to reprint the note here.

Charley.

First of all I am sorry you will find me here this way. I have tried to have done it in a way that will be less tromatic. I am not in any pain at the moment and if I do have it I beleive it will be short.

You know I have not been alright since your daddy past last year. He was a good man and I am sure he is in Heaven with Jesus and the angles. Maybe I will get to be up there to tho I am not sure how that is going to work out. I am trying to figure it out. People say they know what is going to happen but they dont. Not really. Its like how people talk about going to some other contry but they dont know what its like, they only know what they seen on the TV. Then when they get there its probly very nice but its not what they thot it was going to be. Ether way I am not afraid.

If you have not guest by now I am very unhappy. I have realized it doesnt matter what I do I am never going to be happy. Thats because I have only did too things in my life that was importent and that was you and your little baby sister who died before you was born. That dont mean I am not proud of you because I am every day. But every day I get more lonley and scared and some times I cry myself to sleep every nite. You have made your own life with Donna and your own kids and its like a part of me has broke off and floted away. It is like I blue up a baloon and let it go and now its flew up into the sky where I cant

133

even see it no more. I want you and your family to be so happy together and I know you will be. You dont need me trying to be around all the time.

When I was a little girl my mama told me that if you was not with somebody in love with you then your life is not realy werth living. I thot that was true for a long time but now I think something totaly difernet. I think the way to be happy is to make a good thing or to at least make something good. I have made my good thing. I made you. Now I realy just want to be shut of it all.

I know you will not believe this but today I heard my gardin angel talking to me all day. She said the world was changeing rite now. Not like it has done all along but more a big change all at once. She said it was not the end of the world but like a make over. She said the make over was like them games you used to play on the TV them Atores or whatever. You know what I mean. She said its like the game is going a sertan way and then you push a button and you are playing a difernt game. Or maybe it starts all over again or maybe it goes to a difernt cassle or whatever or maybe you have a difrent caracter. I dont know what you call that. All I know is she said it will be very beutiful and you will see it very soon. But it will not be like how I growed up so I would rather just see it from up there. She said the world is like all tangled so some lines will have to be cut.

Anyway my stomache is starting to pain me a little so I will stop for now. I love you so much. You be good to them kids Charley. And to Donna. She will lose wait someday you just wait. Anyway if they let me into Heaven I will tell your big sister what a smart boy you turned out to be. Your daddy alredy seen it but you just know he loved you so much he coudnt harly stand it some times.

134

Love,

Mama Phyllis

     The last two lines were handwritten in black marker at the bottom, almost certainly in postscript:

SHE LIED THEY DONT KNOW WHATS COMEING!
DONT LET IN NO N

N

Lacey Veracruz ate a Fruit Roll-Up and watched her video of Spike the Raccoon and *Li'l Warriors*. This was the Noah's Ark one. It was the new one Mommy broughted her home from work. Auntie Linda and Unca Darryl were in the kitchen. They were talking. Auntie Linda was smoking again. That was okay. Unca Darryl was drinking beer cans. He had seven. Seven, eight, nine, ten. Seven, eight, nine, ten.

Before Auntie Linda watched the TV. It was the news. The news was scary and sad. Lacey saw a woman crying. Two airplanes hit each other in the sky and now the woman, she was crying. Airplanes can stay up in the sky most of the time but if they hit each other they can't. Their wings fall off and then they can't fly.

In preschool today they had a bad time. Except first they painted a picture. That was fun. Lacey painted the apartmenent. She painted it green but really just the inside part was green, in the living room. Lacey's room, it was pink and she had a *Dora the Explora* poster and a Disney princess poster and a Spike poster and a Spider-Man poster. She had four posters and that's why she had a four-poster bed. Mommy laughed when she said that. She didn't know why. Mommy laughed for silly reasons.

Auntie Linda said Mommy was at the store to buy something to eat for dinner and then she would come here. She hoped for dinner they would have mash potatoes and hamburgers and fish sticks.

This video was good but it didn't have much Spike the Raccoon in it. This one had Pooka the Chipmunk and it had Bonkers the Squirrel. Bonkers is funny. He got hit on the head with an acorn and now he's silly. It hurt his head but the other aminals take care of him because Jesus wants us to be kind to the umfortunate.

"So what's the big deal?" Bonkers asked. He made his eyes roll around. That was *funny!* His voice is silly! "So it's gonna rain! All you need is an umbrella! A little water won't kill ya."

"Bonkers," Pooka said. He gets tired of Bonkers sometimes

and then he makes a yawning sound: *Hhhhhh*. "You just don't get it."

"Get what?"

"We went back in the Yesterday Machine, remember?"

"Yeah, so?"

"So this is back before it ever rained on the Earth. When God made the Garden of Eden and the rest of the world, he suspended all the water in the air. Do you know what suspended means?"

"He held somebody's pants up?"

"Bonkers! It means to hold up anything. Sure, suspenders hold up your pants, but a suspension bridge is a way of holding a bridge up. Ya see what I mean?"

"I guess so. There's water in the sky?"

"Yep. There sure was in Noah's day."

"Like in clouds?"

"Good job, Bonkers! That's right! Except the clouds are thicker than anything you've ever seen, even in thunderstorms."

"Goshen! So when's it gonna rain? When it does, is all that water gonna fall on the ground?"

"Yep. It's gonna form a deluge, which is another word for a flood, very soon."

"Uh-oh! So how is God gonna save everybody from the flood?"

"He isn't, Bonkers."

Bonkers was sad. "How come?"

"Sometimes when people get too bad, they have to be destroyed. In Bible times, God punished wicked people with floods."

Lacey knew about floods. Mommy watched a show once about a place that had a flood. It was called Katrina. Katrina was

138

drowned in the flood. Mommy cried when she watched the show. There were houses and cars underwater. The water was brown. People got killed and also lots of aminals. Mommy said they had to send the people in Katrina some blankets. But wouldn't the blankets get all wet? Mommy said "You're right" and then she didn't send the blankets. But she cried for a long time.

Lacey asked why the flood came and drowned all them people. Mommy said floods just happened. She said the weather made it happen but floods couldn't happen in Okahoma 'cause they didn't have no ocean. That made Lacey feel better but then Auntie Linda said something about a tornado but then Mommy threw a spoon at Auntie Linda. That made Lacey laugh! Except then Auntie Linda called Mommy a bad word.

The man on the video had a long beard and a brown dress. His name was Noah. He had a family but Lacey didn't know their names. Noah and God were friends. God was invisible but Noah heared his voice. God said, *"Noah!"* It was scary.

"Yes, Lord?"

"I command you to build an ark."

"Yes, Lord. But why?"

"I will make it rain for forty days and forty nights."

"What's an ark?" Bonkers asked. He was in a bush with Pooka. They were watching where Noah and God couldn't see them. *Good question*, Lacey thought.

"An ark is another word for a box," Pooka said. Why didn't they just say box? People in the olden days talked funny. *Ark! Ark!* It was like a doggy.

God said Noah should build a ark. The ark would be a ship. Noah and his family would ride in the ship and then the flood would come but it wouldn't get them because they were in a big box. That was a good plan!

The front door opened. *"Mommy!"* Lacey went over and gave Mommy a big hug and a kiss. She was holding a bag and her purse.

139

"Hey, little girl," Mommy said. "Did you have a good day today?"

"It was scary," Lacey said.

"She's been really good," Auntie Linda said. "She been watchin' her videos and keepin' quiet."

"Is that right?" Mommy said. She put the bag on the kitchen table and her purse on a chair. "Were you a good girl at preschool today, sweetie?"

"Yes," Lacey said. "I hit Brandon, but, um, he was stealing my crans an' I only hit him a little. Teacher was crying."

"Your teacher was crying?"

"Miss Vaughn had a freak-out," Auntie Linda said.

"I heard a noise. It was all whoooooooooooo."

"That's pretty close. I heard it, too," Mommy said. "I think everybody did."

"Everybody heared the noise?"

"Uh-huh. *Heard* the noise."

"In the whole world?"

"I think so."

"Goshen, that's big." Goshen was what Pooka said when she got excited.

Mommy laughed. "It sure is. Well, I'm proud of you for being such a good girl today, even though you were scared and everything."

"I wasn't that scared. Um, just a little bit scared, like that much." She made a little bit with her fingers.

"Oh, okay. Well, I was kinda scared, too."

"You was?"

"I were. *You* were. Lacey, let go of my leg." Mommy made the "*hhhhhhhh*" sound. "God. Lacey, look, I need to talk to your

Auntie Linda and Uncle Darryl for a while. Go finish watching your video, okay, sweetie?"

"Are we gonna have fish sticks?"

"I didn't buy any frozen food today, honey. The store was too busy. I bought us stuff to make tuna casserole."

"*Mmmm!*"

"I know, it's one of your favorites. Ow, honey, you're standing on my foot. Go watch TV, okay?"

"Um, but I, um, I missed you."

"I missed you, too, honey. I'll talk to you in a bit, okay? I gotta talk to Auntie Linda."

"Okay."

"Thank you, honey. Good girl." Lacey went in the living room and watched the video. She saw the Noah video before but that was before she saw a show about Katrina. It was different now because she knew what a flood was. Lacey didn't know the name of the city where Noah lived but it didn't look like Katrina.

Noah worked hard! He had a hammer and a saw. "I sure wish Elroy was here," Pooka said. Elroy's a beaver. "He could use his big teeth to cut all these trees down."

Bonkers sniffled. "All these beautiful acorns."

"You can keep the acorns, Bonkers."

"I *can*?"

"Sure! Noah doesn't need 'em. You ever see a ship made out of acorns?"

"A ship made out of acorns," said Bonkers. "*Hhhhhhhh.* Now that would be Heaven."

"You don't know the half of it, Bonkers."

"It's not al Qaeda," Mommy said. "You need to quit saying that. You're getting yourself all riled up."

"I am not!" Auntie Linda said. "I'm just tryin' to be

141

prepared, like you oughta be. You got Lacey to think about. Let's say it ain't al Qaeda. It's damn sure some kinda terrorist! And how you gonna feed Lacey if the store stays like that? How you gonna cook if the power goes off again?"

"Linda, we don't live in New York. The terrorists don't give a shit about Oklahoma."

"Mommy," Lacey said.

"I know, honey. I said a bad word. I apologize."

Lacey watched her video. God told Noah to find two of all the aminals, like two horsies, two elephants, two kitty cats, and two dinosaurs. Except mostly they came to him. They came from all over the place and walked into the ark. Noah and his kids put in hay for them to eat. Noah's wife made lemonade because Noah and his kids were all sweaty. It was very hard work to make a boat.

Bonkers tried to help but he got lost and an elephant sat on him. Lacey laughed and laughed. Bonkers was stuck in the elephant's heinie!

"What do you guys want from me?" Shay said. "I'm doing my best. I got enough to worry about trying to keep her fed at all without worrying about freakin' al Qaeda. You have each other. I got Lacey and a job. That's about it."

"You got us," Unca Darryl said.

"And I got you. But that's it. I barely been hangin' on for two years now, y'know that? Most of the time I ain't even got my head on straight. I'd give anything for a week of vacation. But that ain't gonna happen. I'm gonna keep livin' from paycheck to paycheck and finding shoes to put on my kid's feet."

"I ain't tryin' to talk about all that," Auntie Linda said. "I'm just sayin' it seems kinda funny that everybody in America lost their shit at the same exact time. That don't sound like no kinda 'climate adjustment' I ever heard of."

"Climate adjustment," Unca Darryl said. "That's ridiculous."

"Well, I agree."

"They're just lyin' through their teeth."

142

"So what do you think it is, Darryl?"

"Man, I don't *even* know."

"You don't think it's al Qaeda like Homeland Security here?"

"That's right," Auntie Linda said. "Call me names."

"I dunno what it is," Unca Darryl said. "Mebbe...mebbe it's one o' them space aliens."

"Oh, Darryl!" Mommy shouted.

"I dunno, I'm jus' sayin'! Mebbe they got some kinda funky radio or somethin' an' they just beamed it into our heads."

"Why would they do that?"

"Mebbe they're testin' us. You ever think of that?"

"Testing us how, Darryl? A hearing test?"

"I don't know! They're from space, Shay! Leave me alone!"

"Okay, Darryl."

"How'm *I* s'posed to know? Shit!"

It started to rain on TV and all the bad people started running. The lightning was *loud!* Noah and his family were inside the ark. They had a lantern. The horsies looked scared. Lacey sure would like a horsy to ride. "Mommy, I want a horsy."

"I know, sweetie. It's on my list."

Lacey crossed her arms. "I hate the list."

"I hate it, too, Lacey. Watch your show."

Another siren went by outside. Lacey runned to the window. It was a police car!

Pooka and Bonkers rided in the ark. Pooka was shivering! It was raining so hard! "Remind me never to go on a cruise," Bonkers said.

"At least God didn't have to punish everyone on Earth," Pooka said. "It's a good thing Noah was so faithful, or there

143

wouldn't be any people left at all after the flood."

"He's good people," Bonkers said.

"And I'm extra super glad he saved the chipmunks!"

"And the squirrels!"

"Ronnie woulda loved this," Mommy said. Ronnie was Daddy's grown-up name. "Every time there was a fire or an earthquake on the news, he'd practically make popcorn. I couldn't drag him to a movie, but if there was a disaster on the news, you couldn't pull him off the couch with a tow chain."

"That's true," said Unca Darryl. "You remember how excited he got when that tornado came through town? I thought I was gonna have to knock him out with a brick to keep him from chasin' it down the road."

"Some brave hero. Of all the ways he coulda gone, a damn icy road..."

"Come on, Shay. Ain't no sense dwellin' on the past."

"You give me a future worth dwelling on, I'll dwell on that, okay? Do you know, the day before his accident, he almost fell off his mama's roof? He was up there knockin' down icicles, messin' with the antenna so she could see the weather reports better, and he almost fell thirty feet onto a wrought iron fence. Woulda killed him sure as anything. He grabbed onto the eaves and caught himself. His daddy and I had to help him down."

"Shay, that's why I'm tellin' ya, it was his time to go."

"There *is* no time to go!" Mommy shouted. "You mean to tell me there's some calendar up there, sayin' Ronnie's gotta go this day, Darryl's gonna go twenty years later?"

"Oh, honey, don't. That ain't right," Auntie Linda said.

"I know. I'm sorry. I just...You didn't hear all the phone calls I got today. They were comin' from everywhere. I drove around town lookin' for a store that was open, and the whole time I'm thinkin', how many people had a day today like I had two years ago? How many people are out there right now tryin' to figure it all out? Why him? Why me? Why today? What am I gonna do?

144

Why does it all have to happen so stupidly? Ain't no reason for any of it. Ain't no al Qaeda. Not here, anyway. There's no grand conspiracy. There's no *plan*, Linda. No reason. No sense in any of it. Nothing."

"You mind your daughter don't hear you sayin' that," Auntie Linda said. "She's upset enough as it is."

Lacey heared her but didn't say nothing. She was too busy thinking about *Li'l Warriors*. Mommy said the stories in *Li'l Warriors* were true, give or take. "Give or take what?" Lacey asked. Oh, they just kinda fib for fun's sake, Mommy said. Lacey wondered if the flood was a fib. Because here's why: There's lots of horsies in the world, lots of doggies, lots of dinosaurs. Not just two. But if only two aminals from each kind went in the box, that meant all the rest of the aminals drowned. So why did God make a flood to kill all the other aminals? The flood killed the people. God said all the people was bad. But didn't people have kids? Were the kids bad? Why did God kill all the people? Were all the people in Katrina bad? Was Daddy bad?

Lacey couldn't tell Mommy why she started crying. She didn't want to hurt Mommy's feelings. She didn't cry too long, though. She's a big girl.

Reprinted by permission of Global NewsNet, 14 March 20--:

[No Title, posted as "Breaking News"]
From James McMillan

NEWARK, NJ—FAA officials have released few details about this afternoon's tragic midair collision over Newark Liberty Airport. WingWest 1730, a DC-10 carrying 314 people, had just taken off en route to Los Angeles via Phoenix Sky Harbor. Allied 470, a 737 from Chicago O'Hare carrying 207 people, was in a holding pattern two miles away, awaiting permission and a clear runway to land. Communication with the Newark tower indicated nothing unusual until 4:47 Eastern Time, when screams and shouts were heard not just inside both planes but over tower radios nationwide. The atmosphere in the Newark tower became so emotionally charged and in such a short amount of time that tower personnel are still unsure what went wrong. The global phenomenon that caused this disturbance is as yet unidentified.

Gwen Heller, a spokesperson for Phoenix-based Allied Airlines, expressed sympathy to the families of the passengers and crew of both aircraft. "We are devastated to hear of the tragedy in Newark today. Rest assured we will conduct a thorough investigation, and our hearts and prayers go out to everyone affected by this horrible catastrophe." Heller then met with family members and, visibly upset, waved off further questions from reporters.

Peter Jameson, an FAA spokesman from New York, told GNN that pilot Alex Krasner, an Allied veteran with a stellar flight record, began yelling incoherently and steered his plane directly toward WingWest 470. Due to confusion in the tower and aboard 470, the WingWest pilot may never have seen the collision coming. Witnesses on the ground say the DC-10 struck the 737 behind the port side wing at an altitude of about 500 feet. There was an immediate explosion, and both planes crashed into the tarmac within seconds. "We're very fortunate this happened over the airport itself," Jameson said. "If it had happened just a few seconds later, we'd have been looking at large debris coming down over a densely residential neighborhood."

Based on immediate anecdotal evidence, Jameson believes the co-pilot of Allied 1730 fought Krasner for control of the plane. "We've got some very hectic communication between the plane and the tower. I need to hear all the flight recorder evidence before I say for sure, but even then it might be impossible to say. It's sometimes hard to differentiate between all the voices when everyone's yelling." At the moment of impact, Jameson says, "What you'd very likely hear would be a loud boom, followed by a sound of rushing air. That's consistent with several other situations we've investigated over the years."

Early reports indicate Krasner was hallucinating at the time of the incident. "He was yelling," Jameson told reporters. "It was nonsensical stuff, that's for sure. That's really all I can say about it at the present time. I have no indication from the evidence that Mr. Krasner was engaged in any alcohol or narcotic consumption at the time of the incident." Unconfirmed reports indicate the pilot may have said "I know what this is," "there's an army in the sky," and unspecified phrases in Latin. GNN sources were unable to explain these remarks, but they note transmissions were highly garbled and may have been misheard.

One eyewitness who spoke to GNN on condition of anonymity said, "I really couldn't tell you what [Krasner] was thinking. He's been a good pilot for fifteen years. I don't know if maybe he just lost control in the moment, or you know, maybe he had some kind of psychotic break. In a moment of crisis like that, you can say all kinds of crazy things. We don't know what was going through his head. It's a terrible situation, absolutely terrible. Those families are just, you know, it's the end of the world for those people. I can tell you we're going to be sorting this one out for a long time to come."

"We ask the press to be respectful of the families who lost their loved ones here today," Jameson said. "The investigation is ongoing."

The unshaven pilot dropped out of hyperspace on the dark side of the planet. The universe coalesced out of luminous fog to form anime speed lines...hyphens...stars. He checked his instruments and wheeled the starship *Parallax Dragon*, toward Coruscant. Noting the microcosm of city lights covering the entire face of the galactic capitol world, he grinned and observed, "This game is fuckin' *sick*!"

"I'm sick a you playin' it so much."

Ordinarily Amanda would be stranded on Tyler's couch while he played *EverQuest* or *Ultima Online*, but with the Internet down over large swaths of the country, server lag times made MMRPGs effectively pointless. That was okay. Tyler had spent a fair chunk of his last part-time paycheck from Bayeux Entertainment to buy *Star Wars: Imperial Assassin*, the latest epic first-person shooter from LucasArts. It won raves from *PC Game Power* magazine for its graphics and cut scenes. Coruscant alone was so labyrinthine an environment that many players wandered around as tourists, ignoring the plot of the game entirely.

"Come check this out," he insisted. "I'll come in low enough to give you a good look when I land."

"I don't care, Tyler. In case you haven't noticed, I'm living on a pretty detailed planet myself." Amanda indicated Tyler's plastic ice cube of a TV. Firefights raged in Jerusalem. A band of Zionists carrying plastic explosives were stopped en route to Masjid Qubbat as-Sakhrah, the Dome of the Rock, then killed and drug through the streets by their beards. Forty-seven people were dead in Orlando, twelve of them children. One child was beaten to death with a *Little Mermaid* doll. The culprit was alleged to be another child. Rwanda was a hell zone, too unspeakably base to be shown in its gruesome entirety. Five high school seniors joined hands and leaped off the Triborough Bridge. Amanda folded herself into a corner of the ratty couch and drew Tyler's NFL blanket over her bare skin. She wore a pair of Tyler's ratty boxer shorts, her pierced nipples shining like teddy bear eyes against the colorless plain of her sexless chest. She took another toke of her one-hitter and felt the sleepy tingle on her nose that announced a comforting high.

She shouldn't be doing this, she knew. There was a reason now why she shouldn't, a reason still busily accreting inside her. She could feel it now, a growing pearl in her briny oyster depths, a jagged grain of sand evolving frantically into a character boasting billions of polygons.

Tyler had already smoked a thin joint before loading the game. Now he took occasional hits off a second joint, the smoke pouring into his nose like a backdraft. "Sick *ass*," he exalted. His fingers floated over the keyboard and fondled occasional controls, a super slo-mo Rachmaninoff.

She should've stayed over at her mom's. She couldn't take being around her parents right now. She couldn't take being their greatest disappointment.

The eastern horizon of Coruscant flared piercingly white. Far below, a dense linear matrix of skyscrapers stabbed up at Tyler like bayonets. Looking closer, he spotted the veins and arteries of aerial freeways, speeders and cargo vehicles zipping around on untold business. Someday, he figured, this landscape would be folded into a grand *Star Wars* MMRPG, maybe *Galaxies*, maybe something better. Then those whizzing dots in the air traffic below would house individual players. The merest pixel could be a person, infinitesimally far away but as influential on the game as any other player. These simulated worlds had a way of expanding in directions no designer could confidently predict.

"I came over here to talk to you," Amanda said. "I kind of wanted you to talk back, if that's not too much trouble."

"Shit, Amanda," he whined, "I told you. I just bought this. I want to fire it up for a while. I don't bust your shit when you buy a new CD, do I?"

"My CDs take forty minutes. You get stuck on those games, I feel like I'm dating the back of your shitty haircut for a month."

"Oh, whatever," he retorted lamely. "I told you I wanted you to play *with* me."

"Hey, Tyler," she sang, "remember when we used to have

sex? Remember when we used to play with each *other*? Remember when you used to, like, want to see me naked? I'm right here, boy. Come an' get it."

"I'm busy."

"Yeah, that's right. Busy playing your stupid video game. I'm a person, Tyler. You're dating a person. We don't shut down when you're too busy to play us. We go right on living our lives. And sometimes, we get bored and go looking for other players."

"So go looking, then."

"Don't fuckin' tempt me!" She shouted this almost triumphantly, as if she'd decoded a password. He stewed as she scratched at the piercing in her left ear.

Tyler threw the *Dragon* into autopilot so he could face her directly. "Amanda, listen. I don't want to fight with you. I don't like fighting. I'm not good at it. You can run circles around me, I get that. But what are we fighting about? You think I didn't have a fucked-up day, too? Maybe this is how I de-stress, you ever think of that?"

Amanda, stymied and small, took another hit of dope. "I'm cold," she murmured.

He glanced at his monitor, saw he had a few minutes, and went into the bedroom. He came out a few seconds later with the comforter from the futon. He laid it over her with disarming gentleness and kissed her cheek. "Just gimme half an hour, okay? Thirty minutes. I'll head over to Palpatine Square and save the game. Then I'll come watch all this shit on TV with you. Okay? I just can't handle it right now."

"I know," she said. "I'm sorry, Tyler."

"It's okay. I gotta get my head on straight."

"I want my head on straight, too."

"Maybe you should turn off the news. Watch a movie or something. Hey, fire up the Xbox, play some *Halo*."

"Tyler, I don't want to play video games! They're not my thing, okay? God!"

"Okay! So read a book, then."

"I left it in the car."

Tyler swallowed his response; she obviously wanted to watch the news and hate it. Whatever. A guy could drive himself into the bughouse mulling too long over estrogen logic.

"I got beers in the fridge."

"Maybe later."

The *Dragon* banked to avoid the restricted airspace surrounding the Imperial Palace, a pyramid so high and vast it eclipsed the dawn for seconds. Imperial Center Control transmitted a landing vector, which Tyler fed into the ship's navicomputer. For at least a dozen levels, he'd be a contract killer in the employ of Emperor Palpatine. According to the game trailer posted on IGN four months ago, he'd graduate from blasting Bothan spies to squaring off against Han Solo himself. He imagined at that point he'd be talked into switching allegiances, and his ship would join the climactic assault on *Death Star II*. Those nouns and events were more familiar to Tyler Knizek—aka Imperial assassin Bane Verdugoz, aka Elf Commander Witchblayd of Norrath, aka T1g3rb0Mb the Unfraggable—than Rwanda or the Dome of the Rock. He was far from alone in this virtual religion, a peculiarly American Kabbala.

Like all literate people since the invention of literacy, Tyler found himself seduced by virtual worlds. Four thousand years ago, he would have been fully conversant in the Epic of Gilgamesh. He'd lay awake nights around the campfire, imagining the adventures of King Gilgamesh of Uruk, who surpassed all other kings. Six hundred years before Christ, he'd race through the biography of Odysseus. In the first century, he'd know the Torah like the back of his hand. Later he'd know all about John Clayton, aka Lord Greystoke, aka Tarzan of the Mangani Apes; he'd be fully conversant in the later, Lone career of a Texas Ranger named Reid. Every great story is an invitation to immersion in demidivine lives that never were.

Games went back as far, of course; chaturanga, an Indian game played in the sixth century, gave birth to shogi, makruk, and chess. Xiangqi, or Chinese chess, was played centuries before that.

Chess is a battle simulation, a tiny war that seldom leaves corpses. By the end of the nineteenth century, card and board games themed to pre-existing stories hit the market. Now most game designers found ways to synergize with other media. A game, like any other story, is a shared imaginary world, and fiction had become interactive, a public domain in manners other than metaphorical.

Star Trek; *Star Wars*; *Battlestar Galactica*; *The Lord of the Rings*; *Final Fantasy*; *World of Warcraft*; *Halo*; Marvel Comics; DC; Image; *Heroes*; Larry Niven's Known Space; Hogwarts School of Witchcraft and Wizardry; Sunnydale, California; satellite LV-426 in the Zeta II Reticuli system—Even Tyler would be disheartened to realize how many histories he knew as comprehensively as Earth's. He knew more fictional greetings (*aiya*, *bo shuda*, *nuqneQ'*, *nanu nanu!*) than salutations in terrestrial tongues.

Something very like this line of thought passed through Amanda's head as she stared balefully at a nearby figure of Uglúk the Uruk-Hai, one of Tyler's thousand prize possessions. "Tyler," she began, "do you think you care about your games and stuff more than you care about real people?"

"Fuck me," he whined. "Settle down, Dr. Phil."

"I'm not, like, judging you," she lied. "I like books and stuff."

"When you were reading *Golden Compass* I thought I'd never see your whole face again. I was halfway to staging an intervention."

"I know. I just…I don't know if…" She touched the kanji symbol on her back, but it failed to give her strength enough to finish the sentence: *I don't know if we love each other as much as we love our collections.* "I mean…Do you think about me as often as you think about video games?"

"I don't know. I guess." A mugger jumped out at Verdugoz, who reflexively danced back and opened fire. The assailant was a black market droideka, shielded and inordinately facile with its blasters. The noisy business of the city continued in the background, an entire megalopolis on autopilot.

"You remember how psyched you were when the last *Harry Potter* movie came out?" she asked. "You and your crank-spanker friends all dressed up in, like, custom T-shirts an' shit and got drunk and went to see it at midnight. You remember that?"

"Uh-huh." It was taking most of his limited concentration to keep from getting smoked by this damn robot.

"You were so fucking excited. I've never seen you so excited, that's what I thought. Then I realized we'd just had our two-year anniversary the week before. You barely got up off the couch. You get more fired up about Michael Bay commercials than you do about our relationship."

"I do not," he said automatically. "I get excited about you, just in a different way. Like, in my head."

"Where no one can see it. In a black hole."

"Amanda, I love you, okay? Why are we fighting about this?"

"We're not fighting." She took a deep, steadying inhalation off his funky old blanket. "We're not. I'm not yelling or anything. I just want to know what excites you."

"I don't know, I guess like…" He indicated the room and its thousand toys, then stabbed the keyboard to elude certain death. "I guess with you it's more personal."

"I just wonder, like…What if we get married?"

"I don't want to get married, Amanda," he said immediately, clenching his jaw.

"I know, I know, *God!* I'm not saying we *should* get married! I'm saying, like, theoretically, let's say we did get married. Are you gonna get all excited 'cause I made roast beef or whatever? Is that the kind of thing you would ever get fired up about?"

"I like roast beef."

"You know what I'm saying."

He gave her the courtesy of fully considering his answer, partly because he was too busy tossing thermal detonators to form a coherent sentence.

"Listen to me!"

"I am," he said truthfully. The droideka dropped its shields at an ill-timed moment, within the fatal radius of a grenade, and exploded into zipper components.

Verdugoz holstered his sidearm. "Nice try, Dash Rendar," the animated Verdugoz gloated in his sardonic baritone. "Next time try meeting me in person." Tyler winced, anticipating—

"'Dash *Rendar?*'" Amanda repeated, laughing.

"Shut up." He turned down his speakers and trekked to his save point in peace. "Look. I don't know how excited you get at, like, eating fucking dinner at the Olive Garden. Maybe inside you're all bursting at the seams. But I think...I think the whole point of like, going out with somebody is, I don't know, the quiet time. You can, like, share your time with somebody in silence. And maybe they don't get all excited 'cause your favorite movie has a sequel. And maybe you don't spend a month reading all of Jane Austen's shit just to be...partners. I don't like fucking Kidney Thieves records. You don't like My Chemical Romance. But that doesn't mean we don't care about each other."

"Nobody likes My Chemical Romance, Tyler."

He ignored that. "I'm just saying. It's like..." Finding the right metaphor took him so long he had time to save his game and close it out. "It's like, if you asked me what my favorite food is, I'd say a bucket of fried chicken. No big deal, right? KFC's fine. An' it's not like it's all spicy or whatever. It's not, like, exploding in your mouth. There's nothing exciting about chicken. If you're in a car with some guys and they go, hey, what do you want to eat, and some dude goes, hey, let's get some fried chicken, it's not like all the other guys go, 'Oh, holy shit! Fuckin' fried chicken, dude! Sweet!' But I *love* fried chicken. An' y'know why? Not because it's spicy. Not because it's exciting. People love chicken because it reminds 'em of a time they *felt* good. Maybe they were with their family or whatever. When I'm with you I *feel* good. And not because it's exciting or I can't wait to rip your clothes off. I don't have to rip your clothes off. You, like, take your clothes off." He indicated her nude torso. "I like that. I love how we know each other so well we can have other things and still be, like, happy around each other. Without even talking. So what's wrong with that?"

155

It was, by several seconds, the longest speech she remembered him making in two years. She was stupefied—which probably explained the totally retarded thing she said next.

"Do you think we could ever have a baby?" The question, though transmitted at the volume of a hiccup, exploded in the room like a flashbang.

"A baby?" Tyler sputtered. "Are you fuckin' shitting me? Have you seen my apartment, for Chrissakes? I can't even keep my Jeep running. The landlord keeps hounding my ass to move it away from the front of the house. It's leakin' oil like a fuckin' supertanker. A baby? What am I s'posed to feed it with, magical powers?"

"We'd have to get a full-time job," she replied.

"Are you..." The color dissolved from his face like the dots off an Etch A Sketch. "Are you fuckin' pregnant?"

"No," she said, quietly, and coiled even deeper into the blanket.

He leaned back and exhaled explosively. "Oh, Jesus Christ, Amanda! Ya gotta...ya gotta not scare me like that! Oh my God. Shit! Holy fuck." It's true, she could almost see his heart bouncing away underneath his concave xyphoid sternum.

"I just wanted to know if you thought we'd make good parents. If you thought we could be a good family together."

"Amanda," he said, laughing, "I'll tell you the fuckin' truth. If I had me for a dad, I'd shoot heroin in, like, the third fuckin' grade. I'd rather have Courtney Love for a parent. At least she's got millions of dollars."

"I don't know if I could be a good mom," Amanda admitted.

Tyler slowly relaxed. "I don't know. I think you could be a good mom if you wanted to," he decided. "But shit, how much do you want to? Is it something you're really in a hurry to do in your life?" He waved at her topless, tattooed body. "In *your* life?"

Good question, she thought, and lay on her face so he wouldn't see her crying again. He did anyway. He rubbed her back, kissed her shoulder blades, made her coffee, and fired up the Xbox.

Forums > Headlines: Sugar Roses, OK > Religion

truthseeker (Old Pro) – Posted March 14, 20-- 22:07

> I was watching TJ Stonecipher last week, and he said the Dome
> of the Rock had to fall back into Jewish hands before the End
> could come. Then this happens. I tell you, it starts to get a
> little creepy.

Posts: 381 | Location: Oklahoma | Registered: January 07, 20—

OorahSemperFi (Old Pro) – Posted March 14, 20-- 22:09

> Yeah, I can't wait to see what SugarRosesNeedsChange and his
> gaytheist buddies have to say about this! Let them deny the
> power of almighty God now!!!

Posts 3165 | Location: Oklahoma | Registered: March 12, 1998

SugarRosesNeedsChange (Old Pro) – Posted March 14, 20-- 22:11

> Come on, people, let's not get our collective panties in a bunch.
> It doesn't take a genius to realize there has always been violence
> in Jerusalem. What happened today was terrible, obviously,
> but I don't see any proof of supernatural activity.

Posts: 1502 | Location: Oklahoma | Registered: October 22, 1999

OorahSemperFi (Old Pro) – Posted March 14, 20-- 22:12

> Are you ****ing high, Sugar? No proof of supernatural

activity?? There were voices in the ****ing sky! I'll tell you what, I dropped to my knees and prayed in a hurry. And

you're a fine one to be lecturing us about panties, just cuz you happen to be wearing em.

nursebetty (Educated) – Posted March 14, 20-- 22:12
    ooh burn lol!!! ☺ ☺ ☺

OorahSemperFi (Old Pro) – Posted March 14, 20-- 22:12
    Thank you nurse! ☺

SugarRosesNeedsChange (Old Pro) Posted March 14, 20-- 22:14
    Let's derive our homophobic invective from the twenty-first century, shall we? It might surprise you and others of your antediluvian ilk, Oorah, but neither I nor the majority of my Dorothy-befriending brethren wear ladies' unmentionables. My point was it would be wise to withhold judgment on the current crisis until all the facts are in.

OorahSemperFi (Old Pro) – Posted March 14, 20-- 22:15
    quote:

    Let's derive our homophobic invective from the twenty-first century, shall we? It might surprise you and others of your antediluvian ilk, Oorah, but neither I nor the majority of my Dorothy-befriending brethren wear ladies' unmentionables. My point was it would be wise to withhold judgment on the current crisis until all the facts are in.

Holy ****, Sugar, you even defend yourself gay!

Posts 3168 | Location: Oklahoma | Registered: March 12, 1998

nursebetty (Educated) – Posted March 14, 20-- 22:15

OH SNAP ROFLMAO !!!!!!!!!!! ☺ ☺ ☺ ☺ ☺

Posts 99 | Location: Oklahoma | Registered: October 25, 20—

SugarRosesNeedsChange (Old Pro) Posted March 14, 20-- 22:18

At times like these I wonder why I even bother with the court of public opinion. Then I remember how much it amuses my significant other to read over my shoulder and watch as civilization declines before our very eyes. However, in this case, I think it's just barely worth pointing out that no one knows what all those apocalyptic prophecies mean. When Jesus's apostles asked him when the end would come, they were referring to the end of Roman occupation of Israel. Jesus was smart and kept his answer vague. Name me a day, for example, when humanity hasn't been troubled by "wars and reports of wars." The situation for the Jews went from bad to worse, and their temple in Jerusalem was torn down forty years later. As for the end of the Big Scary Book, we don't even know if the John who wrote Revelation was the same John who was Jesus's BFF, and we certainly don't know what all those biblical Japanese monster movie clips had to do with anything.

Posts: 1504 | Location: Oklahoma | Registered: October 22, 1999

OorahSemperFi (Old Pro) — Posted March 14, 20-- 22:18

Sugar, I would think even you would know not to mock the Bible at a time like this.

Posts 3169 | Location: Oklahoma | Registered: March 12, 1998

nursebetty (Educated) — Posted March 14, 20-- 22:18

no doubt!!!!! repent and be saved!!!!!!!!!!!!!!

Posts 100 | Location: Oklahoma | Registered: October 25, 20—

SugarRosesNeedsChange (Old Pro) Posted March 14, 20-- 22:20

I'm not mocking the Bible, good citizens. I find its poetry delightful, and its counsel intermittently inspiring. What I am mocking, and without one iota of hesitation or contrition, is your insistence on overlaying the half-baked prophecies of semiliterate tradesmen two thousand years ago over reports on Fox News. Not everything that happens in the world is the fulfillment of predictions Judakiah the Elder made before the invention of soap. I prophesy a rational explanation will be found for these phenomena. Maybe the screwballs on Godlike Productions are right, and what we're seeing is a government experiment gone horribly awry. Maybe it's space aliens. Maybe, just maybe, it's Allah.

Carl Sagan used to say, "Skeptical scrutiny is the means, in both science and religion, by which deep thoughts can be winnowed from deep nonsense."

Posts: 1505 | Location: Oklahoma | Registered: October 22, 1999

OorahSemperFi (Old Pro) — Posted March 14, 20-- 22:21

Sugar, as my daddy the Master Gunnery Seargeant used to say,

"That boy's as queer as a hockey bat". You take your hatred of God and his rightousness and you go straight to hell you fag!!!!!

Posts 3170 | Location: Oklahoma | Registered: March 12, 1998

O

Zack sat glumly and drank his tenth beer of the night, an impromptu wake raging all around him. The high dudgeon of collegiate emotional intensity warmed his face like a sunburn. Dozens of eyes stared at the TV, many through lachrymal lenses. A student, Brad Kessler, all tangles and zits, sat in Zack's favorite chair and stared at the bandage on his cheek. Zack sat in a guest chair opposite him in a corner of the living room. "Nasty shiner you got there," the kid said, barely managing not to sneer.

"Yeah, how 'bout that," Zack mumbled.

"You might oughta get that looked at."

"I should." Zack had been working on a cover story all night and decided to give it a trial run. "The hospitals and roads were too busy today, though. I had to stop suddenly on the way home. Smacked my head on my own steering wheel like a dumbass, you believe it?"

"That sucks."

"It sure does, Brad. It sure does." Two dozen kids in his apartment. One of those a student he slept with, two more with whom he'd struck up the preparatory dialogue. This whole thing was turning into a minefield. The sophomore nuking Pizza Bites in his kitchen, the one he banged last semester, Amber Tolland—God, she hadn't even been worth it. She fellated him awkwardly for ten seconds, then ran into his bathroom to puke. They fucked the next morning. As he came, she called him Dr. Heath. She hadn't been in his house since that pathetic day four months ago, but now here she was, slamming around the kitchen like she owned the place.

Why did he get himself into these messes? It wasn't his fault. How was he to know the world would happily tear itself apart just as Spring Break was starting? The way he figured it, thousands of professors banged students. They just kept secrets better than he did, except when they didn't: He remembered that Korean math prof who got caught with kiddie porn in his classroom. One minute he's explaining how to multiply compatible matrices, the next he's tripping over an overhead projector cord and some freckle-headed

163

sophomore from the Baptist Student Union helps him scoop up the spilled contents of his briefcase. Next thing he knows, he's in handcuffs. It could happen to anyone, because *everyone*, Zack surmised, was guilty of wanting to fuck *someone*. In a town like this all you had to do was want it. And if you could be taken down for wanting it, then you might as well go ahead and get it.

Had he cheated on Alyssa? Sure. Alyssa, on the other hand, snorted enough Bolivian bouncing powder to stage the Iditerod. We all have our faults. And who paid for all the nose candy? He did. Never touched the stuff himself. A little weed, sure. Booze, obviously. But Zack's only real addiction was new female territory. Why? Because it was there.

He remembered the days when a casual fuck would help it all make sense. Those defrag sex days were long in the past.

"I saw Laura this afternoon," Brad announced, his jaw tighter than the E Street Band.

"Yeah? How's she doing?"

"Pretty bad. She's all banged up, too. Just like you. Somebody popped her in the mouth."

"Unbelievable."

"Yeah, she wouldn't say who it was. Not to me, anyway. She say anything to you?"

Zack found himself staring beams of coherent hate into Brad's accusing eyes. "I haven't seen her today. She's not in my Friday class."

"Huh." Brad took another gulp of Corona—Zack's beer! The balls on this kid! "Well, I just thought maybe she came by your office or something."

"I don't know, maybe she did. Everything was so chaotic this afternoon I really couldn't tell you."

"Yeah, she really looks up to you, it seems like. Might even be a crush."

"Is that right?"

164

"Yeah. Y'know, things aren't so good with her and her dad."

"I didn't know that."

"Yeah, sometimes I think she's, like, desperate for a father figure."

Zack snorted. "Somehow that doesn't sound like me."

"No. It doesn't," Brad agreed, his voice a leather sap.

"Y'know, Brad," Zack drawled, "you students, you practically live in each other's back pockets. You see each other twenty hours a day. And there's a real temptation from that to feel like you're somehow responsible for each other. You're not. And don't think just because you spend all that time around someone, you know what's going on in her head. You're not a psychologist, and someone like Laura, she's not a patient on your couch. People have *worlds* of secrets inside themselves, sometimes even secrets they keep from themselves. So they're sure as hell not gonna let *you* find out about it."

"I hear ya. Still. Small department. Like you say, we see each other a lot. Easy for rumors to get started."

"It sure is. Our own little Hollywood Babylon."

Brad watched the mayhem on TV for a while and formulated his next move. "You know Amanda Quinlan?"

"I don't think so. She's not one of my students, is she?"

"I don't know."

"After a while you all start to look alike."

Brad frowned. "Funny how that works."

"I'm kidding, Brad. Jesus, lighten up. Who's Amanda Quinlan?"

"She's in two of my classes. Real cool, like, tattoos and shit."

"Sounds like fun. You should go for it."

"Yeah," Brad said irritably. "That's not why I bring her up.

165

She's got a boyfriend."

"Oh, sorry."

"Real douchebag."

"Ain't that the way of the world?"

"Yeah. Well, anyway, she said she talked to some guy who's here in town from Hollywood."

"Hollywood, California?"

"Yeah, like movies and shit. Says he works for one of the studios."

"That's interesting. What's he doing here?"

"You know that book that came out about Sugar Roses?"

"Which one?" Zack asked, thinking first of his own.

"The, I don't know, the, like, law book. What's his name."

"Ohh. Turow, Scott Turow."

"Yeah."

"*Court of Law.*"

"That's him. Anyway, they're makin' a movie about it."

"Oh yeah?"

"Yeah. They hired this guy to write the script for it, 'cause he used to go to school here, at SOSU."

"I'll be damned. He's here now?"

"Yeah, like, she met him at the library. She works there."

"I wonder how old this guy is."

"Older, like thirty or forty years old."

"A real sage, huh?"

"I guess."

"A real geezer."

"You know what I mean. Older than us." Brad emptied his bottle. "I guess it only seems like a huge age gap, but." Zack waited. That was the end of Brad's sentence.

"But what?"

Brad glared at him. "It just is. A huge age difference. That's like, the difference between a parent and a kid."

Zack nodded. God, these fuckin' punks. He hated it when college kids were so full of their own fuckin' cleverness they believed they could outdebate Abraham Lincoln. Every semester, it seemed like, he ran into some new junior genius. "I ought to meet this guy. I wonder if he was one of my students."

"He's close to your age."

"I guess so. I started here pretty young. Worked on my Ph.D. while I taught. Yeah," he drawled, "that was back when I thought I knew a thing or two. Thought I had it all figured out. Jesus. I'll tell you what, Brad. I didn't know shit."

"Oh yeah? You knew enough to get your Ph.D., obviously. Enough to stay out of trouble."

"That's true." It was all so damn exhausting.

A cluster of undergrads hugged each other as news cameras panned over indivisible knots of flesh that used to be people, footage courtesy of Al Jazeera, Xinhua, UPI, NHK, WKMG CBS Orlando. The world came down slowly, reluctantly, from a bad acid trip.

"Dr. Heath," Sara Regan asked, wiping sloppy hair from her eyes, "what do you think is going on, anyway? Is this, like, terrorists?"

"I highly doubt it," Zack answered. "I figure it's probably some kind of mass delusion."

"Dr. Heath doesn't believe in the supernatural," Brad said, finally succumbing to the sneer he'd been cooking for half an hour. Zack cast him as the lead in a play last year, and while Brad had decent comic timing, he also had Kissinger's ego. "He's an *atheist*." The surly punk made the word sound like a synonym for *child*

167

molester.

"If it exists, it's natural, no matter what it is. There is no supernatural."

"You don't think this falls into that category?"

"I do not."

"But Dr. Heath," Sara's friend Crystal sniffled, "a lot of us heard voices before the fighting started. Some people think it might be angels and demons."

"Some people have overactive imaginations. Southern Baptists and Dan Brown are fucking up America."

"That's not right," Sara said. "You shouldn't make fun of us, especially now. Just because we believe in things doesn't mean we're making them up."

"I'm not making fun of anyone." *Not yet, anyway,* he thought. *Keep it up, though, Brad.* "Why especially now?"

"Because now is when everything is changing."

"It's the Big Now," Brad agreed.

"The Big Now," Zack sighed. "Funny how every now is the Big Now when you're a certain age. I remember it well."

"This is different," Brad said. "Which you'd see if you weren't so keen on blowing it all off. I can see why you do. You skeptics have a lot to lose this time."

"Is that right?"

"'Course it is. Something like this turns out to be true, you'd have to reassess your whole view of the world."

"I guess I would."

"Angels and demons," Sara repeated.

"Or telepathic space aliens," Zack suggested. "We can't rule out little green men."

"I don't appreciate being treated like a child," Brad snarled.

"Slow your roll, Brad. Have another beer, okay? Nobody's dissing you. All I'm saying is, don't leap to simple conclusions. Some people—not *all* people, *some* people—claim they heard voices in the air. That's not proof, it's anecdotal evidence. It's hearsay. Supposedly some of those voices—again, not all, but some—are in Hebrew or Arabic or Hindi or whatever language the hearer believes is sacred. And it's not, by the way. God doesn't speak Hebrew."

"You don't know that," Brad said. "You don't even believe in God."

"Yes, you do," Crystal said, shaking her head.

"No, he doesn't," Brad insisted. "He told me so himself. He made fun of me when I prayed before a performance one night. Said God wasn't a patron of the arts and I should pray to Paul Allen instead."

"That's fucked up," someone said, the voice of a suddenly mutinous room.

"Who's Paul Allen?" someone else asked.

"Either way," Zack said, shrugging, "it's funny how God always speaks the language we expect Him to speak. But I digress. Power goes out all over the country. Cars die on the road, some of them don't want to start again. Maybe that's supernatural, maybe not. More likely they shorted out. People get nervous. Real nervous. Then, around 3:45, everybody loses their fucking minds."

"All at once. All over the world," Brad said. "That's no coincidence. That's totally supernatural."

"What else could it be?" Sara agreed.

"I don't know, Sara. But that doesn't mean it has to be the voice of God."

"I don't believe it was." Sara hugged a throw pillow.

"You don't? So what was it?"

"I think…" Fat tears rolled out of her eyes, unnerving the assembly. "I think what we felt was total rage. Not from God. From the Devil. From demons. I think the end of the world has finally come."

169

"'Finally?' You're eighteen years old!" Zack snorted.

"I do, Dr. Heath. You can laugh all you want. I think Satan has been set free to tempt us into joining him, just like the Bible said he would be."

Zack couldn't hide his astonishment. College kids!—of higher intelligence than most, and they actually believed this insane shit! "Where'd you get that, some church pamphlet?"

"No, the Bible!"

"Okay, listen," Zack stammered, "when you say Satan, do you mean the scary Alan Rickman lookin' dude with the horns and forked tail?"

"No," she groaned. "Of course not. That'd be stupid. No one knows what he really looks like."

"Okay, you're right," he nodded. "That's much smarter."

"Thank you."

"He's making fun of you again," Brad said. "He doesn't believe in Satan, either. He makes fun of everything decent. I read your book, Dr. Heath. You don't believe in the Revelation. Look at him! He doesn't believe anything he can't see with his own eyes."

"That's not true," Zack insisted. "I believe you get laid, Brad."

"Go to hell!"

"I don't believe in hell, either." Zack celebrated the point scored by cracking another beer. "And y'know what? It's sure funny how you Christians set all your perfect rules aside any time you want to get your junk wet."

"What I do or don't do," Brad said, seething, "is my business."

"This is true. We should stay out of each other's business. I cheerfully take it all back."

"You're leaving out some pretty important details, Dr. Heath," Sara said quickly. "It wasn't just voices in the sky today. People flew planes into each other. They saw Jesus. They started fighting for Jerusalem, just like Bible prophecy said they would."

"Every commentator on GNN can tell you there's gonna be fighting in Jerusalem. You don't have to be Sherlock Holmes to figure that out."

"The problem with not believing in God," Brad said carefully, "or in anything bigger than yourself, is it leaves you without any morals. Nothing's a hundred percent right, and nothing's a hundred percent wrong. Everything's negotiable. But it isn't. That's the trouble with people today. They gotta realize, if God says what they're doing is committing a sin, then that's not negotiable. He isn't saying maybe it is, maybe it isn't. He's saying it's a sin, plain and simple. It's a moral wrong. And okay, so maybe this isn't the end of the world, but y'know, I think you'd have to be crazy not to feel like we're running out of time to commit. One way or another. Pick a side. Jesus wants people to choose sides now, before it's too late. And maybe it already is. I mean, you gotta consider that possibility. One day will be the last day. So what if Sara's right? What if today was it? What if it's already too late?"

"Too late for what, Brad?" Zack sighed.

"Salvation."

"My salvation?"

"Anyone's salvation. Anyone who hasn't shown allegiance to God."

"See, this is the thing I never understood," Zack mused. "For an all-powerful being, your God sure does need my help a lot. He needs money, emotional support. Mobile infantry...Needy! That's one pitiful deity you've got there."

"Dr. Heath!" Sara cried.

"He doesn't need our help, He wants it," Brad said.

"Help with what? Holy war? Is he drafting us into His war against terror? If you're right, then the forces of evil are demons and demigods, Sara. So how does He expect us to help Him with that?"

"I don't understand every part of it," Crystal admitted,

171

"but my faith says I don't have to understand. It's not my job to understand. All I have to do is be there if He needs me."

"The alternative," Brad smirked, "is pretty damn bad. But hey, that's between you and the Lord. I'd try harder to get on His good side. Or maybe you like bein' on fire."

Zack swirled his beer. "Brad seems giddy at the impending destruction of billions of sinners worldwide. Starting with me."

"I think people have a chance to make things right," Brad said, "but I don't believe that chance needs to last forever. And either way, it's not up to me."

"Dr. Heath, please don't reject God," Crystal said. "He loves you."

"I'd say you really oughta get things squared away," Brad smirked. "Guy like you."

"Are you fucking her, Brad?"

Zack's question snapped into the room like a cat from a bad horror movie, hissing and sharp. Only the TV spoke for eons.

"I don't know what you're talking about," Brad said finally, his face reddening.

"I'm talking about Laura. Are you fucking her? 'Cause you're not the only one." Silence crashed into the room like a plane. Zack listened to the tirade coming out of his mouth as if he had no idea how it might have got there. "You don't know one goddamn thing about my morality, Brad, so either *get the fuck out of my house* or stop yammering about how God wants to torture me forever. Okay? How's that for getting things square? That square enough for you? *Brad?*"

The air was incendiary, his question an unanswered live wire.

Shay exited Zack's bedroom door, shut it quietly, and moved to sit at his shoulder. "Lacey's asleep finally," she murmured. "Hey, what's all this? You two manly men about to fight? Ooh, how exciting! I was hoping we'd have more fighting today. Today was just way too mellow for my taste. Should I get some carving knives? Or will switchblades be enough?"

"We're okay," Zack announced, ignoring the wide eyes of stunned undergraduates. "Brad was just learning to mind his manners while he's a guest in my fucking house."

Brad sat quietly, his face going purple. "You're right, Dr. Heath. I apologize."

Zack regarded him balefully. "Finish your beer." Brad left five minutes later. Zack kept his heretical thoughts to himself the rest of the night, finally shuffling to bed around four. Wide awake, he listened to Shay's gentle snoring and the murmur of quiet conversation elsewhere in the house. Lacey slept on an air mattress tucked in the corner, so he couldn't even wake Shay to work out the tension. Goddamn that motherfucking Brad. Talk about opening Pandora's box. Drunk as he was, he knew exactly what the look on Brad's face signified: One way or another, Zack's world was definitely in serious trouble.

Part Two
Εσχηατον

Endgame

Saturday, March 16, 20—
Hail Discordia?

It sounds funny after everything that happened yesterday, but today will be one of the most important days of my life. In the middle of a world crisis, my own personal apocalypse has just begun.

Speaking of the Apocalypse, last night I heard T. J. Stonecipher on GNN talking about how he encouraged his viewers to "immanentize the Eschaton." I didn't know what that phrase meant, and neither did Argyle Greenwood. (By the way, something tells me Little Lord Argyle won't be coming out any time soon. Religious hysteria and sexual honesty don't mix.) Apparently, "immanentize the Eschaton"—go ahead and memorize the phrase, it's fun to say—means to hasten the End of the World *by any means necessary*. Is anyone else as terrified as I am that they actually have a phrase for this? That means somebody might take it serious enough to try it!

08:14A.M. – **0 Comments** – **0 Kudos**

– **Add Comment** – **Edit** – **Remove**

176

Π

Amanda entered the End Times hunched over the toilet, voiding the contents of her stomach and probably the rest of her thoracic cavity as well. At no point in the spasmodic proceedings did Tyler so much as stir from his vegetative state. Wikipedia noted helpfully that morning sickness, also called emesis gravidarum, occurred in fifty to ninety-five percent of pregnant women and was probably caused by low blood sugar after a night—in Amanda's case, a night and most of the preceding day—without food. Amanda learned this a few minutes later online on Tyler's computer. Unfortunately, Wikipedia offered no professional counsel with regard to the slaying of useless impregnating boyfriends. Amanda considered the poetic justice of braining Tyler to death with his own custom game controller, then reluctantly decided she'd better make absolutely sure she was pregnant before racking up homicide charges.

She'd slept like shit the night before.

Wikipedia also advised her that home pregnancy tests were effective within two weeks of conception. Given that she was only a few days late, she wondered if the test would work if she took it today. Meanwhile, she watched TV with the sound off. The networks had, of course, suspended their usual broadcasting in favor of news, partly because the situation warranted it, and partly because insensitive remarks on pretaped sitcoms and dramas would probably get them sued. Had Scott been here, he could have recounted the sweeping precautions taken by Excelsior Studios after 9/11. An action film called *Urban Combat*, starring Sly Stallone as a SWAT commander hunting Sam Neill as his mad bomber brother, was shelved for two years, only to flop like a dead carp upon its eventual release. Shane Black's screenplay *American Jihad*, a hot property at the time, vanished without a trace. Even superhero movies were placed on hold, as cartoon pyrotechnics were viewed as emotionally inflammatory. The same would hold true in the current catastrophe. The usual Saturday morning cartoon punch-'em-ups were replaced by pale, robotic talking heads.

A Cornell physicist named Dr. Allan Sylvan turned up in several interviews, as his atheist tirade *But Dice Do Play God With the Universe* was in its fortieth week on the *New York Times* bestseller list. Amanda skimmed the book approvingly when it arrived at the library. Even in Sugar Roses, the waiting list to read it was over two dozen names long. He appeared now on ABC. Amanda unmuted the sound but kept it low to avoid waking Tyler.

"Dr. Sylvan," the reporter asked, "between your book and a rabid interest in books like *The Da Vinci Code*, is it possible people's faith isn't as strong as we've been led to believe?"

"That's an interesting question," Sylvan answered, his pudgy face cracked by an automatic smile. "*Harper's* investigated this a few years ago, and their results were so surprising I quoted them in my book. Something like eighty to eighty-five percent of Americans identify themselves as Christian. Now, we may not realize it on a daily basis, but that number is extraordinary. Only seventy-seven percent of Israelis identify themselves as Jewish. Funny thing is, we're not as Christian as we believe we are. Only about two out of five of us can name even half the so-called Ten Commandments. One in eight believe Joan of Arc was married to Noah. Nineteen in twenty have premarital sex; one survey said it was 'nearly universal.' Bill McKibben, the *Harper's* writer, went on to say, if we're so Christian, then why do we give so little of our national wealth to charitable causes? He believes the central message of Jesus has fallen on deaf ears."

"Do you agree with him?"

"I do, but that's not my point. I believe Americans are far less Christian in their doctrinal beliefs than they pretend to be, as well as in matters of personal morality. Supposedly less than half of us believe humans evolved from lower life forms. If that's true, then why do most schools continue to teach it?"

"Obviously that's a matter of some controversy," the reporter noted.

"Indeed, but not in half of all American school districts, as we'd expect based on the surveys. I think people believe there *might* be something to evolution, but they're afraid to come out and say so. Over half of us now admit we support homosexual civil unions, yet the Bible is adamantly clear it thinks all gay men should burn in Hell—which, by the way, less than seven out of ten of us believe in anyway. How can you be a Christian and not believe in Hell? Yet apparently, about one in four of us fall into that gap. And remember, that's what people will admit to believing in a poll. My honest feeling is, in many churches in America, the congregation is sitting there smiling and nodding, but they don't believe most of what they hear. They're just adamantly opposed to saying so, because nobody wants to rock the boat. Funny thing is, the preacher's probably wishing he could say something contrary as well."

"Dr. Sylvan, what about the Intelligent Design movement? Do you find anything in that idea that merits further study?"

"Study how? No one's studying it. That's part of the problem."

"How so?"

"Well, I'm rather unique among astrophysicists in that I'm willing to even consider the possibility. We've had such a hard time, we scientists, with all this insane hue and cry from the Christian conservative movement that our knee-jerk reaction is basically to flinch away from it as fast as we can. I'm sympathetic to that reaction, but I think we do ourselves a disservice by dismissing it out of hand. The problem is, so far, the idea that we may have had some sort of Intelligent Designer has been completely untestable, so must of us believe it doesn't fall under the purview of science at all. Which is true, but remember, the atom was little more than an untestable theory when Democritus and Leucippus suggested it around 420 B.C. That doesn't mean there weren't atoms at the time, of course; it just means no one knew how to get down to the atomic level and look for them. I think it behooves us as scientists to find a way to test this Intelligent Design theory and see if there isn't maybe something to it. Unfortunately, the ID movement has been, thus far at least, so nakedly a façade for Christian activism that it hamstrings the whole debate."

"If there is something to it, does ID mark a point of reconciliation between religion and science?"

"Not at all. There can, in fact, be no possible reconciliation between religion and science."

The reporter jerked backward in surprise. "Bit of a line in the sand, don't you think?"

"Hear me out, Janice, please. Religion is, by definition, the worship of the unknown, while science is the unprejudiced search for the unknown. I can't really worship something or Someone if I first have to admit I don't know whether the thing exists in the first place. But I do think there's room for détente between, shall we say, spiritual curiosity and scientific curiosity. It's going to require two things. First, scientists are going to have to broaden their philosophical approach to science, and I think we can do that, as many of us come from religious backgrounds. The harder step, because it demands something of many Americans, is to admit they don't have it all figured out. If people are comfortable reading *The Da Vinci Code*, with its Catholic conspiracy theories and revised biography of Jesus, then surely they can admit God might have a more sophisticated method of creating life on Earth than to mold it out of clay. Life took longer than six days to get here, and fossils aren't elaborate practical jokes. They're real evidence that might tell us something about the modus operandi of an Intelligent Designer, if indeed such a Person is ever proven to exist."

"Dr. Sylvan, where do you stand on the unusual phenomena we experienced yesterday?"

"Well, Janice, I was asked this no fewer than a dozen times yesterday, and I'm afraid I don't have much of an answer for you. See, that's the difference between science and religion in a nutshell. A cleric experiences something unusual like that and says, 'Oh, no problem, I know what this is. I read about it in a book written by some raving nutter two thousand years ago.' Or a prophet, take your pick. While I, as a scientist, say I have a few theories, but nothing that's gelled into even an educated guess."

"And your *un*educated guess?"

"I suppose the prevailing opinion in my line of work is that it was some kind of religious hysteria. This is not beyond the realm of possibility. We know for a fact that patients with temporal lobe epilepsy often experience religious hallucinations—as many as seven out of ten of these people, in fact—and we know symptoms can be spread by mass hysteria. There's a very well documented case of a school where one child vomited but not, it turns out, from food poisoning, and most other children in the lunchroom got sick for no reason at all. Many of these threw up as well, so mass hysteria can have very real consequences. However, I find the simultaneity of what happened yesterday convincing proof there's something else at work here."

"Maybe demons?" the reporter grinned. "Do we all need an exorcism?"

"Well, speaking for myself, I need exercise, but probably not an exorcism. No, I don't think we have imps to blame for this problem, either. But as for what it might have been—you know, Janice, the brain is a very sensitive organ. Tweak its chemistry one way or the other just the slightest bit, and you'd be amazed what can happen. All you need are a few fancy molecules in the right place. Dopamine, serotonin, norepinephrine—these are chemical compounds that we know have major impacts on our mood and behavior. I suspect something happened yesterday that acted as a mass neurotransmitter, but honestly, I couldn't imagine what it might be. If it was God, He certainly works in mysterious ways."

"I believe we can all agree on that," Janice smiled. "Dr. Sylvan, it's been a pleasure talking to you."

"And to you as well."

"I hope we'll have the opportunity to do so again soon. For ABC, I'm Janice McCarthy. Back to you, Charles."

Amanda muted the TV again as Tyler gradually surfaced from an abyssal of sleep. She waited as he stretched and farted in the bedroom, a grotesque accompaniment to a silent Geico commercial. He wandered in and crashed onto the couch like a Scud missile, scratching his nuts through threadbare boxer shorts. "You really know how to impress a girl," she said. "Fashion sense like that."

"Get off my ass," he mumbled.

"Sorry."

"'M'na make some coffee."

"Thanks, I'd love some."

"Mm." Instead of getting up and moving into the kitchen, he stayed on the couch at her side, numbly watching muted news footage. "'Sgoin' on?"

"I've been watching this guy Sylvan, Allan Sylvan. He wrote that atheist book about dice and the universe."

"Uhn-n."

"He thinks we breathed in some kinda neuro-something shit that made us all crazy for a while. Mass hysteria."

Tyler wiped his face so hard the flesh pulled away from his eye sockets. "Huh."

"What do you think? You think we all just went crazy for a while?"

"I don't know, man. I was here playing *Imperial Assassin*."

"You didn't feel anything weird?"

Tyler pondered the question. "I don't think so. 'Sreally just wrapped up in the game."

"Meanwhile I was freaking out and trying to keep people from beating each other stupid. Weird, huh? People are trying to commit multiple homicide in a library, but there's you playing a violent video game, and you didn't even notice what was going on."

"I guess."

"Did you even hear the humming tone?"

"Lea'me alone, a'right? It's early. Have a cigarette."

She couldn't. It was driving her crazy. "I should let you wake up."

Silent seconds ticked by.

He rubbed her arm. "I'm sorry. I know you're just bored or whatever. I dunno. Maybe I'm just used to being fired up. I don't even notice anymore." He grunted. "Maybe all these games are making me a fuckin' psychopath. I'll prob'ly murder you in your sleep some night," he grinned. "I won't even know it 'til they show me on, like, security video at the trial."

"Great," she decided. "It's nice that I have that to look forward to."

Tyler watched an entire iPhone commercial before replying, "I'm not gonna murder you in your sleep, Amanda."

"I know, Tyler."

"Besides, you were acting kinda weird before yesterday anyway."

"I was?"

"Yeah, I dunno. Like…your mind was somewhere else."

She rubbed her forearm nervously. "I've been really stressed."

"I could tell. So how come you didn't talk to me about it?"

"What, are you shitting me? When do I ever even see the front of your head?"

He lay his head on her lap and rubbed her leg idly, his breath swampy on her thigh. "I know."

"Those damn video games."

"I just like 'em, that's all."

"I'm not saying don't play 'em, I'm saying I want to be a real couple."

"I do, too."

"Then why do we never even…?"

"What?"

"You know, Tyler. We don't, like, communicate any serious feelings for each other."

He mulled this over. "You mean sayin' we're in love an' shit."

"Oh my *God!*"

"Well?"

"Tyler!"

"What?"

Her tiny doorknob fists bounced exasperatedly on his shoulder. "I love you, Tyler! Okay? I fucking love you. But you don't even say it anymore."

"We barely said it ever."

"You're right. We barely did. So I don't know. Do you even love me?"

"I guess so."

"No, Tyler! No! That's not good enough!"

"Why? Why does everything always have to be all serious with you?"

Amanda reflected on emesis gravidarum, epidurals, stretch marks, postpartum depression, and an unimagined parade of agonies, indignities, and handicaps. "Life is serious, Tyler. It can be. It is sometimes, I promise. Not everything is, like...I don't know. A game. Not everything in life has a save point. You can't always start the game over."

"Fuckin' metaphors at seven in the morning."

"Shut up," she said, growling impatiently. "It's like...I can feel my life is on the verge of getting really fucking serious. And I know people always think that when they're our age. But...the last few days... I don't know, maybe it's all this insane shit on TV and people jacked in the library and my car dying and seeing everyone scared, but I'm really feeling trapped. Not just as a person, but as part of, like, humanity. It feels like we're running out of time. And life kinda goes on, same as always, but I feel a time coming when it won't. When everything will change so bad we can't put it back. And I don't know if I'm ready to handle something like that. You understand what I mean?"

"I guess so. Some of it."

"I need your help with something tonight."

"Like what?"

"Just say yes, okay? Just say yes without asking what it is. We can do that for each other, right? Just say you'll help me and I can count on you. It's important, okay?"

"Okay." At least he seemed awake now, glaring at her in anxious confusion. "You can count on me. Shit."

"Thank you, Tyler." She stretched to kiss him on his patchily stubbled cheek. "I'm gonna make us some lasagna for dinner, okay?"

"That sounds good. What's the occasion?"

She didn't know how to answer that question. Instead, she unmuted the TV, and together they watched towers of black smoke unspool over Jerusalem. That afternoon she bought three different home pregnancy tests.

From: Jessica Strohmeier
Date: Saturday, March 15, 20— 10:46 AM
To: Scott Glass
Subject: miss you

Hey baby. After we hung up last night I put on some music and thought about how much I miss you. I realized we've kept each other at a distance for a long time now. I don't know why that is, but I know it's mostly my fault. Maybe I felt like if I told you how I felt you'd get nervous and run away. Scott, the truth is I'm so happy for the opportunity you have at Excelsior. I've known you for two years now, and there's a big difference in you now that you have some self-confidence. I like the difference. But I didn't want to tell you, because it seems like I'm saying now you have a high-paying job, I want to be with you. I'm not like that. I'm doing fine by myself. This job is excellent but it isn't all I want out of life. I want to be in a relationship that is strong and can last for years and years. Lately I wonder if that's you or if I should keep looking. I don't want this to sound like an ultimatum because it isn't. If you want us to stay exactly how we are then I will happily go along with it. But Scott, I am a pretty good person to be with. I know sometimes it's comfortable and boring but I think that's because we haven't tried to be special for each other. Does that make sense? I guess what I'm saying is hey Scott, you want to give this thing a try, for real? Cuz I do. Think about it, okay? I'll call you sometime this weekend. Like you baby. Except the truth is I really love you. I love you, Scott. I can't believe I'm telling you that in an email, but I guess that's how we are sometimes. Chicken! Maybe someday we'll have guts enough to tell each other face to face. What do you think? Anyway be good and think about me when you get the chance. Bye!

--Jessi S

P

By leaving the TV off and listening only to his iPod, Scott was able to write fifteen pages of screenplay that morning. The movie would open on a beautiful Oklahoma sunset. The murder took place in April of '87, when Scott was in high school. He knew that period in Oklahoma intimately and sketched it in a few sentences. In a screenplay, dialogue is king, while exposition, "the black," has to be kept short, as most producers don't bother to read it anyway.

EXT. SUGAR ROSES, OKLAHOMA – SUNDOWN

Fiery pastels over low green hills. SUGAR ROSES is the quintessential American small town, clustered around a minor college campus but focused on its forty church spires. Five thousand families eat hearty suppers behind bay windows and unlocked front doors.

Not bad for a first draft, especially since his thoughts were elsewhere. He read Jessi's email five times. He found himself strangely proud of her; it wasn't like Jessi to be that bold in expressing her secret emotions. If only he could take it seriously. After the day she had yesterday, the feds swarming her office, the waves of hysteria, the nightmarish drive home, it was only natural she might go looking for something stable, only to reject it again a week later. He'd lived in L.A. long enough to know any semblance of domestic routine seemed as golden a prize as the lost Ark of the Covenant. There were neighborhoods in southern California, Hollywood absolutely among them, where a lifelong marriage was harder to find than a hooker with a heart of gold; yet Hollywood was the primary publicity machine for both True Love and the perfect fuck. Billions of people worldwide were made to feel like failures for their inability to achieve either. The Dream Factory, sad to say, ruined lives. It spread the cancer of crawling self-judgment.

If the moral watchdogs who blamed Hollywood for the

world's sins and unhappiness really wanted to make people happier with their lot in life, they chose the wrong movies to picket. They should have organized mass DVD burnings of *When Harry Met Sally...* and *Sleepless in Seattle*. Outraged citizens should spit on puffy-lipped effigies of Meg Ryan.

Scott felt no guilt and little horror as he sketched the slaying of Evie Rae Chambers, age sixteen, in her own backyard. It was fun to play God. Miss Chambers had just come back from a trip to Konawa Lake with half a dozen school friends. She wore cutoffs and an Eskimo Joe T-shirt over an electric blue bikini. Her body was found stripped and stabbed thirty-eight times under a cucumber magnolia. Her assailant threw her bikini bra over her eyes, then ejaculated onto her face. The murder weapon was a serrated hunting knife. Obviously, these were details that had to be softened for the big screen; the studio would prefer if he wrote for a PG-13. He wanted to capture the merciless ferocity of the murder on his pages, but there was no point in writing material the studio would never allow a director to shoot.

He thought of the rage he saw yesterday. He considered the violence blazing in every corner of the planet that morning. Sugar Roses, by comparison, was an oasis of empathy and peace, yet even here, every few months a volcano of rage erupted in some quiet citizen, and the result was the end of another life. The violent crime rate here was higher than the national average. It seemed even the watchful eyes of Saving Grace, Inc. and a vengeful Baptist God couldn't stop every bullet or sheath every blade.

Scott grabbed his research folder and looked again through photos of Evie Chambers, slashed in her prime. Black bars covered her nipples and pubis but failed to hide the killer's vicious concentration there. The flesh around her breasts split like sashimi. Blood splatters extended for meters to her right, indicating the killer was right-handed. Her pubic hair was matted in blood, an oil slick in the black and white photos. Her open mouth gave her the look of a hungry, pathetic baby bird. She wore the short, boyish haircut Scott remembered from the girls of his own adolescence.

It was obscene what luck could do. It raped and killed.

188

It perverted a pleasant springtime evening with a beer on the back stoop into the copper stink of animal attack. Scott drew a distinction between God and Luck—God the vast angelic Father who tries to make everything okay, Luck the murdering son of a bitch who keeps God from succeeding. Luck gets everyone killed in the end. Even God steps into the shadows and lets Luck have its way with people. Yes, the killer was ultimately responsible. Sure. But what unseen force put Evie there in the first place? What did she ever do to deserve this monstrosity?

It occurred to Scott that back in 1987, when the town of Sugar Roses was abuzz with every grisly detail of the murder and ensuing trial, the vibe must have been similar to this morning's. Simply walking around town would be valuable research. The sun was shining. Businesses were open. He grabbed a notepad and drifted deeper into town.

At least once a block, he'd pass a stalled car, usually aged or poorly maintained. One of these had run into somebody's living room; the car was pushed aside and the hole sealed with plastic. He passed a black patch where someone started a fire in a pile of trash. Another lawn was covered in bottles, Bud Light and serious booze. Graffiti on a rundown duplex screamed, "I KNOW WHAT YOU DID." Smells drifted by: coffee, bacon, cigarettes, and for twenty unpleasant feet, urine. Even the literal atmosphere of the town had changed. This was not just another bad day after all. It was the beginning of something awful. An ocean was rising.

He ate in a coffee shop downtown—eggs, bacon, brutally strong coffee, damp hash browns and a biscuit, all for five bucks. They fed you here, that was for damn sure. The waitress looked like she came straight from Central Casting. Surly old men picked at wheat toast and gossiped over coffee and yesterday's newspaper. The old men agreed, *them Ay-rabs had to be stopped afore they burned Isr'l to the ground. The president, why, he ought to send in troops, let ahr boys get things done in a hurry. Othawise, them Jews'd wanta come over here, and besides, didn't the Bah-ble say we was s'posed to protect Isr'l in the Last Days?* Eavesdropping in Sugar Roses on a Saturday morning, it was easy to see some people are most content fulfilling their own stereotypes.

He swung by the library in hopes of chatting with Amanda again, but it was closed for the day. Instead he called Jessi, left a rambling message to the effect that he was taking her email seriously—without answering its question, of course—and turned off his cell phone.

He jogged around Madeleine Park. The two-mile track directed him past high school boys fishing, little girls tossing bread crumbs to ducks, and sorority girls trading inanities on benches. A Choctaw family said grace before tucking into a picnic lunch. Blaring orgies of flowers bloomed beneath cerulean skies. It'd be perfect, if the joggers didn't bear haunted looks in their eyes, or if every third snatch of overheard conversation wasn't about bloodshed in parts of the world most people couldn't find on a map.

He kicked a Dr Pepper bottle past the sweeping front lawns of grand manors on Imperial Road. A few of these houses bore the Century markers indicating they were built around the time of Oklahoma statehood. All were quiet as libraries. About halfway to 19, Imperial morphed into Country Club Road, the golf course hidden behind walls of oakleaf hydrangea and beauty berry. Stingless imprecations floated from the tirades of annoyed duffers. Here at least, the world of Everyone But Us was light-years away.

He watched cars cruise by on the highway and scratched notes in longhand. If the world was going to hell in a handbasket, he wanted to write the last great screenplay on planet Earth. It wasn't much, but coming home reminded him how far he went away. He felt blessed by the opportunity. Still, he liked this place, and he wanted to do right by it in his pages. The handful of lazy, simpleminded cops in Turow's book did not an illiterate backwater make.

As he walked north he heard a parade of ambulances outside the hospital. Sugar Roses hadn't finished bleeding.

He poked around Heartland Mall and spent a relaxing if unenlightening hour at Bayeux Entertainment. There he struck up a conversation with the book manager, Phillip, a snarky small-town Oscar Wilde who was clearly as gay as a maypole dance. He didn't see anyone giving Phillip a rough time. Perhaps Sugar Roses, like most of America, was growing out of its vicious homophobia. Phillip pointed him to a book called *Commedia dell'Heartland*, a satire about Sugar Roses penned and self-published by an SOSU professor. Scott read a few pages over a lukewarm Bayeux sludgaccino. The author, a slim figure in an anachronistic aviator jacket, squinted into the sunlight saturating his cover photo. "Dr. Zachary Heath," the jacket read, "is a theatre professor at Southern Oklahoma State University in Sugar Roses, where he was born and achieved the first of three college degrees. He is the author of three plays, one of which (*Ding Dang Doo*) received an Oklahoma Theater Association Award in 2002. His story 'Buyer's Remorse' has been selected for publication in *Southern Humanities Review*, and a poem, 'Villanelle for Alyssa,' was featured in *New Letters* for spring 2004. He is faster than you, he is stronger than you, and he is going to eat you."

"Yeah, I'll give it a shot," Scott said.

"Come by Abilene Sam's tonight," Phillip replied. "The author and I are having drinks together."

"Oh, I don't want to be a third wheel."

Phillip narrowed his eyes. "You wouldn't be. Trust me."

"I ate there last night," Scott said. "It didn't seem like your kinda place."

"Oh, please. I like kicking my spurs up with all the other buckaroos. Besides, our branch of Spago closed years ago."

"Funny. So, the book—any good?"

"I don't see Dr. Heath on any shortlists with Cormac McCarthy, but I think you'll discover he has a certain *joie de vivisection*. He's the bee's knees around these parts." Scott paid for *Commedia*, the coffee, and Decemberists and Neko Case CDs. He returned to the Standard, where he scowled at news and thought about reactivating his cell phone. Why didn't he want to talk to Jessi? Maybe his career in L.A. had been so full of near misses, he didn't want to give her a chance to change her mind. He was reminded of the time he scored a date with the homecoming queen, then didn't answer the phone or go to school for three days so she wouldn't have a chance to renege. In the fullness of time, she ditched him halfway through *Innerspace* anyway—goddamn Meg Ryan again—and disappeared with a running back with the all-too-appropriate nickname Fuckhead. He didn't want Jessi to run off with a guy named Fuckhead, and maybe that wasn't an unfair request.

So instead he called his parents, made plans to see them before he left Oklahoma, and soothed their anxieties about his vulnerable life in Los Angeles. It was the same after 9/11; his mom was convinced cells of angry Muslim terrorists were lurking behind the Hollywood sign, ready to blow the entertainment business's sinful, sodomite, coke-snorting community ass halfway to Allah. As he spoke to her, his voice grew more quiet, his tone more persuasively rational, and his hands shakier from the unnerving suspicion she was right. His dad just wanted to know if he'd met Heather Locklear. He hadn't.

"I heard they're making a *Dallas* movie with John Travolta," his sister announced. "Congratulations. You're in an industry that's making a *Dallas* movie with John Travolta."

"He bowed out," Scott countered. "Too artsy or something. Besides, I'm also in a town that's winning hearts and minds for Jesus."

"Even Jesus doesn't love us enough to go see a *Dallas* movie with John Travolta."

Thus ritually tormented by his loving family, Scott showered and walked the short distance past the highway to Abilene Sam's. He marveled yet again at the establishment's aggressive tribute to all things rootin'-tootin'. Was there a giant wagon wheel in every room? *You betcha, Red Ryder.* A severed buffalo head? *Yes.* Faded photos of the 1889 Land Rush? *Absolutely.* A news story commemorating the lynching of four Ada men in 1909 for the murder of Gus Bobbitt? Sugar Roses wouldn't want it any other way. *This ain't Denny's, amigo, but you can dang sure go find one and eat there if you got a problem with the way we do bidness.* Scott found the place charming, albeit visibly xenophobic and angry, and it seared a perfect slab of dead cow. A cut of beef this big would cost twice as much in L.A., and taste half as good.

He was halfway through a magnificent steak and tall beer

when Phillip and the author walked in. Scott waved them over. "Dr. Heath," Phillip said, "meet Scott Glass, screenwriter and agent provocateur."

"Scott," Zack said, extending a hand.

"Dr. Heath."

"Call me Zack."

"All right."

"I didn't have you in any of my classes, did I? Phillip tells me you're an alum."

"Yes, sir, but I'm afraid I never had the honor."

"Honor, my ass. Seems like all we ever do in that theatre department is theatre. It's become a cliché."

"I wasn't much of an actor. More of a bullshit artist."

"And fellow wordsmith," Phillip reminded them. "You do have that in common."

"I read some of *Commedia dell'Heartland* today. I enjoyed it."

"I'm thrilled you pronounced it correctly," Zack said, his eyes cascading down an underage waitress's legs. "We don't get too many word fans around these parts."

"I'm writing the screenplay version of the Turow book myself."

"Haven't read it. Any good?"

Scott swigged his beer. "Yeah, probably. It's not my cup of tea."

"That's funny. So why are you writing a screenplay about it?"

"From it, actually. I guess because Excelsior offered it to me. It's a real opportunity."

"Contracts signed, all that?"

"Oh yeah. My agent's fifteen percent of ecstatic."

"I'm sure he earned every penny."

"She. Lucille. And yes, she was happy to inform me of such when I called her and told her about the deal I'd made that she never heard of."

"Ain't that the way. At least you have an agent. I have to bomb on my own."

"I meant to tell you," Phillip said, patting Zack on the arm. "Sales of your book are way up today."

"My book? Why?"

"I suppose the good citizens of Sugar Roses want to focus on, as we say in the book business, Local Interest."

"Jubilation. Your gift horse can close his mouth now. I ain't lookin'."

"How's *Court of Law* selling?" Scott asked.

"I can't keep it in the store," Phillip smirked. "The warmhearted denizens of Sugar Roses love buying and hating it. I'm hoping to schedule a book burning."

"They should install that feature on Amazon," Zack agreed. The waitress swung by, dipping low to flash flirtatious, tip-magnet cleavage to all three of them, even the profoundly gay Phillip. She left menus and sashayed off. "God bless America."

"Above the fruited plains," Phillip said.

Scott stifled a grin. "Something funny?" Zack asked.

"No."

"What is it?"

"I'm sorry, I just…It's nothing. I thought you two were an item." Scott stabbed a forkful of steak fries and looked up in time to see Zack and Phillip's faces hardening. "No offense."

"Keep your voice down," Phillip hissed.

Scott froze, his fork halfway to his mouth. "I didn't mean

anything by it."

"We're not an item. Don't be gauche."

"I wasn't trying to be. Like I said, I misunderstood. I apologize."

"I'm not gay," Zack said. "Obviously."

"We're not an item!" Phillip hissed again.

Scott swallowed. "Let me buy you guys dinner," he managed.

"That's more like it," Phillip said.

"You're the man," Zack shrugged. "They got lobster on this menu?"

"So anyway," Scott said. *Commedia dell'Heartland.*"

"You ever written a blog?" Zack asked. Scott shook his head. "Me neither. But let's say you did. Let's say you blogged about Sugar Roses. You're an idiot that way. And maybe you weren't always nice about every little thing. Maybe you were in a bad mood some days. Maybe you were venting. But maybe you didn't worry about it, because you didn't imagine anyone would ever actually read it."

"And yet," Scott grinned. Zack spread his hands. "Something tells me this story ends in tears."

"Not today," Zack grinned. "Today, Phillip informs us, it ends in book sales. Tomorrow, who knows?"

"And yesterday?"

"I was mildly detested." Scott sighed. "Apparently being nice is a big deal in Sugar Roses, bigger than thoughtful, even bigger than true. I tell you this because once your name appears on a movie called *Court of Law*, you'll be right out there with me."

"Hopefully better paid," Phillip smirked.

"You can say that again."

"Why's it gotta be like that?" Scott asked. "Why can't

people just accept the fact that not everything about Sugar Roses is perfect? It's still a pretty likable place."

"Pretty likable is deemed insufficient," Phillip said quietly.

Zack agreed. "This is God's country. They don't see Sugar Roses as a town, they see it as a way of life. Their way of life. God's way of life." He nodded over at the TV on the bar. Local news showed thousands gathering in churches across the Midwest to pray for the return of Baptist normalcy. Fervent wishes for the End Times had finally come true, and now these believers were desperate to cancel the show.

"You should try posting on the *Sentinel* message board," Phillip sighed. "It's like chumming for sharks. Seems like every time, I pull back a nub."

"Wait," Scott said. "I read those. Which poster were you?"

"The good-looking one."

"Trust me," Zack said, "there are people here, even otherwise wonderful people, who lack any sense of humor about themselves. It ends badly."

"This is a lesson you learned the hard way."

"I certainly did."

"And yet, you still created something. They didn't. All they could do was criticize. So in my book, that puts you ahead. No pun intended."

"Ah, the competitiveness of youth," Phillip sighed.

"Yeah, just make sure the check clears," Zack sighed, smiling tightly, and waved the waitress over. After he and Phillip ordered, the three men sat and watched the news a while in silence. Soldiers from IDF, the Israeli Defense Forces, squared off against rebels from Hamas in the Negev. Even with the TV muted, it was obvious reporters were playing up prophetic, apocalyptic aspects to the story.

"Looks like maybe the Good Book knew what it was talking about after all," Phillip said, nudging Zack's elbow.

"Looks can be deceiving. Another day, another disaster."

"You really think so?" Scott asked. "You think this'll all just blow over? I don't think so."

"Not blow over, just keep right on going. They've been fighting over Yahweh's desert real estate for thousands of years. Why stop now?"

"They really want Muslims off that hill."

"They always did."

"Until now, they weren't as bold in their moves toward the Dome of the Rock."

"Yeah, but listen. Any time anything happens in Israel, all the fundamentalists go bugshit expecting the Rapture. It's funny how the prophecy's so vague it could apply to almost anything."

"Dr. Heath, as you may have noticed, is our resident skeptic," Phillip said.

"I prefer cynic," Zack said. "Or, as Ambrose Bierce defined it, 'a blackguard whose faulty vision sees things as they are, not as they ought to be.'"

"I like that," Scott grinned. He noticed a kid with pale green hair listening in from a nearby table. Apparently sardonic discussions of Bible prophecy offended even countercultural Oklahomans. "Count me in," he continued, lowering his voice.

Zack spun his fork in a mock salute.

"Bierce also defined a Christian as 'one who follows the teachings of Christ insofar as they are not inconsistent with a life of sin,'" Phillip smiled. "Glory be, it's as if he were born here in little ol' Sugar Roses."

"What about you?" Scott asked Phillip. "Where do you stand on all this? Are we in the Last Days?"

"We're always in the last days of *something*. 'Tis a consummation devoutly to be wished."

"I'm a rational guy, but I can't explain what I felt the other

197

day. I'm starting to take it seriously."

"I felt it, too.   But I'm certainly not ready to leap past mundane logic to a conclusion just yet."

"Do you believe in God?" Zack asked Scott.

"Well...I'm from Oklahoma," Scott answered, shrugging.

"I take that as a yes."

"I don't go to church, if that's what you mean."

"It's possible to believe and stay home on Sunday morning."

"I agree."

"Phillip's an agnostic," Zack said quietly, "but every week, there he is, uniting with Pastor Dan in a church he has to perjure himself to attend."

"Judge not," Phillip smiled. "My deceptions are between me and the congregation, not the Almighty. God and I merely disagree on certain biological imperatives He seems disinclined to cancel. Either way, my attendance in church is a comfort to my parents in their declining years. It's the least I can do. And I must say I find the idea of a First Cause compelling."

"Same here," Scott said. "I don't see protoplasm duking it out and producing a baby. It just doesn't make any sense."

Zack shrugged. "Nature makes plenty of mistakes an all-knowing God wouldn't make. That protoplasm also gave us mosquitoes and, I don't know, Ebola."

"The Lord works in mysterious ways."

"The Lord works in imperfect ways. There are rough edges everywhere you look." Zack twiddled a toothpick. "You any kind of quantum mechanics fan?"

Scott laughed. "Gosh, who isn't? No, it's on my list, right after I figure out women and the movie business."

"I admit I don't understand it much myself, but it's interesting. And when you study it at all, you find the world we do understand, bizarre as it may be, is an island of rationality. And it floats on this…*meringue* of multidimensional nonsense that baffles the brightest minds on the planet. It's ridiculous. It's insane how impossible this stuff is to comprehend. There are edges to the physics we understand, maybe to what we *can* understand. Light can act like a particle and a wave in the same experiment. We know nothing can go faster than light, yet some particles act like they're talking to each other faster than light. There are eleven dimensions, most of 'em wrapped inside the three dimensions we *can* see. And it doesn't conform to the physics of Isaac Newton any more than a tyrant adheres to his own system of laws. We don't know why. But the one thing we do know is, it doesn't look built by a master craftsman. It's not a simple construction. You're right: It doesn't make sense."

"Maybe it makes a kind of sense we don't have."

"It seems ungrateful to criticize the Creator for being smarter than you," Phillip told Zack, triumphantly stirring a glass of iced tea.

"Oh, whatever. Look, maybe there's an underlying order we'll discover tomorrow. Okay. Maybe it's the perfect design. But to me it always feels like…You ever see one of Frank Gehry's constructions?"

"You're referring to the architect?" Phillip said.

"Yeah, he designed the Disney Music Hall in L.A.," Scott said.

"Exactly, and the Experience Music building in Seattle and a lot of other very cool buildings. I'm a fan. You look at his buildings, and they seem like a tangle of curves. No straight lines anywhere you look. They're like steel clouds. But if you pulled off all the sides and looked inside the building, you'd find geometric order. Rooms with straight sides. Lumber and metal connecting at right angles. Because no matter how chaotic the surface might look, there has to be order at the heart of each building. It's what allows that crazy shape to keep standing. And I think people thought the universe would be like that—chaos on the surface, but with one perfect system of laws at the center keeping it straight. $E=mc^2$. The Second Law of Thermodynamics. Thou shalt not kill. Simple, geometric, unified. But instead, the deeper we look, the more chaotic it gets, and there's a clear division between Newton and everything else. There's a scale, this submicroscopic scale, below which everything goes completely haywire."

"I don't understand."

"It's the difference between Gehry, an engineer, and whatever makes this universe tick. People claim we have an Intelligent Designer, but y'know, nothing about the design seems intelligent to me. This world is horseshit. It's extremely half-baked. It's not the way a perfect God would do it."

"I don't believe you're qualified to say," Phillip shrugged.

"Open your eyes."

"Maybe God is a committee."

"That would explain some of it," Scott agreed.

"I don't know," Zack said, rubbing his chin.

"Look, Frank Gehry doesn't have to start from scratch," Scott mused. "He builds his designs onto a pre-existing design, physics. He knows about gravity and how hard it'll pull on his designs. He knows about, like, atoms and atomic forces and how the ground isn't gonna dissolve under his foundation. He knows the ground is solid and it can support X pounds per square inch and it isn't gonna, like, suddenly turn into vapor. But what if you were trying to build physics on top of *nothing?* No logic or physics at all? No solidity. Isn't that what God did? Maybe what you're saying is exactly what we'd expect from a universe built by God."

"A god who didn't think things through, maybe? Or who didn't understand quantum physics and never bothered to learn it? That's an awfully irresponsible god."

"You say there's a clear divide between the universe we understand and the crazy, chaotic universe it's sitting on. Right?"

"Right."

"So maybe that's the line where God started. Or maybe there was, like, a bigger, smarter, crazier God Who already built everything else, the quantum stuff you're talking about, and the God we believe in built His universe inside of it. Or on top of it. Or maybe there are universes inside universes. I'm not smart enough to know what I'm talking about," Scott said, laughing, "but that doesn't mean the universe can't be smarter than me. Y'know, just because I don't understand this place doesn't mean God doesn't know what He's doing."

"Well, I think it ought to make more sense than it does. Which is nada."

"You guys ever play video games?" an adolescent voice asked from outside their conversation. The kid with the green hair grinned over his cheeseburger. "Yeah, sorry. I was eavesdropping. Whatever."

"How's it going?" Scott asked, feeling defensive.

"Pretty good. Tyler Knizek." The others introduced themselves. "Oh, yeah," Tyler said, nodding at Scott. "My girlfriend knows you from the library."

"Amanda?"

"Yeah, that's her."

"Nice to meet you. Video games."

"Yeah, you play?"

"I dabble. Sports games, mostly."

"I don't play those too often, but okay, so maybe you'll understand anyway. Part of the fun of playing video games is finding and using the weaknesses in the game—things the programmer never thought of, y'know. Mistakes. Like, let's say you're playing online blackjack, and you notice the computer slows down before it offers you insurance every time it's showing an ace but holding a pocket ten. Okay? So that's a glitch in the game. It really happened. A friend of mine noticed it and made sweet bank in less than eight hours. Hackers do it all the time. They saw a glitch in the way Windows handles animated cursors, and they used it to break into *World of Warcraft* and steal a bunch of other people's gold. Which doesn't sound like much, 'til you realize there are players who pay real money for fake *Warcraft* gold."

"Fascinating," Phillip said, wishing they'd get back to

talking about books. He hadn't cracked a physics text or played a video game since Bill Gates had a boss.

"Yeah. It's how games are put together. The programmer, like, he can't think of everything, right? He's gonna make mistakes. And you notice the mistakes by finding places in the game where things don't make sense, where you can, like, fly through walls and shit. Or sometimes the coder even builds those places in on purpose. A lot of games have cheat codes where you type in a secret command, and the game lets you do anything you want."

"So you're saying, God made cheat codes."

"They even call that shit 'God mode.' Or maybe you're seeing mistakes at the quantum level, like maybe He didn't think of everything. That's what I think."

"So God," Zack said, ripping into an order of beef ribs, "is an Asian kid typing for three days straight on a diet of Jolt Cola, Slim Jims and Hot Pockets."

"Red Bull, dude. Get with the times. But basically, yeah. Hey, maybe that's why there are so many Asian people."

"Et voila," Phillip said, rolling his eyes. "Generation Y to the rescue."

A teenaged girl, dark-haired and cheerleader pretty, worked her way through the restaurant with a box of pink flyers. "Hey," she said, reaching Tyler first. "Got an invitation for ya. Hope you can make it."

"Thanks." Tyler took the flyer and glanced at it with obvious disinterest, tossing it aside seconds later. The girl didn't notice, having moved on to Scott's table.

"Hey, gahhhs," she drawled, "how y'all doin' today?"

"We are excellent," Zack announced with fraudulent heartiness.

Phillip rolled his eyes again but turned to her cordially. "And how are you today, young lady?"

"I am super good, thank you for asking. Now, I don't want to interrupt your dinner, but I am invahtin' people to a very special service tomorrow mornin' at Sugar Roses First Baptist Church. Pastor Dan Taylor, y'all know him, he wants tomorrow to be a tahm a community healin', okay? We're gonna have potluck an' fruit pahs an' I don't know what all. There's gonna be good music an' fellowship an', lahk, it's gonna be a really big community event, okay? Not just church but lahk, a festival, lahk, a really big pep rally for Sugar Roses. An' everybody's gonna be there. I really hope y'all can make it. Anyways, here is an invitation for each o' y'all, from me to you, so I really hope you can come an' I get to see you there, okay?"

"Thank you," Scott said, accepting a flyer.

"You are very welcome! Now, I know it'll be a blessing to ya."

"Y'know, I might have to check this out," Zack said, checking her out.

"The Great Cynic sees reason?" Phillip smiled, accepting a flyer. "Will wonders never cease? Hallelujah. Thank you, my dear."

"I think it's time Pastor Dan and I met face to face," Zach mused.

"I sure do hope to see y'all there," the girl said, grinning. She turned to Phillip gleefully. "An' I know you from Bayeux. I see you there all the tahm."

"Indeed? Are you a fan of the literary arts?"

"I sure am. I buy all the *Door Within* books an' *Christy Miller* an' *Sierra Jensen*, I just love them, they are so inspahrin' to me. Robin Jones Gunn is so awesome to me. She is just...unh!" the girl said, a climax of devotion from the diaphragm.

"I'm not familiar with Mr. or Ms. Gunn's work," Zack said.

"It's Missus," the girl corrected politely. "Her husband's name is Ross and she has two children. An' did you know she writes, lahk, fahve books a year? I wish I could be as inspahrin' as her. What a blessing."

"Young adult Christian fiction," Phillip told Zack.

"Oh, God help us."

"He will, sir," the girl replied. "I know that."

"Out of the mouths of babes," Phillip replied, grinning and nudging Zack.

"'Thou hast perfected praise,'" she said, completing the quote. Her smile lit the restaurant like a miracle.

You are happily invited to a special revival
service of

Sugar Roses First Baptist Church

100 North Main, Sugar Roses
Sunday, March 16 at 10:00 a.m.

Enjoy coffee, tea and muffins in the

Fellowship Room, 9:00 a.m.
Potluck picnic lunch to follow at
Madeleine Park,
Broadway & Townsend, Sugar Roses

"Featuring Madge's Famous Baked Beans!"

We invite people of all Christian faiths to join us in
a spirit of praise and fellowship. We come together in
this dramatic unprecedented time to show our love for
Jesus and our loyalty to Our Heavenly Father. Join Dr.
Robert Stuyvesant and our 40 member Choir for music
of worship to lift our hearts. Pastor Dan Taylor will
offer his encouraging sermon 'Victory at Last'. May the
blessings and peace of Jesus Christ lift your heart and
embolden your spirit!

> "So do not fear, for I am with you;
> do not be dismayed, for I am your God.
> I will strengthen you and help you; I
> will uphold you with my righteous right
> hand." -- *Isaiah 41:10*

Σ

"A Pentecostal minister, a Jewish rabbi, and a Catholic cowboy open a cattle ranch," the voice-over said. "It may sound like the start of a bad joke, but it's very real. Here on Dan Straka's ranch six miles outside of O'Neill, Nebraska, the beef of choice is Red Angus. The breed is known for its tolerance of heat and resistance to pinkeye and other eye diseases, but that's not why it's being raised here. These cattle are destined for life in Israel, and one of them might be the harbinger of doom."

Amanda couldn't will herself off Tyler's couch. The harbingers of her own doom lay nearby in a plastic bag. It still smarted how intensely the clerk at Walgreen's glared at her as he swiped the pregnancy test bar codes over the scanner. Thankfully, that and Amanda's withering return stare were the only comments made about her purchase. She wanted this to be decided before Tyler came home, but she didn't want to face the inevitable.

"For thousands of years, the Judeo-Christian faithful have been expecting the appearance—or reappearance—of the Messiah in Jerusalem. Unfortunately, it's believed the Messiah can't appear until He has a Jewish temple to return to, and someone else is in the way. Muslims now control the Temple Mount, including the famous Dome of the Rock. But even if Jews controlled the Temple Mount, a true Jewish temple couldn't be built there yet anyway. That's because the book of Numbers, chapter 19, which describes God's plan for such a temple, requires the sacrifice of a perfect red heifer. For two thousand years, no such animal existed. That's where Straka comes in. Together with his pious partners, Dan Straka is breeding Red Angus heifers like there's no tomorrow—which, some Christians believe, there won't be once the Messiah returns. They believe Christ's return marks the Rapture of the faithful...and the End of the World."

Magic cows! Amanda thought. *People actually believe in this shit! Magic cows! In the twenty-first century!* This is the world her child, assuming she carried one, would be born into—a world where bees go missing and Natalie Portman saves gorillas and nutballs breed cattle to imminentize the fucking Eschaton. A world that was clearly, unstoppably, burrowing up its own ass to the core. How could she possibly subject a new person to the End of the World? She was rapidly coming to the conclusion that things were coming to their conclusion, one way or the other. These maniacs wouldn't have it any other way.

If the Christians made a red cow for the Jews, and the Jews made the triply sacred Temple Mount a vacant lot, and the Temple became a reality, what then? Catastrophe. Not to use the word lightly, Apocalypse. *Let's say the Messiah doesn't come,* she thought. *Jesus stays dead, the Twelfth Imam moves to Dallas and becomes a Presbyterian, and Superjew doesn't move back into the Fortress of Solitude.* If history teaches us anything, it's how far people will go to avoid eating crow. The conflict and bloodshed would be unspeakable. And what if Messiah did come back, but wasn't a Christian? Even worse. Christian fundamentalists would accuse the Jews of lying and their Messiah of identity theft; if the Messiah's a Jew, then Jesus wasn't really the Christ, and that could not be permitted. On the other hand, if Messiah turned out to be Jesus 2.0, then the Jews would fight back just as hard. People wouldn't let go of the traditions and beliefs of two thousand years, no matter how compelling the evidence against them. And whatever the outcome of the Messiah's reunion tour, Muslims would never forgive the reconquest of sacred property—unless, of course, Messiah had the awesome supernatural power required to prevent violent reprisal, in which case it didn't matter because billions of people would die at his hand soon anyway.

Cells like soap bubbles, crushing together, the Big Bang projected in reverse. This was the secret in her belly. She had to know. She couldn't know. She couldn't move her ass off the couch.

"The Temple Mount finally reopened to non-Muslim visitors in 2006," another reporter said in a windblown stand-up, "but prayers of any other religious faith are strictly forbidden here, as are Hebrew prayer books or musical instruments. And that's fine with the Israeli government. After all, Moshe Dayan appointed the Muslim Waqf, or Sacred Trust, curators here in 1967 as a nod toward interfaith compromise. Besides, most Jews are unwilling to venture onto the Temple Mount anyway, because only High Priests were allowed to enter an ancient sanctuary here called the Holy of Holies, and now we don't know exactly where that was. So it's unclear how a new Jewish temple could be built here without risking an act of blasphemous encroachment, but that hasn't stopped a Zionist death squad called 'Revenge of the Babies' from launching a major offensive against Muslim—and Israeli—security."

Jew against Jew. Why not? Welcome to the Black Parade: Muslim against Muslim all over the Middle East, Buddhist against Buddhist in the Nanjing Massacre and the Battle of Shanghai, Hindu against Hindu in Gujarat, and Christian against Christian in Northern Ireland and throughout the European Theatre. Join the crowd, guys. But still, couldn't they have picked a scarier gang name than "Revenge of the Babies?" She hated to think the End of the World would be precipitated by a group that could easily be confused for an episode of *Rugrats*. It might have sounded awesome in Hebrew, but it lacked a certain punch in translation.

Revenge of the Babies...and this time it's personal! Waaaaah!

Thus spurred by coincidence and the ever-ticking clock of Armageddon, Amanda snatched up the Walgreen's bag and locked herself in Tyler's squalid bathroom. She squinted at the fine print on the back of each box and discovered the kits were meant to detect human chorionic gonadotropin, or hCG, in her urine. Surely that was a scarier name than Revenge of the Babies. "I'm sorry, Miss Quinlan," she said out loud, assuming a comforting George Clooney doctor voice, "it says here you have human chorionic gonadotropin. Shall I find you a minister?"

The kits recommended testing herself first thing in the morning, when levels of hCG were at their highest. *Fuck that.* She needed privacy. If she waited 'til morning, she'd either have to hide it from Tyler, or test herself in her tiny apartment. This was the only place she ever felt alone, a sad comment on her relationship with Tyler.

Pee on a stick, Amanda. That's all there is to it. A dipstick, in fact, if that word in the instructions didn't remove any last particle of dignity from the proceedings. It was like getting medical assistance from Sheriff Roscoe P. Coltrane.

Boxers down. Toilet seat cold on her lily white ass. The all too prosaic aquarium trickle. And finally, as if to herald the impending birth of another glorious human existence, she reached between her thighs and poked a dipstick into her pee.

209

She closed her eyes and counted. "Ninety-nine. A hundred." She opened her eyes and consulted the cheap plastic oracle:

"Fuck."

When Tyler came home, he found Amanda tangled in his sheets, bundled in his sweatshirt, and crying on his pillow. She explained there was a part of him inside her now, too. He enveloped her, holding her tightly as they wept for a life they'd created and needed to end.

BadAmanda

Online Now!
Last Updated:
March 15, 200—

Send Message
Instant Message
Email to a Friend
Subscribe

Gender: Female
Status:
In a relationship
Age: 19
Sign: Aries

City: Sugar Roses
State: Oklahoma
Country: US

Signup date: 10/16/0-

Blog Archive
[Older Newer]

The specific blog entry you're trying to read is currently set to be private, and only the blog owner can see it.

[back]

T

The sun rose, cool in a clear sky, and the birds sang their morning prayers. Scott awoke early and couldn't get back to sleep. He jogged and showered before the hotel staff put out the first Little Debbie Cakes and complimentary coffee. The news was even worse than last night, clenched hands and held breaths, thousands more dead, the Savior delayed. The world was tearing itself apart in an explosion of tribalism, warfare, and fundamentalist bloodlust. Oh, and last night, the president dreamed he was handed a sword by a king on a glowing horse. He testified as such in an early morning speech from the Rose Garden, then declared China and Saudi Arabia infidel nations and enemies of peace. GNN had a field day.

Scott reread the invitation to First Baptist and decided to check it out. He was up anyway. It'd be a good opportunity to see the town united in crisis. Besides, he was raised around Baptists. The language and pleasantry of his family's religion slumbered in his cells.

He strolled down Main Street past dim shop windows and the clink of dishes inside minuscule diners. Dusty pickups filled every parking space. Those seniors who weren't churchgoers congregated here, glowering through misanthropic fellowship over bituminous coffee and grease-stained Sunday *Sentinel*s. Eggs and bacon, hash browns, dollar coffee—there were no crêpes or mochaccinos to be found on this street, and the patrons of these diners wouldn't be caught dead at Cuppa Joe's. Coffee wasn't meant to cost four dollars and come in a bowl, it was served in a dusty brown cup the bored waitress flipped and filled without asking, just as God intended. Foam is for shaving, and Splenda ain't even a word.

Physically and figuratively, the First Baptist Church was the center of Sugar Roses. The original church was among the first buildings in town, predating the original post office just south. Growth and increased donations in the mid '80s allowed for the construction of a two-block complex including a memory garden, a full kitchen, and an activity center with band stage and basketball court. Nowadays the church even maintained a colorful website for its eight hundred regular members. Jesus had a web presence, if not always an earthly one.

Scott arrived fifteen minutes early, but the thousand-seat church was already filling. The structure and its forty-foot spire shone like ivory in the spring morning sunlight. A cross section of Sugar Roses paraded up the ramp to the church's open doors. The sign out front, an ongoing record of Pastor Dan's homespun sense of humor, greeted the faithful: "SERVING THE COMMUNITY SINCE 33 A.D." Although he was dressed in khakis and a polo shirt, Scott didn't feel underdressed; some men wore suits, but others were in blue jeans and work shirts. He was greeted by three different people on the way to the door. A greeter bid him official welcome and pushed a church bulletin into his hand. His eyes adjusted slowly to the dimness inside.

Phillip approached and shook his hand. "You made it."

"We sinners have to stick together."

"Speak for yourself," Phillip said. "I'm born again."

Phillip sat by an older couple very near the pulpit. Scott elected not to follow. It'd been years since he was in a church for anything other than a wedding. Thankfully, the old protocols soon reasserted themselves: shaking hands, sincere smiles, and the clutching of forearms. Elaborate wood arches surrounded staggered platforms at the back of the hall. Benevolent Christs gazed down from brightly-lit stained glass windows in the east-facing façade. Scott found a seat near the back. The hard wooden pews were as uncomfortable as he remembered from his youth. Even the hymnals seemed the same, *Sing Joyfully* in cheap golden leaf on bright red covers. The Bibles provided, however, were no longer the seemingly inviolate King James but the New International Version. He found he missed the Elizabethan thees and thous of the classic translation. The church's eldest members limped in cautiously behind walkers or portable ventilators and cleared their throats in phlegmy gargles.

He'd barely glanced at the bulletin when a pudgy but handsome man in his late thirties touched his shoulder. "Good morning."

"Good morning," Scott replied, standing awkwardly.

"I'm Dan Taylor. Don't believe I've had the pleasure."

"Scott Glass. It's my first time here. I was born and raised Baptist in Ardmore."

"Oh, wonderful. Yeah, I'm an old friend of Keith's, the assistant pastor there. Excellent music director."

Scott flinched. "I have to admit, it's been a while. I've been living in L.A. the last few years."

"Oh, that's okay, no shame in that. How you likin' it out there in sunny Los Angeles?"

"It's like living in a theme park. It's fun the first day, but it gets a little crazy."

Taylor chuckled. "I imagine. Well, listen, I'm glad you could make it this mornin'. We hope it'll be a blessing to you."

"I'm sure it will."

"Come by the picnic after. Get yourself around some honest-to-goodness Oklahoma vittles. We've got some good cooks around here."

"I will, Pastor, thank you."

"Call me Dan. I'll see you there."

"Dan." He sat back down as the pastor moved through the crowd and greeted each newcomer, of which there were several dozen. Scott pondered the irony of how tragedies only increased people's faith in God's love. It reminded him of the "God Bless America" banners and bumper stickers so ubiquitous after 9/11, a time when God was clearly looking elsewhere. He didn't know whether such unquestioning devotion inspired or depressed him more.

Amazingly, Zack came in just before ten and found a seat across the hall. Scott tried and failed to catch his eye. A young brunette and her daughter came in with Zack and sat at his side. *Funny*, Scott thought, *he never mentioned a wife or girlfriend*. Zack seemed anxious to confront Pastor Taylor; the brunette kept

215

soothing him back into his seat. Scott could only grin as he visualized Zack announcing he'd accompany her to church. She must have imagined hell was freezing over. Maybe it was.

A pretty redhead sat at a Rembrandt digital organ. She launched into the prelude, "Joyful, Joyful, We Adore Thee" from Beethoven's Ninth Symphony, a tune Scott knew well—though, ironically, from its appearance in *Die Hard*. Although the piece was played in instrumental form, the bulletin provided Henry Van Dyke's retrofitted lyrics: "Ever singing, march we onward, victors in the midst of strife." Scott considered it a shockingly upbeat choice after the events of the last few days, but he soon relaxed into its Yuletide familiarity.

The congregation settled as an avuncular man in an extra-large suit, the assistant pastor, jogged to the front of the room for call to worship. "Hey, good morning, everybody!" he sang. "What a beautiful sunrise God provided for us today! Did you see it?" Scattered voices confirmed his assessment. "Yeah! Can I get a *woohoo*?"

"Woohoo!" the congregation repeated weakly.

"I just find that so encouraging, when things haven't gone my way or I'm kindly depressed, to see the beauty of God's creation and know He is active in the world. And that's what we're here for today, friends, encouragement. I know it's been a difficult week, and I know folks are hurting and fearful. But we're gonna change all that today. Pastor Dan has a message that's gonna lift your spirit up to the heavens. We need it! Lemme hear a *woohoo*!"

"Woohoo!" the congregation parroted.

"I'm sorry, I couldn't hear ya! What'd you say?"

"*Woohoo!*"

"That's right, woohoo for the Lord!"

It suddenly occurred to Scott that the churchgoer most famous for his use of "woohoo" was Homer Simpson, a questionable role model at best.

"We're gonna get encouraged today!"

"*Woohoo!*"

"Anybody out there need some encouragement?"

"*Yeah!*"

"Me, too! So let's give it up for the Lord!"

"*Yeah! Woohoo!*"

"Okay! Before we get started today, we got some quick announcements to make. I know Pastor Dan has a lot to talk about this morning, and I'm looking forward to hearing it, so I'll be as quick as I can. Now as some of you know, Sister Becky Farrell was in a bad car accident the day before yesterday." There were shocked mutters; apparently most people didn't know. "Her car died on I-35 as she was turning off at Highway 19 when the tone hit. It looks like maybe she was planning to get some gas there at the Raindance." It was the only permissible explanation for why a good Baptist might turn toward the Raindance Casino on a Friday afternoon.

"Anyway," the big man continued, "the story we got is some fellas hit her from behind, and when their car died, too, they went runnin' off on foot." The congregation muttered its outrage. "I know, it's terrible. But meantime, OSP got their license number and there shouldn't be any problem finding them boys. That's the good news. The bad news is, Sister Becky was in surgery most of yesterday for a serious spinal injury. We don't know what the outcome is gonna be other than poor Gary is fit to be tied. I can't even imagine. So as you talk to the Lord this week, say a prayer for Gary and Becky, and let's get her a big ol' miracle. I don't think Gary's even left the hospital for a second, so I'm sure his family could use some covered dishes. My wife and I are taking him some leftovers from the picnic this afternoon, but I don't know what they're doin' about feeding them kids. Thank God they were all at school and not in the car with her. They could sure use our help in this time of need."

This was part of what Scott missed about church, the family feeling of a support group. It was also a benevolent cage. He stifled a smile at the Big Brother subtext implicit in these announcements.

The choir filed in, forty strong, from a side room and shuffled into place. The choir master led a rendition of "Majestic Sweetness Sits Enthroned." "Had I a thousand hearts to give, Lord," the congregation sang, "they should all be thine." Scott mumbled along, unable to remember the tune and self-conscious about his rusty church-singin' voice. The organist played Bach's Arioso, Scott dropped a few bills in the collection plate, and Pastor Dan smoothly took his place at the lectern.

"Good morning."

"Good morning," the congregation replied.

"I know most of you probably expected me to come up here today and talk to you about Revelation. Why shouldn't you? I almost did. I told my wife so late she didn't have time to change the church bulletin. I been watching the news all yesterday just like you have, and it's all anybody seems to be talkin' about. The End of the World. Rapture. Armageddon. Or maybe they're finally motivated to talk about the trials we've been expecting for years. If so, give thanks to God. It's about time somebody paid attention to what's in store for the earth. But the Lord didn't direct me to talk about Revelation this morning, and I believe I've figured out why. The truth is, there's a lot of disagreement on Revelation, even in the church. I don't think it's my place to tell what all those Bible mysteries mean. We got people coming in here today from all kindsa Christian faiths. Maybe we got people in here today who don't belong to any kinda church at all. They sleep in on Sunday mornings." Scott noticed Zack flinching across the room, placated anew by his companion.

"That's okay," Taylor continued. "We're glad to have 'em. If that's you I'm talking about, please don't take offense. I'm delighted you're here. We want to do our best to make you feel welcome. In fact, we hope you'll see fit to come by our church picnic at Madeleine Park after the service. We promise to feed you and share some encouragement with you. But in the meantime, I gotta tell you what the Lord directed me to pass on to you today. I think this morning might be the most important sermon of my career in God's service. 'Cause look, the way things are going, it might be my last chance to speak to you as a congregation. I'm convinced, friends, the End is in sight."

Pastor Dan glanced away from his notes, then paced back and forth as he continued. "My sermon today is from John chapter 4, the Samaritan woman. Now, one of the things that's happened over the last few days is preachers of all stripes are arguin' about what it means to be a Christian. Are all Christians gonna be saved? What about Christians who don't believe in the Rapture? That's a good question. If the Apocalypse is comin', you don't want to be on the wrong side. I know we all want to get saved. And maybe this is the last chance we've got to get it right. So I been lookin' at the Gospels real hard this weekend to see what Jesus had to say about salvation, and wouldn't you know, like a lightning bolt, the Lord spoke to me directly and pointed me to this chapter. Did He speak to me in words? No. He did somethin' better. He spoke to me in the language of the heart."

Scott smiled, remembering the warm certainties of his childhood.

"At the beginning of John chapter 4, the heat is starting to come down on Jesus and his apostles. The Jewish Pharisees are starting to feel threatened by Christ's message. Why? Because Jesus preached a way to salvation that didn't involve Jewish ritual. So to get a little breathing room, Jesus decides to go north, up to Galilee. Between Judea and Galilee, there's a strip of land called Samaria, and the people there are descended from Assyrians mixed with some Hebrews. They worship the Jewish God, but they also worship Greek gods like Zeus. The Jews all despise the Samaritans. They have a racial and religious prejudice, and believe me, when the Jews of Jesus' time hate somebody, they don't fool around. They go out of their way to avoid being *seen* next to a Samaritan, let alone talking to one. So in verse 4, when Jesus 'has to go through Samaria,' there's a back story there. They had this other road that went around Samaria to the Jordan River. It might have even been a shortcut to Galilee. So when Jesus 'had to use' the road through Samaria, that's not geographical, it's spiritual. God required him to go.

"Now, Jesus goes to the well, and it's the sixth hour, the middle of the afternoon. The Bible says he was 'tired.' Some say 'weary.' The Greek word here comes from the word for a beating, so we'd say he was 'beat.' It's the hottest time of the day. So here's this Samaritan woman drawing water, but why is she the only one there? Well, most Samaritan women drew water from the well first thing in the morning, when it was cooler, and also 'cause it was a good time to socialize. But this woman's here by herself. We're gonna find out why in a minute. Jesus sends his disciples into town to buy some food, and they don't have any objection to that. But think, now. They're gonna buy Samaritan food, from Samaritan people, and eat what they were brought up to think of as unclean. So why's that? Because Jesus already worked on the apostles. His message was heard. They've been relieved of their bigotry and hatred. See, unlike the Pharisees, they're not snobby or elitist anymore. They're not too good for other people. Jesus is gonna push things even further here in a minute.

"He asks the Samaritan woman to give him some water. Now, the Scriptures don't tell us her name—some people think it's omitted on purpose, to make her represent a whole group of people—but the tradition in the Russian Orthodox Church is to call her Photina. I'm gonna go with that, 'cause I want you to think of her as a real person. I want you to imagine what she looked like. She's not a young woman, 'cause she has a history. Maybe to a Jew she looks…different. Maybe her hands are all twisted from years of work. But she's about to receive a gift no other Gentile has been given to that point. She's about to have the longest conversation with Jesus of any single person recorded in the Gospels. Imagine that. A non-Jew. What a blessing! What would you give for personal face time with Jesus?" A few congregants wiped away tears, imagining.

"Jesus says, 'Will you give me a drink?' Now, if I were her, given the way Jews treated Samaritans, I might say, 'You've got some nerve, buddy.' And really, she's not as polite as she could be, is she? She says, 'You're a Jew and I'm a Samaritan woman. How can you ask me for a drink?' Jews don't talk to Samaritans. But she doesn't just say 'Samaritan,' does she? She says 'a Samaritan woman.' The fact that she's a woman is also important, because Jewish men don't talk to women in the streets. It's like some Middle Eastern countries now. Women are thought of as second-class citizens. And some of this, I'm sorry to say, was religious tradition. The Law of Moses didn't treat women like equal citizens, and believe me, the Jews took that idea and ran with it. So now we got three kinds of prejudice at work here:

220

racial, religious, and gender. Jesus has risen above all that. What a wonderful example.

"So they start bantering back and forth about water, but remember, he's asking her for a drink outta her bucket. Now, I hope I don't offend anyone here, but he's offered to drink outta what amounts to a segregated water fountain. That just wasn't done in Jesus' time, and she knows it. But how many Christians in America, in *recent history*, were limited by foolish bigotry and blocked themselves from the company of wonderful people? How long was Christian charity held back by simpleminded hostility and fear? We have a better example than that. We shoulda known better."

Scott noticed the pastor had Zack's full attention now. The brunette at Zack's side noticed, too. The pastor checked his notes and continued.

"Now look ahead to verse 17. She says, 'I have no husband,' and Jesus says, 'You're right when you say you have no husband. The fact is, you've had five husbands, and the man you have now is not your husband. What you've just said is quite true.' See, that's why she didn't want to draw water when all the other women were there, in the morning. She didn't want to deal with all their criticism and scorn about her choices or misadventures in life.

"Now, if you ask me, we're starting to get a bit personal about all these husbands. I imagine Photina might want to take offense. But she realizes: How could he have possibly known all that? We've never met! He's never been here before! I mean, whoa! Now, we don't know why she was married five times. We don't know why she was shacked up with some guy who wasn't her husband. But the Jews only allowed people to be married twice, no matter what. Most Jews would've ended the conversation long ago, but even if they hadn't, this would've been a definite deal breaker. So we're talking about sexual prejudice now, the hatred of someone for their sexual or romantic life. And Jesus, once again, rises above that."

Scott saw Phillip's back stiffen.

The pastor cleared his throat. "She says, 'Sir…I can see that you are a prophet.' And she asks Jesus a deep, important religious

221

question. She says, 'Our fathers worshipped on this mountain'—that'd be Mount Gerizim nearby—'but you Jews claim that the place where we must worship is in Jerusalem.' Now, why does she ask that? Does it come outta left field? Not at all, though some people claim she's just tryin' to change the subject away from her checkered past. But that ain't right. The Jews and Samaritans argued over the right place to worship—the home of God's temple, in fact—for hundreds of years. It was a major rift between them. So now that she has access to direct knowledge of God and His Son, Photina wants to settle this once and for all. She wants to make sure she and her people are worshipping God the way He wants, and she's convinced Jesus knows the true answer. But look how he responds: 'Believe me, woman, a time is coming when you will worship the Father neither on this mountain nor in Jerusalem. You Samaritans worship what you do not know; we worship what we do know, for salvation is from the Jews.' Now, think about that. He says Samaritans worship a god they don't know. That's true, 'cause who's ever met Zeus or Apollo? They don't exist. And the Jews worship what they do know, for salvation is from the Jews, and the Jews of that time really *knew* him. They knew *Jesus*. But that ain't clear enough, so he says, 'A time is coming and has now come when the true worshipers will worship the Father in spirit and truth, for they are the kind of worshipers the Father seeks. God is spirit, and his worshipers must worship in spirit and truth.' Now, he didn't say the Jews are right or the Samaritans are right; he says so far, neither of 'em are right. But things are gonna change. From now on, it ain't about what kinda church you go to. That ain't what's important. It's about spirit and truth—about making a change in our emotional nature. It's a change in the way we get along. From now on, you and I, Jesus and Photina, we can all have conversations where we seek the spiritual nature of God *together*. We don't need some elitist rabbi to guide us or to force us to conform to an ancient law. We need direct spiritual communication with God and direct, truthful conversation with each other, on equal terms, with an open heart."

A quiet unease had penetrated the church. The congregation sensed it was being corrected, and the air felt cold and sharp with electricity.

"Photina's amazed by this. Awestruck. What she's seen

222

and heard is something no one has ever seen before, in Judea or Samaria. She can barely get a word out. She says, 'I know Messiah is coming. When he comes, he will explain everything to us.' What a careful response. Can you see how she's hinting? 'Cause what he just told her *is* an explanation. She's hinting he might be the Messiah, and she's giving him a chance to respond. This Photina is one clever lady. I like her. What a fascinating person. What an interesting person to engage in a conversation. It'd challenge my mind. Maybe yours, too. And she's brave, too, incredibly brave, because she knows she can be stoned if people misinterpret her reason for being there. I like Photina. And Jesus does, too, 'cause he announces who he is to her, for the first time in his earthly ministry. He hinted around about it with a rabbi in the previous chapter, but now he declares himself openly to her in no uncertain terms. He says, 'I who speak to you am he.'

"What a privilege. Oh, my heavenly God. Can you imagine? I mean, Lois Lane thought she was special for knowin' who Clark Kent is. But Photina just found out Jesus is the *Messiah*, the Savior both Jews and Samaritans have been waiting for, for hundreds and thousands of years. Hey, but check this out: The Greek language didn't have punctuation the way modern English does, so it's actually possible to translate this verse as, "'*I Am*,'" in quotation marks, 'is who speaks to you.' And 'I Am,' you remember, is the meaning of the Hebrew name Yahweh, the personal name of *God Himself*. Oh, my Lord. It must have been like a lightning bolt hitting her full in the face, a nuclear bomb going off in her heart. If that were me, I'd have a heart attack right there and die. I couldn't take it. But she winds up spreading the message of Jesus to her fellow Samaritans, and she convinces them so well that later, when Phillip comes to Samaria, he's able to convert the whole capital in a single day. Praise the Lord. Hallelujah.

"But look at verse 27: 'Just then his disciples returned and were surprised to find him talking with a woman.' They do notice. 'But no one asked, "What do *you* want?" or "Why are you talking with *her*?"' They may have been surprised, yes, but they were ready to live a different way. They were finally putting prejudice behind them. They were ready to invite and include other people. Y'see? They couldn't let racial, religious, gender, or sexual prejudice push them away from the spirit of God anymore, 'cause they recognized the example set by Jesus. They were ready to change." The pastor shut his Bible and paused to collect his thoughts in the all-too-silent church.

"I suppose you're all wondering what this has to do with the last coupla days. Well, I asked God what I should talk about today, and this was the story He put in my heart like it was branded there. And when I studied it, I understood why. One fella calls it 'the gospel in miniature.' It's the message and power and irresistible attraction of Jesus, all in a nutshell. And as I look around this Sunday morning, brothers and sisters, I believe we're headed toward a point of no return. And if the End of the World isn't happening right now before our very eyes, then it'll happen in our lifetimes. I'm convinced of that. The world can't take much more of the evil we've been putting it through.

"I say 'we' for a reason. For too long, certain factions in Christ's church have wanted to tell you the key to salvation is separation from the world. They want us to divide other people into two camps, Good and Evil. You're either with us or against us. If you believe something different from what we believe, in our church, then you need to be cut out of the conversation. We talk about America being a Christian nation, and it is, but we really only want it to be *our* kind of Christian. The Founding Fathers were deists. If the Christian elitists I'm talkin' about, now, these modern Pharisees, had their way, then Thomas Jefferson wouldn't get a vote. Ben Franklin, randy old cuss that he was, he'd be shamed and excluded. And if religious conservatives had their way, slavery would never have been abolished. My friends, we must open our minds to a better Christian faith. We must open our eyes and hearts to see what Christ did in his own life, and apply it to our own.

"Now, you say, 'Pastor Dan, that all sounds well and good, but I can't go around loving everybody. The Bible doesn't allow it. There are sinful behaviors I'm not allowed to associate with. The Law says women are subservient to men in the church. So who are we to argue with the Law of the Bible?' But Jesus said the greatest commandments are to love God and love one another. In a true Christian's heart and mind, the Law is superseded by decency. Christ's message, my friends, is that decency and compassion transcend the Law. Jewish law said Jesus couldn't talk to women in the street. Jewish law, the Law of the Bible, said only Jews were chosen by God, and they couldn't have contact with people from any Gentile race. If Jesus put the Law ahead of compassion, then none of us would be in this church today. We recognize, as history and humanity progress, we get acquainted with new kinds of people, who in turn expose us to new ideas and moral viewpoints. Maybe the steady march of science comes up with something that changes the way we view the world. That's okay, 'cause the spiritual Christian approach to other people, the spirit of love and inclusion, is *not challenged* by any new discovery or invention. I don't care *what* we find out tomorrow, or what form of tribulation these End Times may take, there will never be a reason not to love other people. Jesus said it—he lived it, every day of his life—and I know in my heart it's the truth.

"When the Jews in Jesus' time talked about a Messiah, and for some Jews it's still true today, they mean a political and military savior who can lead them to global supremacy. That's salvation to them. The same goes for many Islamic zealots in the Muslim world. But when Christians talk about salvation, they mean Jesus died to erase the debt of our sins and will come back to lead us into Paradise. But look at what Jesus himself said about salvation: 'A time is coming and *has now come* when the true worshipers will worship the Father in spirit and truth, for they are the kind of worshipers the Father seeks. God is spirit, and his worshipers must worship in spirit and truth.' That's the kind of salvation the Jews had in their very midst, only few of 'em could see it. They didn't have to wait for the End Times, and neither do we. It's here now.

"So here's the deal. We can go on feeling superior to other people around the world, even other Christians, or we can make a commitment right here and now to reflect the true spirit of Jesus' ministry. We can commit to loving one another. Instead of driving each other away with hatred and judgment, we can welcome each other with the love of Jesus Christ. Instead of hiding away to protect ourselves, living our lives in a constant state of panic and paranoia, we can give each other the benefit of the doubt. We can earn the best of each other by expecting the best. Instead of dwelling on the past and all the bad cards we've been dealt, we can look forward to the blessed future Jesus promised as a free gift. Now, I know fearful times are coming. I know storm clouds are shadowing the face of the earth. This old system has come to its nightfall. But it's time to be each other's sanctuary, commit to each other, and let the warm, loving spirit of Jesus be the everlasting salvation he intends it to be. As Joshua said to the people of Israel, 'Choose for yourselves this day whom you will serve. But as for me and my household, we will serve the Lord.'"

Pastor Taylor flipped to a bookmark near the back of his Bible. "Or, as Paul told the Romans in chapter 3, verse 21, 'A righteousness from God, apart from law, has been made known, to which the Law and the Prophets testify. This righteousness from God comes through faith in Jesus Christ, to all who believe. There is no difference, for all have sinned and fall short of the glory of God, and are justified freely by His grace.' Are you ready for grace? Are you ready to live in the inclusive, forgiving, open-hearted spirit of Jesus? Then the time to decide has run out. Take your stand. Whatever darkness falls, we must shine the light of God's truth and the spirit of Christ's love and salvation. Oh, praise Jesus. Praise him always. Amen."

All Our Tomorrows: The Future of Computer Gaming

By Kevin Li

Excerpt reprinted by permission of PC Game Power *magazine, March 20— issue*

...When objects in computer games are no longer polygon shells but virtual three-dimensional constructs, they'll behave the way we expect physical objects to behave. The same holds true for characters, both players and NPCs. Designers are already adopting new software that allows the body of a character to fall or react to blows in realistic ways.

Jason Klass, a designer for Monolith, thinks this realism could become a problem for gamers. "I don't know if we'll go the photorealistic route, not completely anyway. It's one thing to shoot an obvious animated character. I don't think anyone lost any sleep over plugging the demons in *Doom*. But what if you had to shoot a photoreal human character in the face? Doesn't that cross some kind of moral or ethical line? What if it became less fun for the player? What if players start suffering combat stress? The question we really need to start worrying about is, 'Would killing believable characters, human characters, desensitize a game player to real world violence? What if it made violent behavior in the real world more likely?'"

Klass also sees a potential for increased strain on designers. "It's one thing to play God in a game like *The Sims* or *Starcraft*. It's another to create a realistic city, complete with millions of very believable people, and then drop a nuclear bomb on it as part of the story. Right now we have graphic tools that can make those scenarios possible. You only have to watch your average summer blockbuster to see what computer graphics can do. The limiting factor now is the average home PC. Complex graphics eat cycles, and the computer only has so many to go around. We don't anticipate that problem in the near future." Indeed, if advances in home computing power continue to follow current trends, the ability to generate and display photoreal graphics in a game room is mere decades away, perhaps even less.

The long-term goal, of course, is total immersion. Imagine walking through Middle-Earth, having extended conversations with fantastic creatures, feeling gravel under your feet, and hearing the calls of strange birds. Now imagine the game has an open narrative, in which the decisions you make can alter the story for both you and other players. Imagine a game, in other words, indistinguishable from actual existence. If that seems implausible, consider this: Of the ten million bits of data generated by your eyes at any moment, only sixteen are extracted and processed fully by the brain. Information gleaned by other senses requires even less of a stream.

"I don't think we're that far from perceptual reality," muses Nobuko Saga, lead designer on Eidos's highly anticipated *Bushido FTL*. "I imagine it'll be possible in my lifetime, and I definitely expect it in my daughter's." The way Saga sees it, there are three significant hurdles:

- Physics – the limitations of existing technology,

- Cost – the ability of a home consumer to afford said technology, and

- Time – the real human hours needed to imagine and craft such a game.

Klass insists these obstacles will be meaningless within thirty years. "The computer power available to us goes up exponentially, while the cost of new equipment goes down. Soon we'll have computers that can do the work of a million designers, including the imagination required to devise a compelling game. We'll have computers as smart as whole civilizations. For that matter, a computer could easily replicate parts of the real world it already knows about. There could be two Parises, one real, one not; but good luck trying to tell the difference from inside. I wouldn't be surprised if the difference between reality and simulated reality starts to blur. I could live out my autumn years on a paradise planet, and the best part is, it wouldn't be long at all before I forgot it wasn't real." He smiles. "I can live with that. Humans have an amazing capacity for willing suspension of disbelief."

ϒ

Phillip offered Scott a ride to Madeleine Park, but he opted for a walk. It gave him time to think. He couldn't help but see the pastor's theme, "Commit to Love," as a sign from above. After pondering this a while he sighed, flipped his cell phone open, and turned it on. Jessi answered in a huff. "It's about time."

"I know," Scott said. "I was thinking."

"Oh yeah? What were you thinking?"

"I was thinking about your message."

"Uh-huh."

"And at first I was thinking…maybe this isn't the perfect time to rush into things."

"You creep."

"And then I thought…" Scott laughed. "Well, see, then I went to church."

"Excuse me?"

"I did. I went to First Baptist Church. You got a problem with that?"

"No, it just seems so out of character for you. I thought you were more of the 'spiritual but not religious' type."

"Call it research. The point is…I'm ready to go for it. If you still want to. I'm sorry I wasn't brave enough before."

"For what, church?"

"No. For you."

Her voice immediately lightened. "Oh, my God, Scott. I wasn't ready, either. Not really ready, y'know? Too many possible bad things."

"Exactly. And look, it is a bad time. It's probably a horrible time to commit to anything, but maybe this is the perfect exception. I want to do this. I love you, Jessi. I want to see if this works as a full-time arrangement."

"You make it sound like Human Resources."

"I guess it is, in a way. Aw, let's do this, babe. What do you say?"

"Mr. Glass, sir, I won't let you down."

"Terrific. Let's find you a desk." Her only response was to giggle adorably.

They listened to each other breathe. "You okay?" Scott said finally. "I watched the news for a while, but it didn't say anything about L.A. I don't know what's going on there."

"We had a bad night. There was rioting in Carson and out toward Terminal Island. Not as bad as the '92 riots, not so far anyway, but it got kinda hairy on the police side. The LAPD's starting to get that 'repel the invaders' mentality again."

"Oh, that's not good."

"You're telling me. I'm scared to leave the house."

"Then don't."

"I have to. My fridge is down to ketchup and mustard."

"You should—*No*," Scott said, stopping in his tracks.

"But I have to, Scott."

"No. Don't go in to work tomorrow."

"Scott, come on."

"I'm serious. Call in sick. Say you're stressed, or your car won't start." The certainty of sudden knowledge pounded in his head like a migraine. Something awful, something terminal was about to happen. He couldn't begin to imagine how he knew, but he sure did, as clear and cold as mountain runoff in April.

"My boss is gonna be running around the office like a maniac. I have to go in."

"Jessi. This is…something. I need you to stay home tomorrow."

"Are you okay?"

"I'm fine."

"You're acting weird."

"Promise me you won't go to work."

"Why are you acting like this?"

"I don't know," he admitted. "Just promise me, okay? Please? I think it's important."

The line hissed for uncomfortable seconds. "Okay. Just tell me what's going on."

"I can't, Jessi. Listen, I'm at the park. There's a picnic I gotta go to."

"A picnic? What kinda town is this place?"

"I know, Jessi, okay? Will you please just stay home?"

"It's like Grover's Corners. What's next, ice cream socials? First church, now this. If you're not careful, Scott, people will confuse you for a respectable adult."

"Please don't start. I'll call you tomorrow. I love you, okay?"

"I...love you, too," she said, savoring the words. "I'll be home."

"'Bye."

He took a quick walk around the track while screening other messages. Joel Adamov's assistant called to check on script pages. That poor bastard, a skinny geek from Corpus Christi, worked harder on Sundays than most people worked on Mondays.

Madeleine Park covered a hundred and twenty acres, twenty devoted to a quiet botanical garden. Covered pavilions surrounded it; the lodge perched on a hill above. First Baptist rented the lodge and nearest five pavilions. Kids played with Frisbees and leashed dogs. Their dads grilled hamburgers and rallied a pickup baseball game for after lunch. Scott found Zack and Phillip at a table away from the main group. The brunette and her daughter were there as well.

"Hey, sinners," Scott grinned.

"Innocent until proven guilty," Phillip said. "Allegedly."

"Nice suit."

"This old thing."

"Scott, this is my friend Shay, and her daughter Lacey." Shay looked up at Zack coolly, offended by the finite *friend* designation. Scott shook hands all around, congratulating Lacey on her pretty dress.

"I should've brought her some park clothes," Shay said. "An hour from now, she'll look like a landfill." She dug out half a dozen coloring books to keep the girl occupied.

"Kids," Scott smiled, knowing nothing about it. "I was surprised you actually showed up, Zack. Then you forgot to corner Pastor Dan."

"He surprised me," Zack admitted.

"Me, too."

"Even for the always unconventional Pastor Dan," Phillip said, "it was rather an unconventional message."

"Love your neighbor?" Scott grinned.

"Love all your neighbors," Zack smiled. "Love everybody. Love like Haight-Ashbury."

"His name is God, and He approved this message. I like it."

"I do, too."

"I'm hoping it made an impression on you," Shay told Zack, nudging him playfully. He smiled tightly but said nothing.

"I uh…Well, I called a friend of mine to eat with us," Phillip said, fiddling with his tie. "I hope no one minds." No one did. "So, Zack, will you be darkening the doors of Sugar Roses First Baptist henceforth? The good pastor seemed to think there won't be an overabundance of future Sundays. It might be a fine time to start hedging your bets."

"Pascal's Wager," Zack harrumphed. Scott and Shay looked confused. "Blaise Pascal. French philosopher, mid-seventeenth century. He admitted the existence of God was a fifty-fifty shot, but he still said you should believe in God because the potential rewards are so high. If you believe in God and He exists, you go to Heaven. Infinite gain. If you believe and He doesn't exist, you lose nothing. But if you don't believe and He sends you to Hell, you lose everything. Best case scenario for an atheist is you don't believe and He doesn't exist, in which case you gain nothing."

"Uh, but doesn't that assume there's a Heaven?" Scott replied.

"And a Hell," Shay agreed. "I think it takes a lot more than believing to win that bet anyway."

"Exactly," Zack nodded. "The Wager makes too many assumptions. It sounds good on a paper-thin, superficial level, but do most Christians even believe in Hell nowadays?"

"They believe," Phillip said, "because they don't think they're going."

"Or because they think I am," Zack agreed. "People hit me with Pascal's Wager all the time, but it always strikes me as cynical."

"Is life a bet to see how much we can get in the afterlife?" Shay asked. "No."

"Exactly," Phillip said. "There's got to be more to it than that."

"I don't know what I think is gonna happen when I die," Scott said. "I guess my Wager is, whatever does happen, it'll make it all worthwhile. But, you know, I don't believe I have to go to church to show God how much I love Him."

Zack wished he could pop a beer, but no one else was drinking. Instead he cracked a soda and hoisted it at Lacey in a mock toast. "It's like those bad action movies, like *The Mummy's Revenge*, where there's a scary temple deep in the jungle, and someone says, 'It's so dangerous no man has ever returned.' Okay, so then how did they know about the temple in the first place? And that's death, right? The Great Mystery. Shakespeare's 'undiscovered country.'"

"'From whose bourn no traveler returns,'" Scott added. Zack toasted him as well.

"I don't live my life the way I do because I'm scared to die," Shay said, "but I'll tell you what, I take calls all day from people who are. People who want to go to Heaven so bad because their life, well, sucks. And I get that part, 'cause my life hasn't been a ticker tape parade, I promise. I think people want to get saved from the past, not the future."

"Very true," Phillip sighed. "Or from themselves."

Zack handed Lacey a crayon. "I've been thinking a lot about what that kid at Abilene Sam's said the other day."

"Who?" Scott said. "The green-haired kid? I know that guy's girlfriend."

"Yeah, the computer game freak."

"I think they prefer 'geek.'"

"Whatever."

"You're so sweet," Shay said, nudging him. "You make friends everywhere you go."

"It's the atheist way. Look, he was talking about God as video game designer, how He coded a universe with glitches in it."

"It sounded very *Matrix*-y to me," Scott said. "Black cat crosses your path twice, it's a glitch in the program."

"The simulation," Zack corrected. "In *The Matrix*, people do exist, they just have, I don't know, doppelgangers in the virtual world. But what if people don't exist? What if they're only the simulation?"

"Look out," Phillip drawled. "Zack's about to get all Stephen Hawking on us again. Beam me up, Scotty."

"Simulated by who?" Shay asked.

Zack grinned. "God, of course. The Designer. The Great Cosmic Asian Kid."

"I don't like that."

"Why not? I find it kind of elegant."

"I have a hard time believing we're nothing but characters

in a computer game," Phillip said. "This world is far too complex. The fashion alone."

"Compared to Pong it is, sure," Zack agreed. "But have you seen video games lately? Football games look like real football games. The players look like people, not like clock radios or trilobites. Now project that rate of progress forward. I can imagine it all too easily."

"I don't know," Scott said. "It seems a bit bongwater to me. I think, therefore I am."

"Maybe. But I did some Googling last night and found this guy, some Oxford professor, name of Bostrom, thinks there's no fundamental reason not to believe it. He says it won't be long before computer simulations reach real-world levels of complexity. Then there's this other guy, Kurzweil, who predicts it'll happen in our lifetime. In Lacey's lifetime, computers'll be as smart as everyone who ever lived put together; and who knows how much richness of detail they'll be able to handle? So as far as the experts are concerned, it's only a matter of time before computer games are as detailed as everyday life. Maybe as detailed as the universe; but really, that doesn't matter, 'cause all you have to do is create six billion characters who *think* there's a rest of the universe."

"Oh, come on. Doesn't that mean the six billion characters are each running their own simulation?" Phillip asked.

"Manner of speaking, sure. Yeah, they're all running a variation on the same construct."

"That's too much."

"Not for one of those mega-super-duper-computers of the future, it isn't. Or maybe there's a virtual universe, but it's based on physics that can only go so far down. I don't know about that. The point is, Bostrom says if computers can run one hyper-detailed simulation, they can run billions. For every player who's running, I don't know, '*Galaxy of Warcraft*' or whatever, two more are playing '*Halo 15.*' *EverQuest* will seem to really go on forever. In Bostrom's future, billions of computers'll run billions of simulations; in which case, even if there is a real world, there's only one, and your chances of being in it are tiny."

"Relative," Scott mused, "to the number of possible simulations you could be in."

"Right. The odds are much higher that you're in a video game than the one chance in billions you're not."

"Spacey," Shay decided.

Scott crossed his arms and concentrated. "Okay, so let's say we are in a video game. Seems a bit premature, but fine. Let's say everything we see here is tucked away in a HAL...*10,000*, okay, and physics are really just simulated game physics. Was Friday a glitch in the game? And if so..." He found himself unnerved by where this took him. "Is it possible for a glitch or a, what would you call it, an architecture problem to be so serious it could cause the simulation to grind to a halt?"

"I can't imagine why not," Phillip said. "It happens to programmers all the time."

"Yeah. 'Does Not Compute,'" Zack agreed.

"So what are you saying?" Shay asked. "Like, the End of the World?"

"More like...Game Over," Scott corrected.

"Wars happen everyday," Shay replied. "Planes crash. Jews and Arabs can't get along. This is nothing new."

"People don't hear voices in the sky everyday," Scott admitted. "Not airline pilots. Presidents don't announce personal revelations from the White House. Y'know? Ordinary housewives don't throw chickens at each other in grocery stores. Not en masse. This is new. This is...I don't know. It really feels like maybe we can't come back from it this time. It feels like...I guess it feels *final.*"

Shay shuddered. They were silent for a time.

"So how would you know if you were in a simulation?" Phillip wondered.

"That's the problem," Zack replied. "You wouldn't. The game'd be so well designed that it might even be in your nature, the nature the Designer programmed for you, to resist the very idea of being in a simulation. *I'd* design it that way. It keeps things more interesting when the characters are fully committed to the world they think they're in."

Phillip smoothed his tie again. "So you build into your characters a knack for self-deception."

"Yeah, they run their own simulations, over and over, like fractals," Zack agreed. "Refining their own world."

"And then what?" Shay asked. "You build into 'em a desire to worship you, like God did?"

"If he did," Phillip sniffed. "I sometimes wonder."

"No," Scott replied, "I think you'd build into 'em...a desire to do *interesting things*. That way they wouldn't just wander around like zombies. That was a problem with the old Nintendo games. The non-player, AI characters existed for no other reason than to wait and tell the player things when he got to them. Nowadays, they have their own agendas, their own lives. They don't care what you do. They battle each other."

"Exactly," Zack agreed. "They have software now that can draw whole armies and pit them against each other, with no human controlling the battle. It's how they did *Lord of the Rings*."

"It's like when they make *Court of Law*," Scott said. "They're not gonna come here to shoot. It's too expensive, and frankly, not glamorous enough, so—"

"They came here for *Twister*," Shay pointed out.

"Yeah, and look how that turned out. No, Excelsior'll send maybe a handful of guys, and they'll take pictures and I don't know, lidar readings and whatnot, and they'll build a virtual Sugar Roses in the computer. Or they'll go to Vancouver and paint in the edges. And I'm telling you, even locals won't know the difference. Except it'll be prettier, y'know, more...dramatically lit."

"Virtual citizens," Phillip said. "Virtual Phillip, with thick, luscious hair."

"Aw, shucks," Shay said. "I was hoping for work as an extra."

"We could pay you for your likeness and image," Scott

suggested. "Not that I have any say in the budget whatsoever."

"Thanks a lot."

Zack was watching Lacey draw. "People are interesting," he said, "so you need virtual people for your virtual world—but it's their *flaws* that make them interesting. You don't want a whole world full of perfect people. If you're the Designer, I mean. You don't want six billion Adams and Eves. You don't want people getting along. You want Napoleons and Alexanders and Hitlers. You want to see armies collide, even when the species evolves to the point where they know it doesn't make sense anymore. But see, what you *don't* want is, you don't want armies firing nuclear weapons at each other. That'd kill too many of your virtual people, destroy the environment, and make the game a depressing bust. That's the trick of being a designer: How far do you let your characters go? How crazy do you let them get? A hundred years from now, will we be firing, I don't know, black holes at each other? Are people gonna have time bombs that actually blow up time?"

Scott flinched. "That implies the simulation is designed to run forever. But what if it isn't? What if you build in a stopping point? I mean, eventually you're gonna want to know the outcome of the game. You're gonna want to know who won. You probably have a finite lifetime yourself."

"Huh. This guy Bostrom," Zack said, "he thinks a common form of simulation would be to start the clock on physics or evolution again and let it play out, a kind of...'Take Two' on the universe. Or maybe you design the world the way it was in 1700, make sure your ancestors are in it, and let it play out. Let the game show your family as it might have been. So now you've got virtual, semi-accurate versions of the Designer himself, or the Designer's great-great-grandfather. And if that's true, and we're the outcome of that species of simulation, then the Designer looks like us."

"Give or take," Scott said. "He's prob'ly a brain in a jar."

"Or She is," Shay noted.

"In which case, we were made in Her image."

"I wonder," Phillip said. "Would a Designer like that create an afterlife as well?"

240

"I would," Shay answered.

"He would if He wanted one," Zack agreed. "It could be a kind of secondhand wish fulfillment. 'Course, the virtual characters would have no idea what that afterlife looked like, unless you allowed some virtual Orpheus to cross back and forth."

"There'd be places where your simulations could touch," Shay said. "Live world meets dead world, or fantasy world. Magic portals, like...like the wardrobe to Narnia."

"It seems to me," Phillip said, "that if you knew they were virtual characters—that is, if you were the Designer—then there'd be no reason to be especially nice to them. You could give them virtual diseases, let them die in acts of God—pardon the expression—even send them to virtual Hell. You wouldn't care."

"Unless you got attached to them," Shay said. "If you think about it, I'm Lacey's designer, and I wouldn't let anything bad happen to her. Would I, sweetie?"

"No," Lacey decided, and went back to her coloring.

"Of course not," Shay answered. "I know people who fell apart when their Tamagotchis died, let alone a real person. Or a simulation of a person. A human being, y'know?"

"It'd all depend on the personality of the Designer," Phillip agreed. "How much He began to empathize."

"I don't think He'd be empathetic at the start," Scott said. "He might grow to care about us, but by then He'd have to interfere directly in the game to affect the outcome. And maybe He wouldn't. Or maybe...the code, the game architecture, wouldn't allow it. He wouldn't have the option of changing His mind once the ball started rolling."

"In a way," Zack said, "you're talking about the deist God."

"No," Scott argued, "I don't think so. The deist God you're talking about created physics and then stood back and watched. A game designer God created physics, right—okay, yeah, but then He *wanted* to affect the outcome but He can't, or He affects it every once in a while but He doesn't micromanage it."

"How do you make a God like that happy?" Shay said. "How

do you worship that God?"

"For that matter, do you?" Phillip added.

Zack answered slowly. "I think it's unfair to assume God isn't already happy without our warm regards. A lot of self-actualized people enjoy playing games. They don't *need* to play, they *want* to. They like the competition. But if the games didn't exist, I mean…they'd be happy some other way, right? But maybe they get emotionally involved in the games they do play. The stories they're running. I cared a great deal about the characters I wrote for *Commedia*."

"As if they were purely fictional," Phillip smirked.

"They were! Give or take. They certainly had 'lives' of their own. Obviously Shay cares about Lacey, who isn't a simulation but, you know, Lacey's running outside her control. Not total control, anyway. Scott cares about the movie he's writing."

"No, I don't, to be honest. But I will care if it allows me to write the next one."

"Simulation as trial run," Phillip noted, "but that opens a whole 'nother possibility. Maybe you create a simulation but don't expect it to work. You want to work the kinks out before you design the simulation for keeps, so you expect the early versions to run a number of generations and then dissolve under the weight of their own…*absurdity*."

"Oh, I'd hate to think we're just practice," Shay frowned.

"It doesn't mean we couldn't be successful on our own terms," Zack said, "even if the simulation crashes a hundred years from now." He frowned again, his default expression. "Or tomorrow."

"So let's say the Designer does enjoy being worshiped," Phillip continued. "What form of worship does He want? Does He want us to behave? Is morality even an issue anymore? If we're nothing but the characters in a video game, then who cares if we're good to each other?"

"*We* care," Scott insisted. "Our responsibilities are still to each other."

"But not to God anymore," Shay answered.

"I think the way you worship a God like that is, *Be interesting*," Zack said. "Bostrom made a good point. The thing that'd give that God the greatest pleasure is if His sim is just motoring along, with armies in conflict and serial killers and natural disasters and all that good shit. Sorry, Lacey."

"It's okay," the girl said, happily coloring Bonkers bright green.

"If you keep the planet busy and fighting with nobody dropping a doomsday weapon, then Game Designer God is ecstatic."

"So what do you think Friday was?" Scott asked. "A glitch?"

"I don't know," Zack admitted. "Maybe designer input."

"'Designer input?'"

"Or maybe the game was designed for an impatient user. Yeah, like, hit the F2 button to add a giant hurricane. If things get really boring, or you want to move the game to another phase, hit F7 for 'Noises in the Sky.'"

"Armageddon mode," Phillip smiled. "Lovely."

"More like 'interesting,'" Zack corrected.

"Well, I don't believe a word of it," Shay said. "Sorry. I feel real. I think, therefore I am. Scott is right. I don't feel my thoughts coming from outside. I feel 'em in here, in my head. In my body. I believe in God the Father, not...God the User."

"If God is just running a simulation," Zack argued, "then evil really happens for a reason. People, you know, *die* for a reason. Death and evil are entertaining. You know this, Scott. You work in an industry that doesn't make a dime on G-rated movies."

"This is true."

"It explains why there's such a disconnect between the Newtonian world we live in," Zack mused, "and the quantum world buried underneath it, y'know, a world that doesn't make any sense to us. It explains why the universe before the Big Bang was so different from the universe after it. It explains why God seems all-powerful but doesn't interfere. It explains...the persistence of evil. It could even explain why an all-knowing God might devise a perfect plan, then give us free will so we're sure to muck it up. I think this Bostrom guy is onto something."

"Because we're perfectly imperfect," Scott said.

"We're perfectly entertaining," Phillip corrected. "Matt!" A thin man in Sugar Roses High School gym shorts jogged up from the track nearby. "Scott Glass, this is Matt Lumley, the music teacher over at the high school."

"Glad to meet you."

"Zack. Shay," Matt said, waving hesitantly.

"Good to see you, Matt," Zack said, shaking his hand. "You don't venture out into the sunlight too often."

"Well," Matt said carefully.

Phillip grabbed Matt's arm, caressed it briefly. "Matt, come over here a second. I want to uh, bend your ear about something."

"Okay. Hey, somebody save me a burger."

"No way," Zack told him. "You didn't go to church. We Baptists aren't allowed to associate with known sinners like yourself." Matt started to reply, but Shay saved him the trouble by punching Zack's arm. "Ow!"

"You pagan," she laughed. Matt and Phillip went into the garden, and an anxious conversation began.

Scott recalled his misunderstanding of the friendship between Phillip and Zack. "Those two," Scott ventured, nodding at Phillip and Matt, "are they, uh, like...you know...?"

Zack and Shay looked at each other nervously. Zack inhaled and exhaled through his nose. Shay just shrugged. "We all have our secrets."

"Yeah, don't ask, don't tell," Zack agreed.

Hamburgers and hot dogs appeared and vanished like loaves and fishes. Zack saved plates for Matt and Phillip. He was finishing his own second helping when Scott noticed a college-aged couple staring bullets at them. "Who's that over there?"

Zack noticed them, too. He wasn't happy about it. "Brad Kessler and Laura Reese. Two of SOSU's finest."

"Wasn't she a student of yours?" Shay said.

"They both were."

"So why are they glaring at you like that?"

"Oh, just ignore them."

"Ignore them? She just flipped me off at a church picnic."

"They're not here for the church picnic. They're visiting the garden. Let 'em visit."

"Even if they're coming this way?"

Zack glanced up sharply. "Terrific."

Laura edged toward them like a gunslinger. "Is this her?" she demanded.

"Come on, Laura," Zack began, raising a hand as if to ward her off.

"She asked you a question," Brad snapped.

Zack stood carefully. "Is that how it's gonna be, Brad? Here?"

"What's going on?" Shay asked. Scott stood to get out of the way, his arms loose at his sides. He'd seen enough Hollywood bar fights for his Spidey sense to know when to evacuate.

"Let me handle this."

"Your old man," Brad said, slamming the syllables home, "made a stupid decision."

"Old news," Zack announced.

"I don't think so. Laura doesn't think so. Look at her mouth, fucker."

Shay reddened. "Hey! My daughter is here. Watch your mouth." Brad shut up, but now all eyes noted the swollen bruise on Laura's face.

Laura sniffed. "You had no right."

245

"Brad, this isn't the place. Look around."

"Where *is* the place, *Dr.* Heath? Maybe you don't know *your* place. Maybe you don't know when to keep your stupid hands off her."

"I'm sorry, Brad, okay?"

"No, it's not okay! Look at her!"

"You weren't sorry to *me!*" Laura yelled, tearing up.

"I oughta kick your—aw, no, you had to bring a little girl! How's that feel, Heath? Hiding behind a little girl? You oughta be ashamed of yourself. You oughta lose your job!" Brad turned to Shay. "You don't know what he's done! You don't know who he *is!*"

All Shay could do was flick her eyes between them like a Wimbledon spectator.

"I think we both know the outcome of this won't be good for anyone," Zack said quietly. "I'm willing to make amends. I wish we could deal with this like adults."

"Yeah, that's just it, Dr. Heath. We *aren't* adults. We're kids. People are gonna say you took advantage."

"I didn't make her do anything. I couldn't. You're being an ass."

"Oh, whatever!" Laura cried.

"Laura, you know what went down." Zack phrased himself cautiously, struggling to avoid the exposure of another gross mistake.

"I know you, you, were in, like, a position of responsibility."

"Oh, don't start that. Jesus."

"I know my grade could be affected."

"Your grade is fine, Laura. For God's sake. Let's keep this in private."

"Is this what I think it is?" Shay demanded.

"*Not here*," Zack declared harshly, clenching his jaw. He

246

focused on Laura. "Look. Come into my office next week. We can make this okay. I can do what you want me to do. We can make it all right."

"No! You can't make *me* all right!" she bawled, exploding in tears. "I loved you!" The garden fell silent. A fair percentage of Sugar Roses' population watched in judgment as a tonnage of communal awkwardness descended, an invisible mudslide.

Zack diminished. "I'm gonna go," he said finally.

"This isn't over!" Brad warned.

"I know," Zack admitted.

Lacey huddled in confusion. Shay patted her absently. "It's okay, *pobrecita*. He's going now," she promised, glaring up at Brad and willing him to do exactly that.

"I guess I'll see you at the house," Zack murmured.

Shay couldn't look at him. "Yeah."

"Thanks a lot, Brad."

"You brought it on yourself, *Professor*."

Zack nodded, adding only, "Ain't none of us heroes."

Brad and Laura watched Zack leave. "I'm sorry," a tearful Laura told Shay.

"Right in front of my daughter," Shay muttered.

"I know. I'm sorry." Laura turned to Brad, who held his fighting posture. "Come on, Brad. Let's go. These people are— I'm really, really sorry."

"Is that Spanish girl okay?" a nearby Baptist wondered audibly.

As Laura pulled Brad off and Zack disappeared around a bend, Scott found himself alone with Shay and Lacey. Among the situations he longed to be in, this surpassed shellfish poisoning and dysentery by mere inches. "And now back to *Happy Days*," he finally managed.

Thankfully, Phillip and Matt returned a few minutes later to bail him out. Even better, they were disinclined to ask what they'd missed. They had concerns of their own, and ate burgers in relative silence.

Pastor Dan caught Scott sneaking seconds on homemade peach cobbler. "That's Dora June's," he grinned. "The Lord done blessed her with a genius for pastry."

"I've gained seven pounds since I got here," Scott admitted. "I'm gunning for ten."

"You can do it. Hey, is that Phillip I see over by Shay Veracruz?"

"And Matt Lumley," Scott replied. *Oops.*

"I know Matt. He's the music teacher over at SRHS, ain't he?"

"I think so."

The pastor nodded. "You mind if I come over and say hi?"

"Uh, no, I could use the company, actually." *More like reinforcements.*

Shay struggled to hide her discomfort. "Well, hello, there, Shay," the pastor said. "Hello, little Lacey."

"Pastor Dan!" Lacey hollered.

"Hello, Pastor," Shay smiled.

"Phillip. How you doin', there, fella?"

"Extravagantly well, Pastor."

"Well, I am sure glad to hear it."

"Matt Lumley. I saw those students of yours performing *Carmina Burana* two years ago. My wife and I sure did enjoy that. Them kids did a real bang-up job."

Matt smiled but still seemed completely unnerved. "Thank you, Pastor. I don't think we embarrassed ourselves too badly. Thank you."

"No, they really were impressive. We could sure use your skills at the church."

"It's an idea," Matt said carefully.

"Pastor, I've been meaning to talk to you about that," Phillip said. "You mind if we step away for a few minutes?"

"Uh, no, not at all."

They didn't go far—out of the congregation's hearing, but not out of Scott's—which sharpened his discomfort at being left alone with a taciturn Shay and a four-year-old girl. Phillip spoke to the pastor as if expecting a gunshot. "Pastor, I needed to...I meant to say...Oh, forgive me. I wonder if you meant all those wonderful things you told the congregation this morning."

"Of course I did. Why?"

"I wonder if you've considered all the places it might lead you."

"If love is leading, then hey, I want to go on the trip."

"I appreciate that. But what you're saying is—Pastor, it sounds so good in principle. It does. It sounds exactly like what people like me have been longing to hear. But you don't see where it's taking you. I mean, maybe the church liked it and maybe they didn't. You understand? Maybe they see you'll be opening your doors to...an element they wouldn't be comfortable around."

Matt said nothing but looked desperate to run for the hills.

The pastor nodded at both men. "Phillip, I've already gotten an earful about this from folks like Danny Murcheson. That poor boy ain't got the sense God gave a goose, kept on muttering something about abortion and 'God's gonna punish.' He's as crazy as a peach orchard boar, but y'know what? That's his own thorn of the flesh. It's his imperfect nature to deal with, just like I deal with mine and you with yours. I don't want to say the message I spoke to you this morning was a revelation. It didn't come from outside my head like those voices on Friday. But I did hear it. I heard it in every part of my being. I know it's what God wants me to do. It's how He wants me to live. Now, I can't speak for every member of the congregation. God'll reveal Himself in their hearts, too. He will, but I can't promise you how they're gonna hear that message when they receive it. But I look at how Jesus lived, the people he hung out with. Sinners and tax collectors. Adulterers. Samaritan women. Gentiles. I can't shut my eyes to that anymore, Phillip. The message of the Gospel is inclusion, and yes, I am ready to stand by that."

"Okay." Phillip closed his eyes. Matt touched his arm lightly. Phillip nodded and said, "Then, Pastor, I guess it's time I told you: I'm…gay." Matt's eyes flicked to his shoes. Pastor Dan looked unsurprised. "I've never told anyone that, not even my own mother. Maybe four people know in the world. And as much as I love my life, I don't want to exist in isolation anymore. I have—" He glanced at Matt, who finally nodded. "I have Matt, and that's wonderful. But what you said this morning—I'm excluded from the network of my town, Pastor. All I do is fake my way through things. I'm lying. My whole adult life has been fraudulent. I feel like a con man. I want to live in my real world, not a prison I throw up inside it. Not some stupid…simulation. I hope I haven't shocked you, Pastor. I could really use your support. I hope that's possible. But if not…I understand."

Dan Taylor shifted in his shoes. He knew he'd volunteered for a lot more of this, and he decided it was for the best. "Phillip, I've known for years."

"Beg pardon?"

"I didn't know about Matt, of course, but I knew you were… what you are. I just figured you weren't acting on it, which is how I accepted it. But Phillip, I meant what I said this morning. It's gonna take some adjustment for me, too. But yes, I support you. Of course I do. I love you. Jesus loves you. God made you the way you were born, and it's up to you to be the man He intends you to be. How's that sound?"

Phillip planned his response as a handshake. Seemingly against anyone's will, it turned into a hug. Phillip blinked away tears. "Oh, Pastor Dan…You're gonna catch holy hell for this," he laughed.

"Won't be nothin' holy about it," replied Pastor Dan.

Scott smiled behind a can of soda. The twenty-first century had finally come to Sugar Roses, and just in the nick of time.

Zack never went home that night. He called Scott from the

bar at the Standard Hotel, staggered into the lobby, and checked into a room two doors down. The night manager asked Scott to help him upstairs. "It's the End of the World," Zack laughed raggedly. "And about fuckin' time."

Part Three
Αρπαζω

Rapture

DR ALLAN SYLVAN:

My friend and colleague, Dr Nick Bostrom, believes we might be nothing more than simulated entities designed and perhaps maintained by some higher intelligence. If so, we may be laboring under the influence of synthetic memories that have been input into our minds. Nick further rationalizes away the problem of evil by suggesting our memories of unfair treatment are likewise simulated, and that no actual evil was permitted to have happened to any of us. Dr Bostrom's ability to say such a thing causes me to suspect he may himself be under the influence of a charmed life, and good for him.

-- *But Dice Do Play God With the Universe*, p. 417

Φ

"Mommy?"

"Yes, sweetie?"

"Why were you crying?"

"I was sad, sweetie."

"How come?"

"I was mad at Zack."

"You were?"

"Uh-huh."

"Is he bad?"

"No. He did a bad thing, sweetie, that's all. He made me disappointed."

"What'd he do?"

"He lied to Mommy."

"Oh."

"He's very sad."

"He's sad all the time, isn't he?"

"Yes."

"I wish he wasn't."

"I do, too. But I don't think me and Zack are gonna see each other anymore."

"You're not? Am I gonna see him?"

"I don't know, sweetie. Maybe."

"Why did Zack tell a lie?"

"I think it's because he's so sad. He doesn't know what to do sometimes. And I think he drinks too much."

255

"Why does he do that?"

"He misses somebody."

"Do you miss somebody?"

"Of course I do, sweetie. Every day."

"Is it Daddy?"

"It sure is. Do you miss him, too?"

"Yes."

"I bet he misses you, too."

"Daddy's dead."

"I know, sweetie, but I bet he still misses you."

"You mean up in Heaven?"

"Exactly. Where the angels live with Jesus."

"Mommy, when are we gonna see Daddy?"

"I don't know, sweetie. We've got lots of other things to worry about before that."

"How come?"

"We're alive."

"What do we have to worry about?"

"You have to worry about cleaning your room and learning your ABCs. And I have to worry about getting a new job."

"How come?"

"'Cause the old one is driving Mommy crazy."

"I like it when you bring home toys and coloring books."

"I know, sweetie."

"Where are you gonna work now?"

"I think Phillip's gonna see about getting me a job over at Bayeux. They give out stuff to take home sometimes, too."

"Like toys and stuff?"

"Mostly books, but yeah, sometimes they give out DVDs, or video games."

"I like video games!"

"I know you do, sweetie."

"Is it gonna be better than your old job?"

"It sure sounds better, doesn't it?"

"Yes."

"I think it is."

"Are we gonna be happy?"

"You know what? Yes. I think we are. I think we're gonna be just fine."

"Mommy, how come everybody was mad today?"

"Well, some of them, like that redheaded man, they were mad 'cause they found out Zack lied."

"Lying's bad."

"It sure is."

"And how come the other people were mad?"

"They were scared, sweetie."

"Of what?"

"They don't know what's gonna happen."

"What *is* gonna happen?"

"I don't know, sweetie. We'll just have to wait and see."

"God could tell us."

"I bet He could if He wanted to."

"He doesn't want to?"

"I guess not."

"A lot of people talked about God today."

"It's Sunday, sweetie. People go to church on Sunday."

"Not in church. In the park, too."

"Like Zack and Scott and Phillip and Matt?"

"Uh-huh."

"You understood what they were saying?"

"No. But Zack said God isn't really real."

"He said that?"

"Uh-huh."

"He said that to you?"

"No, he said it to Scott."

"Well, sweetie, that's just his opinion. He shouldn't have said it around you."

"I wasn't mad."

"It's his personal business."

"I don't know."

"People are worried, sweetie. That's all. They're making things up to be worried about."

"Okay. Mommy?"

"Yes, sweetie?"

"Do you think God is real?"

"Of course I do, sweetie. I know God is real."

"How come?"

"Because you are."

PASTOR T. J. STONECIPHER:

Argyle, I've heard a lot of insidious nonsense about what the phenomena on Friday might've been, and I want to dispel any misunderstanding. It was not just another bad day. What you heard was no mass delusion. Ensuing events made that clear. What you heard was not post-traumatic stress disorder. It was not the announcement of invasion from outer space. It was a call to atonement. It was the Last Trump, a summons for supernatural armies. "From His mouth comes a sharp sword," the Bible says, "so that with it He may strike down the nations, and He will rule them with a rod of iron; and He treads the wine press of the fierce wrath of God, the Almighty." I believe that. I know it in my heart. The Apocalypse of God is upon us.

X

At six a.m. on the day it all changed, Scott grabbed his iPod and a Standard Hotel towel and headed for the street. He jogged for twenty MP3s and returned sweating and cold. On his way through the lobby, he spotted Zack at the complimentary breakfast bar. The man looked like he woke up in front of a jet turbine. "You had your phone off," he mumbled. "I thought about asking you to breakfast."

"Leave the snack cakes," Scott said. "That frosting is made of candle wax anyway. Let's go hunt some waffles."

"You probably ought to check your messages first."

"Who's gonna call me this early in Sugar Roses?"

"You haven't seen a TV?"

"No," Scott said, grasping the tone of Zack's voice. "Oh, shit. What happened?"

"Let's go upstairs. You can see for yourself." The TV in Scott's room was manic with special bulletins: Revenge of the Babies, allied with three other Zionist militias, had reached the western gates to the Dome of the Rock—Bab es-Silsileh, the Chain Gate at the Wailing Wall, and Bab el-Hadid, the Iron Gate at the Western Wall. In shaky video footage, the Dome of the Rock flickered behind pillars of dust and smoke. Modern armies blasted away at each other in the shadow of enigmatic antiquity.

"Jerusalem," a field reporter yelled. "As one Jewish midrash would have it, the navel of the world. This is where three great civilizations began and intersect. Yet there is nothing civilized about this morning's attack on the Temple Mount. Israeli officials tell us the situation is critical. From where we're standing, the force of this afternoon's attack appears all but unstoppable by conventional means. We've seen hundreds of casualties over the last two days. The Isareli Army is reluctant to unleash its full might on fellow Jews, especially when collateral damage could rob the world of its most beloved religious treasures. The UN is pleading for a ceasefire, and minutes ago, a White House spokesman indicated the US could act unilaterally to prevent a full invasion of the Temple grounds."

"Holy shit," Scott gasped. "It's all over."

"Yep, F7," Zack agreed. "But it gets worse."

It had. Saudi sheiks responded to the president's remarks of the day before by refusing to sell oil to U.S. companies. The Press Secretary told the Washington Press Corps this amounted to an act of war. China vowed to support Saudi Arabia in its "defense against the greedy fanatics of the West."

"By which they mean us," Zack explained. The Chinese were mobilizing forces in Xinjiang province near Pakistan, and the Department of Homeland Security was in the process of organizing for Threat Condition Red. Within hours, the whole country would be at a standstill.

"Zack, you gotta be kidding me."

"Nope."

"Are we really gonna do this? Is this who we are?"

"Apparently. But listen, man, I should have told you first: Look for local news. American local."

"Told me what, Zack? What could possibly be worse than Armageddon?" Scott roamed the dial, each report more feverishly terrifying than the last. On CNN Headline News, a familiar, pink-lit skyline staggered and bloomed into flowers of fire. The integrity of Scott's bones deserted him; he slumped to the edge of the bed and stayed there, his jaw hanging loosely. The horrors of rubble and slaughtered children had found him again.

"What you're seeing," the commentator said, "is home video footage of disaster in Los Angeles. This morning, a little before three a.m., a series of explosive charges went off under major freeway intersections. In Hollywood, the 110 where it meets the 101, only minutes from some of America's most glamorous landmarks. In Downey, at the 5 and 605. And in Culver City, just north of Los Angeles International Airport, the intersection of the 10 and the 405. Early police reports indicate numerous casualties. The traffic in this sprawling city has been crippled. Rioting near the harbor now threatens to spill north and west, and authorities are overwhelmed."

A police car sang by the camera, its cherry top flashing. Dawn touched the Hollywood sign. The air travel ban was still in effect, so the video was shot from street level: cars overturned, bodies flailing under jagged lumps of concrete, a woman crying. A shot from the GNN office on Cahuenga panned east two blocks from the Capitol Records Building, that reassuringly silly stack of LPs on Vine, to an Irwin Allen disaster movie on the 101. Twelve-car pileups. Molotov cocktails. A phalanx of riot police. His city, Los Angeles, awash in shock and awe—or, as reporters sometimes called the feeling, terror.

"Oh my God," Scott said. "Jessi." He scrambled for his phone.

"I'll be in my room. Gimme a call when you're done. We'll commiserate."

"Okay."

Zack gripped his numb shoulder. "I'm sorry, man. This hasn't been a very good weekend for us, has it?"

Scott suppressed an angry thought: *Zack blew his life apart all by himself.* There was no connection between his stupid mistake and explosives under a freeway. "I'll call you," Scott said. "I'll probably need emotional support."

"Least I can do," Zack said, shutting the door behind himself quietly.

Scott ignored seven messages and reached Jessi on half a ring.

"Scott! Oh, shit!" she yelled.

"Are you okay?"

"Yeah, I'm home. What the fuck, Scott! The country's falling apart, starting with L.A."

"I know. I'm watching it on TV."

"I don't know what to do!"

263

"It's okay. Calm down. Just lay low. Stay inside. Make sure your doors and windows are locked."

"I'm so scared." She could barely get the words out.

"I don't blame you. Have you seen Jerusalem?"

"It's on fire. All those crazy Christians were right. I should be in a church. I've got sins on my conscience. Some of them are with you."

"You're all right. We'll get through this."

"I wish you were here. I need you so bad. Friggin' China, Scott!"

"I'd be headed to the airport right now if the FAA hadn't shut down all flights."

"Screw that," she said. "I'd be coming to you. I want out of here."

Scott remembered ominously empty skies in the days after 9/11, the quiet on the streets, the way pedestrians froze when any sound drifted by overhead. He remembered the days it felt like everything had changed for the rest of all history. That change was happening now. It was visible in every face on the screen. Faith and trust would be history in America. No one could see those images, so close on the heels of Oklahoma City and Manhattan, and not lose hope for the future.

"I don't want to be in L.A. right now," she continued. "It feels like one big target."

He tried to inject an unexpected smile into his voice to calm her down. "You're in South Pasadena, Jessi. Nobody cares about that. Even L.A. rioters wouldn't touch the Rose Bowl."

She laughed, a quick hiccup. "Oh my God."

"Do they know who did this?"

"Which part are you seeing?"

"The freeways."

"Too early to say. Some friggin' maniac. Rioters. Terrorist

cells. Godzilla. Who knows?"

"Thank God it was early in the morning. I can't believe what I'm seeing, Jessi. This footage is utterly insane." *Jerry Bruckheimer, eat your heart out.* He remembered thinking the same thing as the North Tower fell. Then he remembered feeling like shit about it for days.

A familiar enclosure loomed on GNN as a stream of ambulances raced down Santa Monica Boulevard. "Holy shit, there's Excelsior. The place is empty. The studio'll be shut down for weeks."

"You haven't heard about Argent Zurich?"

"No," he answered, his stomach clenching. "Oh my God. What about it?"

"I assumed you knew. *Shit.*" She started crying. "One more thing, I guess. Nobody was hurt, so they haven't really talked about it."

"What happened? When?"

"This morning, just after the freeways."

"A bombing?"

"No, baby, a fire. Some asshole burned down the building."

Argent Zurich owned and paid for Excelsior Studios. Excelsior Upgrade owned and paid for his life. "Are you shitting me?"

"No, Scott, I'm sorry. My office burned to the ground. I don't know if either of us have a job anymore. It's probably still on fire."

So many years. A dream at last fulfilled, only to be snatched away by a speed-addled psycho tossing Molotov cocktails at hallucinated monsters. *And for what? For fucking what?*

"Did they catch him?"

"No, but they know who it was: A.Q.U.S.A. He must've sent another letter. They think he's a nutjob who wants to start

265

his own al Qaeda cell. He's probably some loser mixing gasoline and orange juice in his mom's smelly basement, but the overpasses exploded last night, and sure enough, he saw an opportunity when he woke up this morning. All he needed was for the police to be anywhere else. With the freeways backed up, the fire department never even tried to put it out. I have no office, Scott. I have no friggin' *job*. No more cute little posters in my office. No more margarita lunches at Acapulco Buffet with Gwen and Kelli. I'm lucky I wasn't killed."

"Argent Zurich," he said dully. "Excelsior Studios. Oh, this can't be happening."

"I know, honey," she said. "I'm so sorry. We're both in a world of hurt."

"It'll shut everything down, worse than 9/11. There won't be a new project approved for months, if not years. And that's if the studio's still standing when I get home. Not to mention all this shit in China. Fuck, I'll probably be drafted."

"You think?"

"I do. Geez, I hope not. The closest I ever got to combat was *Saving Private Ryan*."

"This has to calm down. It has to."

"We're broke, hon, a month from now. We're both unemployed."

"I know, Scott. I'm sorry. Baby…How did you know not to go into work today?"

"What?"

"You said not to go to work today. You insisted. Remember?"

"I remember," he admitted. "I don't know why I said it. I really, truly don't."

"You knew something was happening."

"I've been…" It was hard for him to say. "I just felt it. Like, all of a sudden. Kind of knew it. In my head. I'm not really sure how."

"You hear voices?"

"No, it's like…like I remembered it, like I learned it a long time ago. But it hit me really hard, like, like I was trying to remember something for days, like a tune or an old school friend or something, and then suddenly I knew it. Only it came out of nowhere. I don't know. I've never felt anything that *hard* before."

"Supernatural," she said.

All he could do was sigh. They were quiet a very long time.

"Hey, guess what," he managed finally. "Our whole lives just got cancelled." He chuckled ironically.

"Pretty awesome, huh?" The paradox was, confronting it somehow made it tolerable. They could cry about it later. For now, it was minute to minute.

"I can't do anything here. God, we're so screwed." He gathered his thoughts. "Okay, listen. Can you make it to your parents' place?" The Strohmeiers lived in Scottsdale, Arizona, a suburb of Phoenix, six hours east of L.A.

"I don't know. It'll depend on whether I can find any gas stations open. Right now everybody's hiding under lock and key, with loaded guns in their hands. But yeah, once I fill my tank, I think I can work my way over on the 210."

"Okay. Then pack your valuables, just enough to fill your car. As soon as you're able to leave your building safely, head east. I'll rent a car and move west. It'll take me a while, but I'll meet you in Phoenix as soon as I can."

"I love you, baby. Hurry, okay? I don't want to be alone in all this."

"You won't be. I love you, too. *I love you*. We're gonna be okay."

"I hope so."

"I know we will."

"Thank you," she said. "I really needed to hear that."

"I'll talk to you soon." He called his family, reassured them, made noises that suggested he was fine. He wasn't, of course, but the news kept reminding him how much worse it could be. Millions were dead, around the world, everywhere.

The president issued a measured statement warning China to mind its own business. In Jerusalem, courtesy of automatic weapons and RPGs, God's decisions were finally being made for Him by a fiery collision of homicidal zealots. The Scott who called Zack an hour later had the weight of despair in his voice.

"I need waffles, Zack. Regular waffles. Maple syrup. Just a simple, American, five-dollar breakfast. Then gallons of vodka."

"I know exactly how you feel," Zack admitted. "Have for years, actually. Yeah. So…is your girlfriend okay?"

"No, she's fucking petrified. I'm meeting her at her parents' place in Arizona."

"Good idea. I'm sorry you won't be staying here."

Scott nodded wearily. "Maybe no place is safe anymore."

"I guess you must've heard about your evil corporate overlords."

"I was *this fucking close*." The vast unfairness of it agonized.

"To what?"

"Success, y'know? Hollywood. The Great American Dream. A swimming pool, and palm trees."

"It'll happen again. Even President God Complex isn't gonna take on a billion Chinese infantry. A year from now, all this'll be a distant memory."

"You don't mean that."

"I'm trying," Zack said quietly. "I really am trying."

Scott shut off the TV. "Nah, I'm done with L.A., and I'm pretty damn sure it's done with me. The last thing anyone's gonna worry about for a while is an Oklahoma courtroom drama."

"You should bring your girlfriend here, man. Oklahoma's

boring. Nothing ever happens here. There are times when, you know, that's a serious advantage in life."

"Yeah, it's certainly not L.A. or Manhattan. But I was here when the Murrah Building fell. It can happen again. We're all in twenty-first century America now, like it or not."

"Come on, homeboy. Take a shower. Change your clothes. We'll hit IHOP and send you on your way."

Scott nodded. "Yeah. I'm glad you're here, man. Thanks."

"I'm here, Scott, because my life is in the shitter."

"That is true," Scott said, and laughed for agreeing.

An hour later, numbed by ridiculous tangles of tragedy everywhere they looked, they sat in a plastically indistinguishable IHOP, poked at waffles and omelets, sulked. The restaurant was almost empty. The waitresses glared at each remaining customer, willing him to leave so they could go home to their families.

Scott drained a cup of coffee and signaled for a refill, ignoring the homicidal looks from the waitstaff. "So. This problem you got. The coed."

"I'm trying not to think of it as a problem."

"What else could it possibly be?"

"I don't know. I brought it on myself. Obviously a shrink would say I wanted to get caught. Maybe I needed a change. Maybe this is the opportunity I've been needing."

"An opportunity to do what?"

"You know, to finally get outta Dodge."

"You don't like Sugar Roses?"

"Oh…you know. One town's very like another, blah blah blah. The truth is, Sugar Roses doesn't like me."

"Apparently some of it does. Apparently some of it likes you a lot."

"Very funny. There's a difference between getting laid and

269

getting liked. Even I know that."

"Sorry."

Zack sighed heavily. "The good thing about tenured academia is I can always take the option of resigning. It looks bad for the administration if they fire me, but they can't let me keep my teaching position when the shit hits the fan. And it will. Ohh, it will. That's inevitable now. But they will let me quit. Hell, they'll even write me letters of recommendation to other universities, as long as I go quietly. I know one guy who fucked up all the way to Yale."

"I could see you on an Ivy League campus. Corduroy jacket, elbow patches, the works."

"Nah, I don't see that happening to me. Maybe if my goddamn book sold. But I will get work somewhere. Teaching. I'll be fine. Another lush student body, ripe for the picking."

"So you know why you did it?" Scott asked.

"You mean Laura?"

"No. I mean Shay, what you did to her. She really seemed into you."

"I guess she just wasn't what I wanted. Aw, poor me. But the woman I do want is probably boning her little mutt of a furniture salesman in Shawnee as we speak, so...It's time I got over it, huh?"

"I hear Scottsdale is growing in leaps and bounds. It's an awesome town. Good colleges. You should check it out. We could write a book together."

"You're actually moving?"

"I am. Yeah, I'm done with the movie game. I can live with where I got, y'know, like, how close I came. I think. If Jessi and I work out. If I can keep my creative juices flowing."

"A book deal, huh? That might be nice," Zack mused, smiling and rubbing his chin. "It's hot out there, Phoenix. Bikini country. Plenty of eye candy, I bet."

"Yeah, they might be too smart for you out there, though.

270

You've gotten too used to preacher's daughters. They don't put up enough of a fight to keep your skills sharp. Anyway, think about it, will ya? I could use a self-destructive friend in the neighborhood."

"I will, man, thanks. I don't know. Maybe it's better if I bid farewell to my reign of undergraduate sexual terror."

"Ya think?"

Zack chuckled. "I'm forty-seven. I guess it's time I grew up, huh? Besides, you see one disaster waiting to happen, you've seen 'em all." He gazed at Sugar Roses as if in his rear view mirror. "Five years ago, my life was going just the way I wanted it. It was. I was happy in this town. Successful. In love. Then it all just... dribbled away. You make one mistake, one stupid mistake, and all of it turns into rivers of shit. Every part of my world felt apart in half a second. I mean, I never got over the slam of it. I really never did. It punched the life right outta me. I'm a grown man, and it beat the joy out of me like I was a heartbroken high school kid. I started drinking and fucking 'cause I didn't know how else to respond. It felt like the right thing to do. I don't know. They say everything happens for a reason. You believe that?"

"I really have no idea."

"Brilliant answer."

"I think people need to believe *they* really matter."

"They do, but deep down, it's only on the surface. Life's a joke."

"Hey, at least you find it funny."

"I'm perversely entertained by God's twisted sense of humor."

"I thought you didn't believe in God, twisted or otherwise."

"I don't. But y'know what? I do believe the world is evolving toward some zenith of comic perfection. Every day, a brand new punch line, each one funnier'n the last. And I can see I'm just part of the comedy. My whole purpose in life is a pratfall."

"It gets better, Zack, I promise. Please have faith. Fall in love. I think maybe you have to stop making the same mistakes

271

over and over. So one day you go to shoot yourself in the foot, but you notice you've thrown away all your extra bullets."

"I did fall in love, Scott. I did, and I know I should have told her instead of panicking and doing the stupidest possible thing. But sometimes, man, the love you have just…vanishes away. She fucking loves you and then suddenly, you turn around, it's poisoned itself completely into bullshit. You never saw it coming. You had everything and now it's all gone. Am I feeling sorry for myself? Hell, yes, I'm feeling sorry for myself. I'm sorry I couldn't be trusted. Anyway." Zack gazed out the window. "Enough of that. Onwards and upwards."

"Exactly."

Zack gazed out the window, stumbling for words. "On the edges, y'know. I can feel it. I can. I don't know what it is yet, but… it's coming. I know that. I feel it…building up."

A chill ran up Scott's spine. "What is? What do you feel?"

"I can't see it. A purpose."

"You're just scared."

It took Zack quite a while to answer. "I can feel it."

The word popped into Scott's memory, unexpected but absolutely true: *Supernatural.*

Zack smiled. "Look at this guy." A stubby figure shuffled up Townsend Avenue, unruffled by the cyclones of chaos. "Buddy Sims, Sugar Roses' beloved village idiot. I made a crack about him in *Commedia*, and the town fucking crucified me for it. Funny thing is, I like the guy. Why wouldn't I? Buddy Sims is a lovable guy. Every time I see him, he's grinning like he just won the Publisher's Clearing House Sweepstakes. Socrates was out of his goddamn tree. The unexamined life. Shit, sign me up now."

"Look at it this way," Scott said, shrugging off other, less rational thoughts. "This is all a computer simulation, Zack. A video game. We're not even here, remember?"

A tiny smile lightened Zack's expression. "Aw, you're just saying that to cheer me up."

The waitress jogged over, color drained from her face. "Y'all, I'm sorry, but we're closin' up. I can box this up for you if you want."

"Right now?" Zack said.

"We just heard on the radio. They's a war with Saudi Arabia started, all them Arabs. The president just said it. They're sending troops in to get all that oil."

Scott gaped. "This can't be happening. It'll enrage the whole Muslim world."

"I gotta get home to my babies, y'all, please. I need to close down my station."

They were reaching for their wallets when the shooting started half a mile away.

PASTOR KENNY RAY THIBODEAU:

I don't know what's going on. I don't claim to have any special gift in that area. Even skeptics, even you, Argyle, are feeling the rise of something awesome in this world. Something glorious. Something terrible and transformative and it's just bigger than anything we've ever known before. I couldn't tell you what it is. I don't know. It's more important than I am. All I know is God has blessed me with the opportunity to shepherd a small part of his flock, and right now what I'm telling them is get yourself right with the Fellow Upstairs and the fellow next door. That's all you really can do....I don't know, maybe this is the End of the World. Maybe the Rapture's going to happen in five minutes and we're all going to be carried up to Heaven. I hope so. I know it'll be true someday. But in the meantime, I want God to do His thing on His schedule, in His own way. He's the boss. He's the King of Kenny Ray. I ain't about to go shaking my presents before Christmas morning.

Sugar Roses Hospital is conveniently located on Townsend Avenue, just north of a row of the nutritionless variety of chain restaurants that tend to land people in the aforementioned hospital. Amanda and Tyler arrived early, around 9:30, but had to wait for almost ninety minutes. She knew from the Internet this would only be a preliminary visit. The "baby" in her uterus was a mere collection of cells; she had cast off bigger parts of herself cutting her nails. So why did this feel so damn sinful, so murderously wrong? Even in a busy hospital this dangerous morning, with gurneys and doctors flying past in all directions, she felt as if eyes in the waiting room were flaying her alive. Tyler kept fidgeting and tugging the strings of his hoodie. "I wish I brought my iPod," he muttered.

"Are you shitting me?" she hissed. "Pull it together. I need you to focus."

"I know, I'm just bored and freaked out."

"Tyler, don't be fucking useless, okay? I need you here *now*, in the moment, connecting to the real world. This is serious shit. We're responsible for this."

"I know."

"God, this is horrible. If my mom ever finds out I'm gonna drive off a bridge."

"They oughta have better magazines."

"Tyler!"

"Okay! Shit, I'm sorry!" He glared at his battered Chuck Taylors. "I just…I still kinda wonder if we're doing the right thing."

"What? You wonder *now*? Jesus Christ, Tyler, we've already been through this. You agreed, we were way too young to be decent parents. I can't imagine you changing any diapers, can you?"

"I don't know."

"Tyler, I cannot be having a baby right now. Okay? I just can't. It wouldn't be fair to the kid. Look at the world we live in.

We're about to go to war. It's all fucking coming apart."

"I know."

"So what're you giving me all this, like, moral uncertainty for?"

"I just wish we didn't have to, that's all."

"You think I don't? Shit, you think I'm not having second thoughts?"

She'd already worked through all the ramifications. She knew she was doing the only possible thing. Didn't that make it right? It was even the right thing for the kid she might have later, a kid who deserved parents who could afford her and were mature enough to care for her properly. The kid would be a beautiful girl, loved and supported, protected from the world and all its bullshit. She believed in this. She knew it in every part of her body. So why had she filled three locked blog entries with storms of grief and self-loathing?

The medical receptionist who took Amanda's information treated her like she left a slime trail. A nameplate reading "JESUS" and a *Li'l Warriors* calendar explained why. There were colorful Bibles in every magazine rack. "I can't believe all these Bible-thumping douchebags," Amanda groused. "It's like, who invited you to make plans for my uterus? I don't tell you how to get off for the first fucking time in your whole frigid life."

"Amanda."

"What? I'm pissed."

"Okay. But maybe you're not pissed at *them*."

"Don't even start, Tyler! Seriously! I cannot fucking handle this right now."

"Okay! Jesus."

Her eyes selected this inopportune moment to start pumping tears. "Thanks a lot, Tyler."

A middle-aged woman tapped her angrily on the shoulder. "Excuse me, but could you two please keep your voices down? Your language is horrible."

"I'm sorry," Amanda answered. "Could you go soak your head in fucking poison?"

"Oh, my God," Tyler moaned. "They just want to go home. We're in a damn terror alert."

"They can go home in fucking half an hour. That's all I'm asking. Half an hour of the world's time. We can start this thing over, have a chance at a life."

By ending someone else's, Tyler thought, but said nothing.

"Quinlan?" the receptionist snapped.

"Perfect," Amanda muttered. Tyler helped her to her feet. "Yeah, I'm here."

"The doctor will see you. Right this way, please." Judging by the knotted expression on the receptionist's face, "Right this way, please" was medical jargon for "Feel free to die now."

The doctor was female, early forties, with a mole on her chin. She had a habit of twirling a ballpoint pen in her fingers. Amanda found herself staring at it, mesmerized. Maybe that was the point, to be hypnotized, less willing to make an ugly scene. "I'm Dr. Tendulkar. I'll be helping you through the procedure. I understand you believe you are pregnant."

"Yes, ma'am."

"How late are you?" The doctor had a soft Indian accent, which unintentionally drained her clipboard questions of mercy.

"Just a few days, but I've started having morning sickness. I took four home pregnancy tests."

"They were all positive?"

"Yes."

"I'm going to take some blood just to be sure, but let's assume you are correct. And you've decided to terminate the pregnancy?"

"Um, yes, ma'am." Amanda asked herself why she talking like she was in the principal's office.

"You know this is a very serious decision."

"We've talked about it a lot, together. We're too young. We don't make any money. We might not even wind up together." *Tyler*, she thought, *please don't look at me that way.* "I want to be a mother when I know how to be a good one."

Dr. Tendulkar spun her damn pen again. "All right, very well. You're both over the age of consent, so the decision is entirely up to you. I am, however, obliged to offer you free adoption counseling."

"I can't be pregnant," Amanda whispered, fighting the tearful itch in her eyes. "I can't. I just can't go through nine months of that, only to give it away, or have it in the middle of a damn nuclear war. I gotta take care of it now." After a thoughtful moment, Dr. Tendulkar nodded. Her pen stopped its orbit with the click of a Japanese fan.

"Let's take some blood." This was followed by another long wait while Tendulkar and a male nurse readied ultrasound equipment. "Here's what's going to happen," the doctor said. "We're going to see exactly how far along you are and make sure you're a suitable candidate for a medical abortion. This means we can terminate the pregnancy without resorting to any surgical procedure. But first we have to check you for sexually transmitted diseases. This will require a Pap smear." She turned to Tyler. "You have the option of being in the room for this procedure, if that's all right with Miss Quinlan."

Amanda nodded. "Okay," Tyler answered, barely audible.

Tendulkar regarded the couple sadly. "Very well. Then we will schedule you for another short visit next week. The actual procedure will require little time." The word *procedure* was starting to nauseate Amanda. She wondered how long the queasiness would last, how much of it was physical, how much of it was guilt. "You will be given juice to drink. The juice will contain Methotrexate, a substance which effectively ends further growth of the fetus. At this point, you will no longer have the option of changing your mind." Amanda nodded, having read this online. "I will explain to you what you must then do at home. I assure you, it will be uncomfortable. You won't suffer a great deal in the way of physical discomfort, but many patients find it emotionally difficult."

"I understand."

"The home procedure will be deeply unpleasant. I wish to emphasize this. Also, I'm sure you know many patients come to regret their decision to terminate a pregnancy. I do not wish to influence you in any way. However, I need to be certain you are aware there are options."

"Yes, okay, *please*, can we just get this over with." Amanda held her breath, unable to plead her case rationally. Long seconds ticked on the clock.

"Very well," the doctor nodded, and set her pen aside. "Let's begin."

Tyler patted Amanda's hand, his own breath stuffy with tears.

Something chattered outside. The doctor looked at the nurse. "What was that?" the asked casually.

"I don't know." They heard screaming. The air barked, a single chop hard enough to rattle the walls. Amanda's teeth clacked together. It felt like God clapped.

"Did that sound like a crash?" the male nurse asked, and opened the office door. Just then a fist punched the building. The rest Amanda saw as if in a movie, one long mad transformation, an ecstasy of nonsense.

Every town has its story, its own particular view of the End of the World—every town, every street, every person. This is how they felt the Rapture come to Sugar Roses, a few lives, one building; but the Rapture was cosmic. It was bigger than anything and deep down inside.

Outside in the parking lot, Danny Murcheson stood by the bed of his pickup. The Megatron, the god in his head, was screaming for the unholy sluts and the baby-murdering doctors to get theirs. He threw a tarp aside, revealing enough secondhand weaponry to level a police station. Or the Alamo. Or a hospital. *They been killing them babies*, the Megatron insisted. *Time to fuck all these murdering bastards up hardcore.* "Jesus saves!" Danny screamed. "*God forgives! Heroes kill!*" The armaments rested on a hard blocky mound.

Danny carried a Luger P .08 tucked in his belt, a Tokarev

TT-33 holstered at his right hip. His shoulder holster carried a .38. In his yellow right hand was smoking steel pride, the M2 automatic carbine he fired to take out the security guard at the main entrance. The guy was down before he knew what hit him. *Served him right for being in the wrong place on God's morning.* It was long past time the Lord got even. Danny's next move was to toss a smoke grenade windward, obscuring his position. Then he hoisted the prize of his collection, a Milkor MGL grenade launcher with six rotating chambers, each loaded with a 40 mm antipersonnel grenade. With this, he carried hell in his hands. The launcher fired two rounds in less than a second, punching into the side of the hospital, rocking the world. The screaming came bloody and perfect.

He'd already scouted this corner of the building. He knew the filth that festered inside. Here was where godless doctors dealt out death to helpless children, probably raping or fingerfucking the whores who came to kill their own babies. Everyone inside that ward deserved to die. It was as simple as that. They deserved to be tortured to death, drawn and quartered, sliced apart like a fetus. He fired another shot and marveled at the power he'd been given.

The morning sun glinted off the new yellow-orange cast of his skin.

Buddy Sims stood fifty yards away and gaped as the hospital façade collapsed. He understood only that he'd been called there. *This is it,* Jesus told him. *This is where you'll be needed, my friend. I told you there was hate in this world only good love can fix. My love is perfect, Buddy, and now I'm gonna join it with yours. We're gonna do perfect things together.*

"I don't know what to do," Buddy said.

I'll tell you what you can do. 'Be strong and courageous and bold,' the voice sang. *'Be strong and courageous and bold.'*

"Away with your fear, for God will be near," Buddy sang. "Be strong and curvaceous and bold."

That'll do, the voice laughed. *You'll do just fine, Buddy. I know how much love you got in you. I know 'cause I put it there. Now you just gotta let it all out.*

"Someone's shooting!" the male nurse yelled, and it sounded like a truck hit the building. The nurse stepped back and swatted his own head, accidentally driving window glass deeper into his flesh and hand. A splash of blood ribboned the office door. Tendulkar screamed.

"What?" Amanda asked. "What's going on?" Another blast. Amanda toppled. Tyler threw himself over her on the way to the floor. Dr. Tendulkar leaped toward the nurse, who was slumping down the wall to cold linoleum. Dust filled the air. A taste of burnt plastic. Shards of glass hit the ground. Everything in fragments. Time was jumbled and sharp. The world had gone jagged.

"What's going on?" Scott asked. "What is that?" He and Zack stood in the IHOP parking lot and watched a tree of black smoke bloom.

"That's the hospital," Zack said.

"What is it, on fire?"

"No, let's go, man. Get in the car."

"The car? Why? What the hell are we doing?"

"I don't know."

"What are you doing, Zack?"

"I don't know, man, I gotta go see!"

"Zack, come on, man!" Zack was already starting the car. Without even knowing why, Scott got in and slammed the car door. "Just stay out of this, will ya? The police can handle it!"

"The police aren't there, man. We are. It's two blocks away!"

"It's none of our business," Scott said weakly.

"You're wrong," Zack said, shaking his head. "So get out if you want. But I have to go. I *have* to go. *Now.*"

"Why do you have to go?"

"I…" Zack shook his head angrily.

Scott froze. "Oh, my God. Zack, is this what you meant? When you saw something coming?"

Zack grinned at him madly. "I don't know, man. I don't... Maybe. Yeah. I feel like..." He struggled to form the words: "It's my turn, okay? Are you with me?"

"Your turn? No, I don't know what you're talking about. Why *you*?"

When Zack answered a few moments later, his voice was so small it hardly sounded like his own. "We get these chances, y'know...We're given chances to do the right thing. Make things better...This is mine." Now he almost whispered. "I've been told this is mine."

Scott had one final chance to leave poor Zack to his lunacy. He stayed in the car. That moment passed. "Go." They lurched onto Townsend.

Buddy marched toward the hospital. *"He's there by your side, to help and to guide. He's with you wherever you go."*

"911 Emergency Services, how may I help you?" The voice was barely audible, garbled behind a chorus of high-pitched tones on the line.

"There's shooting at the hospital," Scott screamed into his cell phone as Zack drove like the madman he probably was. "We can see dust and smoke."

"In Sugar Roses?"

"Yes, ma'am."

"We'll send someone over right away." The police department was on South Providence, the other side of town, but Sugar Roses was small enough that officers would arrive within minutes. "Sir, can you see the hospital from where you are?"

"Yeah, it's bad," Scott told her as they pulled into the lot. "There's smoke everywhere. Bodies by the door. One of 'em might be a cop." And that's when he saw the man with the guns, a little man pacing behind a battered, tarp-covered truck bed.

"Holy shit," Zack said, spotting him instantly and braking to a halt. "I know that guy. Look, it's Danny Murcheson. I used to play high school ball with his dumb country ass. He could barely find the plate. Now he's armed to the teeth. Who made that guy a terrorist?" Scott pulled him down behind the dash as the car idled in place.

Danny fired a grenade at a parked ambulance. The grenade rolled under the vehicle, then tossed it off the pavement with a thunderous bark. A second later, gasoline burst into flame. Another two grenades, *thump thump*, arced through the smashed lobby doors.

"I know this guy," Zack marveled. "I can't believe I know this guy."

Amanda shook her head to clear it. The receptionist's voice screamed "Go away!" from outside in the hall.

"We've got to get ou—" Amanda said, and the walls projectile vomited gravel and dust. Bricks and glass burst like a fireworks display. Pennies filled her mouth, copper pennies. She watched the linoleum rise up and smack her in the head. Heat and darkness. Rips of pain stabbing her left leg, confusion, inversion.

Tyler's body fell next to her, limp as a blanket. She shoved him, called his name, and he rolled over woozily. He'd bitten through his tongue. The pain was everywhere. He coughed blood and dust. A baby cried in the gloom.

There were whispers in the darkness—she felt them in her head—but with everyone screaming and crying, Amanda couldn't make out what they were saying. Her leg buzzed with pain. Shock descended.

Danny fired his sixth grenade through an upstairs window. The room dismantled itself in a bloody gray torrent. The baby wasn't crying anymore.

Buddy Sims watched from a hundred feet away. "Believe and obey, each hour of the day, and trust Him with all of your

283

heart," he sang under his breath.

There it is, Buddy. You see it?

"I see it, Jesus. Here at the hospital."

They're gonna need you inside big time, Buddy.

"Some kinda terrorist is shooting a gun."

You let me worry 'bout him. There's some people inside there. You just go in and help.

"I can do it."

I know that.

"I sure do feel scared, though."

I know it. But they ain't nothin' to be afraid of, Buddy. We got this. Ain't we lookin' out for you? Ain't we always been?

"Yessir. I love you, Jesus."

I love you, too, Buddy. Now let's go in there and get this thing done.

"Yessiree, Bob." Buddy marched across the open parking lot and entered the hospital.

"He's still shooting," Scott mumbled, electric charges thrumming his body.

"Scott, get out of the car."

"Turn around, Zack."

"No." Instead he risked a better look, popping his head up over the dash.

"This is crazy," Scott said, cracking the car door open.

Danny reached in his truck and pulled out a loaded, sawed-off Remington 870 Wingmaster shotgun. He also grabbed a shoulder pack loaded with 2-¾" shells. Beneath the guns, Zack spotted the base of yellow bricks, at least a hundred pounds worth, that Danny had stolen from three construction sites. Danny tossed the tarp back over the truck bed, surveyed the front of the building, and marched a few steps forward on the heavy tread of Danner police boots.

"I'm serious, Scott," Zack insisted. "You need to get out of this car."

"What're you gonna do? The cops are on their way." Sirens cried in the distance.

"No time. No *time*," Zack insisted.

"Why's he yellow?"

"He's been poisoned. He was handling TNT."

"Oh, no. Those bricks?"

"Exactly."

"He's gonna try to kill everyone."

"I know. That's why I'm here."

* * *

Danny fired a shot into the building and caught the receptionist running for better cover. She tumbled and wept, her waist spilling outward, an eel's nest of gore.

The power burned in Danny's brain, a live wire. The Wingmaster stabbed in his arms. Soon he'd get back in his truck and drive straight into glory. The Lord of Hosts would welcome him home, crown him with power, them send him back into the world. This was all made to happen. This was all Danny's whispered prayers come to pass, the kingship and destiny promised God's Fist. He heard a car revving its engine behind him. He turned, a smiling hero, to welcome more targets to justice.

"I hear singing," Scott murmured.

"Get out of the car!" Zack demanded.

"Okay." It was time. Scott staggered through the open door on numb legs and dove to the asphalt. "God," he said, dizzily. "I feel it now. I feel it all coming." *This was all made to happen.* Danny's gun flared again. The windshield cracked. The last time Scott saw Zack he was laughing, a cabernet stain in full bloom on his shoulder. Scott kicked the passenger door closed and slid behind an ambulance. "Jesus," he whispered. It might have been a prayer.

Danny jumped in his truck and immediately raced toward the building. He was screaming devils' curses: "The Megatron has spoken! Feel the might of God's Fist!"

Zack gave chase, accelerating faster than the heavy truck. His bumper met the passenger side of the truck at forty miles an hour, shoving the front fender sideways. He could feel the impact stagger his car. The airbags exploded. A thud of pain punched him in the chest, the taste of blood filling his mouth. He managed to shove Danny's truck aside just far enough to roar past the building. Instead it sheered into a parked SUV. The jolt was too much for the detonators stowed inside the truck. A black rose unfolded in the air, enveloping Zack's car in a shock wave of fire. Twisted metal swarmed in the air, hissing like wasps.

Scott stepped out from cover just in time to feel the shock wave of heat on his face. He stood and gaped, then slumped to the ground and wept for his friend. The world smelled like scorched hair and gasoline and spun around, spun around, gray.

Buddy emerged from the hospital into black smoke, a child in his arms. The child was warm, alive but unconscious. Her mother lay tangled nearby.

"Help us, please!" an Indian doctor cried, dabbing at glass wounds on a male nurse's face and throat. The shooting had stopped, and now the cries of casualties were heard in the wreckage.

"I can help you," Buddy promised. "My best friend is showing me how."

Amanda looked at Tyler, whose greenish bangs sagged over his eyes like a veil. "We shou'n'a been here," Tyler mumbled, wincing against the pain of broken ribs.

"We had to," she replied.

"We shou'n'a had to."

286

"I know."

A lumpy blond stump of a man in cargo shorts and a *Sentinel* T-shirt appeared at the shattered office door. "Y'all need help in here?" he asked, his thick forearms blackened with dust.

"She knees hell," Tyler muttered, waving the stumpy man over. "Gedder ahn 'ere." His tongue hurt like murder.

"My name's Buddy," the man said. "I can help."

"You go first," Amanda told Tyler, touching his arm.

"You gone be all right," Buddy said. Amanda realized Buddy was that retarded guy who delivered newspapers. "Jesus told me they's help comin' soon."

"Okay, then," she managed.

"I'll be back for you," he promised Tyler. "I gotta carry this poor girl outside. She got a broken leg. They's a little bitty baby who needs her to be okay."

"How'd you know?" Amanda asked. Buddy shrugged, an embarrassed smile widening his face.

"Please help Aaron as well," the doctor said, indicating the male nurse slumped against the wall. "He needs first aid immediately."

"We are in a hospital," the nurse managed, his blood wet and awful on his scrubs.

Scott carefully picked himself up off the asphalt and took stock. His right hip was bruised and his eyebrows were gone. The redemption of Zack Heath—and Zack's resolve in his climactic moment of purpose—struck Scott as something of a miracle. He'd only met Zack a few days ago, but already knew he would miss the man terribly.

Noise from the hospital drew his attention. Doctors helped patients from the lobby and into the cool smoky air. Scott limped over to help. Along the way, he recognized Tyler in the arms of a stocky retarded man—"Buddy," Zack called him. "Help is coming," Scott yelled, as police cars and ambulances pulled up behind him.

"They's people hurt everywhere inside," Buddy said.

"Okay." Scott moved in, ducking through gaps in the façade into darkness and dust.

"We need help!" a softly accented voice called from the offices to Scott's right. He jogged through the smoke and confusion. In the darkness, an Indian woman knelt over a male nurse, his chest and neck pulsing with blood. Scott rummaged for bandages to cover the nurse's wounds, and they helped him outside. The doctor tended the nurse's cuts. Scott turned back and noticed a wounded young figure on the curb, a woman he was happy to recognize.

"Amanda?" Tears streamed from her eyes.

"We broke it, y'know?" she moaned. "But none of us meant to."

Outside in the parking lot, Buddy froze in place. The time had come. The planes were in the air. Humanity was pulling the pin on its own sorry culmination. A Voice said, *Buddy*, and Buddy knew Who it was without asking.

"Yessir?"

I'm about to do something you won't believe.

"I'll believe it."

Something magical and perfect. I want to make things better in the end.

"I know You can do it. I know that. You coulda done it any time You wanted."

No. It wasn't time before, Buddy. The game wasn't over.

"You was playin' a game?"

Something like that. You ready?

"I'm ready."

Feel your insides. It's hot in there, isn't it?

"Yessir, it is."

288

I put something in there. Now close your eyes. Let it come out.

"Oh my God," Buddy breathed, and the planet fell sideways, exploding around.

A Figure appeared in his mind, a Figure beyond his ability to process. The Figure was everywhere, making the world happen, making it real, loving it into motion. The Godhead set Buddy's body on fire, but the fire was cool, the fire was everything cosmic and cold. Buddy's hair stood on end, its sandy color draining away. The Figure opened Buddy's heart in a twist of ecstatic release. A tide of love flooded creation, and everywhere, divinity glorified the world.

The Rapture came for everyone, a weary cosmos reborn. There were carriers all over the world. This is only how it came for Sugar Roses. The other stories wait to be told.

God's euphoria spread at the speed of love, a constellation of multiple exploding stars of inexhaustible joy. Policemen staggered in a psychedelic daze. The flashing lights of black-and-whites burst like supernovae.

Scott could feel the wave of transcendence coming and wept. The merest whispers of air on his arm excited every pleasure center in his brain. He lay on the pitted linoleum of the hospital lobby and hugged himself, laughing. He would never feel nothing again, the miracle of perfect communion burning all his old logics away.

Amanda's eyes opened, the throbs of pain gone from her body. Tyler joined her and kissed her, a glorious wedding day kiss. If she lived, she saw fully, then her baby would live. She was not about to argue with miracles. The purity of all that love warmed her like a sunbeam.

Buddy sang, a divine melody, though the words he sang were mysterious, even to him. The song was coded, a program, buried deep in the matrix of the world. The light of holiness burned in his mind.

All those waves of love continued for hours. Around the world, people died as they always died, even that morning—some of violence, more of old age, but every last breath was surrendered with blessed tranquility. Food and music were sweeter. People healed a bit faster. They made love in twos and threes, every climax a touch of the Godhead. No planes fell from the sky. The zealots of Revenge of the Babies, and all the other soldiers who stood in their misguided way, knelt in the sacred dust of the Temple Mount and prayed as a family. All the armies turned around and went home. Messiah came beaming and rageless, his arrival an oratorio in the sky. No one hurt or felt lonely. No one hungered or cried in despair. And for a quarter of a rotation of the planet Earth, all was kindness thereon. Love was all things, all moments, the dark past defeated and atoned for.

It was not a delusion—or more to the point, it always had been, and would be again. And if that was the End of the World, then at least it burned in Rapture after all.

Coda
Ἀποκάλυφις

Deus Extra Machina

Ω

The Designer watched the simulation tick down to one last optimal moment—a forced ending, to be sure, but an ecstasy richly deserved. The game could end now if the Designer so willed it. Culmination was built into that dream of a world from the outset.

But then, an uncomfortable epiphany: What if the Designer was nothing more than an element in yet another simulation? What if everything the Designer knew was itself a delusion, an intermediate level of fantasy? And if that were the case, then what would the Designer's purpose be, if not to Design and run this very simulation? What if ending this game incited the end of the Designer who made it? What if winning or quitting the game led to purposelessness or even oblivion? What, indeed, followed life in the Designer's own level of simulation? There was no way to be sure, no top level, no absolute World.

It was safer to play the odds wisely, conservatively. The Designer tweaked a number of irksome parameters in the game, added others to make it more interesting, and let it play on.

Author's Note

I'm indebted to the writings of Dr. Richard Dawkins and Bishop John Shelby Spong. Christian agnostic that I am, I'm free to recommend both with equal fervor. I also challenge the reader to check out the work of Dr. Ray Kurzweil, who believes a kind of transcendence will be common in our very near future. He refers to this paradigm shift as the dawn of "transhumanism," but he might as well call it the afterlife.

I'm grateful to Michael West for his inspiring trans-Baptist perspective and intellect, and to Sean Boyd for lighting a much-needed fire. I'm also thankful to Judd Morse and a handful of MySpace readers for aiding and abetting the murders of my darlings. Chris Clark and the Olympia Writers Workshop Roundtable were, you'll pardon the expression, a Godsend; the book is vastly better for their labors. My research included a visit to the First Baptist Church of Olympia. If Pastor Bob Sievers ever reads this, I hope he finds common ground.

I wrote *Lightfall* a year before I met Buddy or Amanda Stevens, so no comparison is intended for the characters "Buddy" or "Amanda." Love love love, Stevenses; and many thanks also to the great people at Fear Nought, to whom Buddy was thoughtful enough to introduce me.

Two very different geniuses, Imogen Heap and Bruce Springsteen, kept me inspired throughout the birth of this novel.

Dr. Nick Bostrom is a real person, assuming he's wrong, and his theories should be studied in detail at simulation-argument.com. He believes there's a one in five chance we're all characters in a vast simulation. I think he's too conservative, but I find the idea that none of this is happening a transformative comfort. Pastor Melissa Scott is also real, as is her thrilling biography, and the coral reefs are really getting herpes. The day this novel was accepted for publication, I learned some male frogs now create eggs in their testes, probably thanks to chemical fertilizers. We are quickly, irrevocably slipping toward a world we can't predict.

Christian Carvajal